The Melting Season
& Other Stories

Ira Sukrungruang

The Melting Season
& Other Stories

Copyright © 2016 by Ira Sukrungruang

Published by Burlesque Press
www.burlesquepressllc.com

ISBN: 978-0-9964850-2-9

Book design by Daniel Wallace

Cover image by Aaniyah.ahmed

Acknowledgments

This book would not have happened if it weren't for the folks at Burlesque Press—Jeni and Daniel Wallace. They saw something that I did not, and I am eternally grateful for their comments, their commitment, their encouragement, and most of all, their friendship.

And love to my brothers across the bridge, KC Wolfe and Jon Chopan, who strive daily to make a better art, who see the potential and power of the written word, and who, when they were my undergraduate students those many years ago in Oswego, NY, read different versions of these stories and were the inspiration for many of them.

And to my University of South Florida family. And to my City University Hong Kong family. Students, you drive me to the page each and every day. You give me energy. You give me inspiration. Without you, I would not write.

And to Deedra. Because.

Grateful acknowledgment is made to the following publications in which some of these stories appeared, sometimes in slightly different versions:

Animal: A Beast of a Literary Magazine: "The Bartender" titled "Mr. Feathers, " part of "Panhandle: A Fusion"
Ascent: "Ordinary World"
Cedar: "The Valet" titled "The Longevity of Art," part of "Panhandle: A Fusion"
Conclave: "Threatlessness"
Crab Orchard Review: "The Man with the Buddha Heads"
Eclipse: "Bright Land"
Em: "Pick a Path Adventures"
Fairy Tale Review: "Family: A Fairy Tale"
Fiction Fix: "Tell Us What You Want"
Fifth Wednesday Journal: "Happy Ends"
Hobart: "Bridgeview Heights Mall"
Our Stories: "Forecast"
Passages North: "The Dishwasher," part of "Panhandle: A Fusion"
South Dakota Review: "Tip"

Table of Contents

for Kassidy and Kourey, my girls;
Daisy and Keita, my dogs;
but not the cats, never the cats;
and of course,
for Dee, who holds my heart in her pocket

1

Always start out with a larger pot than what you think you need.

–Julia Child

Family: A Fairy Tale

Illustrations by Kassidy Wollert

1. Puberty

The boy did not know that when he ate the seeds that out from his belly button would grow a vine. He decided to show his mother who was busy with his winged sister. She was always busy with her, a handful of a girl, who had taken to flight

only a few days before. Now his sister refused to still her wings, the way she refused to still her mouth when she learned speech. The boy complained to his mother about the vine in his belly button.

"It's only a vine," his mother said. "I told you not to eat the seeds."

"I told you not to eat the seeds," his sister echoed, whirling around the boy's head, naked as a peach.

The boy told his mother that he did not want to go to school with a vine in his belly button. He did not want the other boys to see his vine. He feared the locker room taunt. He feared being shirtless when he changed into his gym suit. Worse yet, what if he was to be "skins" in the basketball game, and then it would not be just the boys who would see the vine; it'd be the girls too, and then who would want to be the girlfriend of the boy with a vine sprouting from his navel? The boy wanted a girlfriend. He imagined this girlfriend daily, and she was beautiful the way princesses in fairy tales were beautiful. He did not think a girlfriend would want a boy with a vine in him. He told his mother this, who was trying to net his sister.

"This is your own doing," she said. "Those seeds. I told you."

"Those seeds," his sister said. "Seeds, seeds, seeds."

The boy thought that this would be a matter in which a father might be useful. He was, regrettably, without one. He wondered if his father suffered the same predicament when he was a boy, whether he too had a vine sprouting from his belly button. He wondered how his father would have handled the situation. Perhaps, the boy thought, he inherited this. He asked his mother whether his father had a vine.

"You don't have a father," his mother said. She kept swinging a net and missing.

"No father, no father," his sister said.

Frustration grew in the boy. Frustration and a vine. The boy decided he would not leave the house, would not go to school to get ridiculed by boys, would not be rejected by a girlfriend he desperately wanted. Instead he lay on his bed and closed his eyes, and wished hard for the vine in his belly button to disappear, wished he would disappear. He thought, if he were to have a vine grow from his belly button, let it cocoon him in green, let this vine wrap its tendrils around him, let him be devoured.

2. NOT ICARUS

It only takes one bug in the eye to deter you from any form of flight. She can tell you this.

She can attest to the inconvenience of having wings. You

do not know pain until you encounter a bee sting on your eyeball. It is not a pleasant experience. These wings of hers—What a novelty, they said. A gift from heaven, they said. But they—whoever they are—have not possessed an enlarged right eye-

ball, have not experienced a throbbing swell, as if a heart pulsated on her face. She cannot cover a swollen eyeball with makeup. She cannot cover a swollen eyeball with sunglasses because sunglasses cannot fit over a swollen eyeball. So what happens? What happens is she walks around school with a swollen eye and wings that seem to hit and knock everything over.

White wings in the library: bookshelves tumble like dominoes.

White wings in art class: dipping into watercolors.

White wings in gym: stilled wings are not wind resistant in sprints, and Mr. Pauly said flying was cheating.

White wings in Language Arts: Mrs. Babcock has nick-named her the white albatross of trouble.

White wings on the school bus: always in the rear view mirror, always sitting alone.

She hates her wings. She does.

But she finds herself in the air. All the time. Such is life. What brings pain, brings pleasure. She soars the skies, looking at the earth from the vantage of birds. She does not test Icarus's fatal flaw—such a stupid boy, like all stupid boys, like her brother—but when you have wings, when you use them, you are literally above it all. You feel as if you can fly toward

4

the sun without repercussions. You are larger because the world below you, the people below you, become microscopic, become ants in tiny ant hills. And from here, you can see the trouble of the world approaching, like that storm in the distance, the clouds that have darkened the sun and sent the ravens into flight.

3. THE BLENDED LIFE

The father is unseen. Most fathers are. But this father blends. If he is among the hedges, he becomes the hedges. If he is among the shrubs, he becomes the shrubs. It is an unfortunate circumstance to be unseen. It is most unfortunate to be unseen and a father. The unseen father is blamed for many woes. The unseen father is at fault. His absence is reason for turmoil.

But the father is not absent. Never absent. He was there when his daughter sprouted wings. He was there when his son 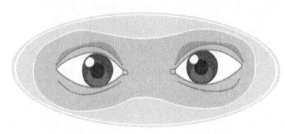 grew a vine in his bellybutton. He was there. Silent. Always watching. From his blending life. He is even there, today, when he watches the mother sit at the kitchen table one afternoon with hardly another breath left in her. Oh how she keeps everything together. Oh how she feeds and nurtures. Oh how she mothers. A cup of tea steams in her hands. Her shoulders slump in exhaustion. There are not many still moments for the mother, the father notices, and to see her sedentary reminds him of a time when she was not a mother, and he was not a father. When on an autumn day, she saw him among a white wall.

"I see you," she said.

He did not say anything. He assumed it was not him she was speaking to. But her eyes, they were aimed at him. Aimed at the white wall. Aimed at him against the white wall, is the white wall.

"I see you," she said again. "Your eyes, they're very brown."

How odd it might have seemed to be only a pair of eyes on a canvas of white.

"You've been watching me," she said.

The father, who was not a father yet, did not know what to say. He spent his whole life blending into things. He spent his whole life going unnoticed. It was a lonely life, but one he had come accustomed to.

"You have beautiful eyes," she said.

This is how love starts. This moment of being seen.

But it happens. It always does. Love changes. Roles change. And suddenly he found himself a father and began to fade. And, she, this woman at the kitchen table, became a mother and her life became about mothering.

"I know you are there," she says. She sips her tea.

"I am," the father says. He is the transparent kitchen window.

"I know you are always there," she says.

"I am."

"Coward," she says.

"I am."

And the father expects her to leave, to say something harsh and turn her back, forget him the way the world forgot him. But she does not. She remains. She sips her tea. She says nothing else, as if he is gone. As if he does not exist. Because he doesn't. Not to her. Not to this family. He is peripheral in all things. The outsider looking in. He knows this. Knows she will not leave. Will never leave. It will be the father who steps away first. Who enters the dark forest. Becomes the forest. Becomes the leaves quivering in a tree.

4. THE ENVIOUS LIFE

Once upon a time, she had a name.

Once upon a time, she was young.

Once upon a time, she was not Mother.

But do not ask her to recall that life. That life has receded.

There is nothing special about her. She does not have wings. She does not have vegetation growing from her navel. She does not have the ability to hide. Quite the opposite. She is always in sight. Always in service. The magic she possesses is that she does not have magic.

Day in, day out, she sees yoga moms in yoga pants going to yoga classes with yoga mats tucked under their sinewy yoga arms, and she envies them. She envies their lives. She spends a lot of time envying.

Once upon a time, she did not envy.

Once upon a time, she was envied.

Like those lost years before she became Mother and was a woman with full hips and even fuller desires. Like those years when she dreamt of swimming among the dolphins and marlins, those years of study to be a marine biologist, a life of the sea and salt. Like those years when she took in lovers, when she rushed them out of bed, when she controlled who had claim to her wants and needs.

Now she is landlocked.

House-locked.

Like this afternoon, when she was tidying up the living room because her son left sticky sap on the windows and her

daughter has begun to molt. She was wiping the window when she noticed a boy sneaking around the blue house across the street. He was a young boy, with a full head of curls like fiddleheads. The boy was older than her son, who was about to go to college in botany, but young enough to turn heads of envying mothers like her. Her eyes followed him slink among the roses then climb a trellis of purple clematis into an open window on the second story. And there she saw her. Another mother. Another mother who was not her. This mother was without clothes. This mother was pale and pink and plump in the right places. This mother was naked and beautiful—the way her red hair fell over her bare shoulders, the way her luscious lips stood out from her face, the way gravity did not prey on her parts.

Envy snaked through the mother's body then, snaked and coiled and constricted. Envy made her touch her own body, as if she was touching the mother from across the way, who tangled herself around the boy, her long legs wrapped around his hips, her hands touching with frantic urgency his shirtless torso. The mother found herself touching her own face, ignoring the cracks and wrinkles and blemishes, ignoring the dark sags under her eyes. She touched her own chest under her oversized tank top that read Best Mother embroidered in pink thread, and felt the sag of her breasts. She slid her hand under the waistline of her sweats and touched the places no one had touched in a long time and her head hit the window and her breath fogged it up. And when she came, she did so in tears. She did so in quiet sadness.

The blinds came down across the way.

"Damn," she said.

The window was streaked with tears and smudges.

"Damn," she said again and began to wipe the window.

The sun cast longer shadows across the yard and she knew it was late afternoon and she knew it would not be long before her children came home. She could hear them now, their voices ringing across the distance, the name she has come to hate.

Pick a Path Adventures

No one thought Louis Wangchakorn was capable of taking Big Dennis down. No one thought Louis was capable of anything. He didn't have it in him. He was an Asian straight-A kid. Not Bruce Lee Asian. Not ass-kicking Asian. More like the Asians in movies about school.

Before any of this, Louis started off as a weak kid. A scrawny, skeletal kid. A skeleton like the one hanging up in Louis' fourth period biology class, the one his teacher Mr. Hinkel kept bumping into. That skeleton shook and rattled. That skeleton was held up by string and a coat hanger.

And Big Dennis was big. No one gets a name like Big Dennis because he's small. If we were to dissect Big D, cut him up like a frog in Mr. Hinkel's class, each leg would be two Louis-es. Both arms would equal one. His head, his gigantic, massive head, would be a contorted-into-a-ball Louis, and his stomach, massive like the sphere at the Planetarium, was at least, no joke, at least six. One Big Dennis equaled twelve Louis-es. We're not talking Mr. Fitness big. Big like his stomach is a planet unto its own where the microscopic people dwell, hiding from spring rains in Big D's belly button.

So during recess, everyone thought it was a joke when Louis decided to do the thing no one thought he was capable of. Even the lunch monitors didn't expect it. They watched for ten seconds like someone was birthing a baby in the middle of the playground in Hyde Park, some fascinating abnormality. Who would expect this? Who would ever expect Louis—our skeletal, bookworm, Asian Louis—flying through the air and clamping his mouth onto Big Dennis' throat, biting and holding on like a lion, a runty lion, and Big Dennis waving his arms like a slow motion picture? And throughout all of this, no one caught on to the seriousness of what was unfolding. The dark realization of it all: that Louis had become a vampire in broad daylight, in the middle of Chicago, in the middle of swings and a slide and a teeter-totter. That Louis had chosen his first victim, Big Dennis, who slowly, like a falling Redwood, crashed onto one knee, then the other, then onto his cushioned stomach, Louis still at his neck, biting and drinking.

*

Louis was a deep thinker. He held onto things. He remembered when he was seven and his mother and father took him to the Forest Preserve twenty miles out of the city and the sun was coming down over a meadow, over the largest sky Louis had ever seen, and as it got darker and darker out came the lightning bugs, the lampyridae. Hundreds of them. Thousands, really. For Louis, it was the most beautiful sight he had ever seen. He ran into the meadow and wanted to catch all that light. Keep it for himself. When Louis turned to look at his mother and father, his arms out to the sides, it appeared as if he had made the lightning bugs rise.

When he came back, he asked his parents why they glowed.

Louis' mother, a history professor at a community college, shrugged. "I know about King Louie, Louie. Not bugs."

Louis' father, currently unemployed, said, "Well, Louis, lightning bugs have specialized cells that contain luciferin which makes an enzyme called luciferase. For the bugs to light up, the luciferin combines with oxygen and the luciferase speeds up the lighting reactions. They do this to attract mates, friends if you will, and these friends will go on to make new friends."

11

Louis didn't understand most of what his father said.

"It's funny," said Louis' mother, "that the thing that makes these bugs glow contain the word for the devil. Don't you think that's interesting? Lucifer. Light bringer. In some books about King Louis, they said that Lucifer possessed him, made him build the Palace of Versailles at the expense of his people. Oh, Louie. Poor misguided Louie."

Louis watched a lightning bug hover near his mother's neck. Then it settled right below her ear, right where her hair ended and her neck began. She smacked it hard, smacked it dead, and then wiped it away. What was left was the glow of the lightning bug's guts, shimmering dust, smeared fluorescence. Louis held on to this, too. Especially this. Because the one thing he remembered most, the thing that he couldn't forget was that he wanted to bite his mother for swatting the lightning bug. He wanted to lunge at the glowing spot at her neck and bite her. Hard. Like he had never bitten anyone before. Which he hadn't.

*

When Louis was ten, he read 7.1 books a week. Out of the 7.1 books he read, 4.2 of them were *Pick a Path Adventures*, flimsy paperbacks where at the end of each page the reader had the power to control the destiny of the characters. *If you do this, flip to this page. If you want to do that, go to that page.* Louis consumed these books. Here, he had control. Out in the walking and talking world, Louis was passive. Decisions are hard for kids like Louis. They do what they're told. They don't deviate. But in his adventures, in these books, Louis had choices. If he made the wrong choice he would simply go back and make a better one, one that changed the outcome of the story. This is the reason Louis devoured 4.2 *Pick a Path* books in a course of a week, 218.4 a year. There were seemingly infinite ways to end a story. And no matter what happened, it was Louis' decision.

Pick a Path Adventure number 117. *Oh Boy, It's a Vampire.* The main character in the story was not Asian, but he was much like Louis, invisible. This boy lived to study and did all the right things. Immediately, as he read, Louis became the boy in the book.

It was Louis walking home during a thunderstorm, Louis who heard footsteps, loud and irregular, like a man who skipped on the third step. It was Louis who made the first choice.

Pick a Path Choice #1: Should he run or confront his assailant?

Louis whipped around. Drops of rain fell to the sidewalk. One of his books flew out of his arms and across the concrete. It stopped in front of a man in a trench coat and the wide brimmed hat of an undertaker.

"Why are you following me?"

The man picked up the book and came forward. One, two, skip. One, two, skip. Louis froze. There was something odd about this man, not just his awkward walk. Something that scared and fascinated him. A foot away, the man titled his hat up, revealed his ice-cold eyes, handing the book back to Louis.

"Do you believe in ghosts, boy?" the man rasped.

PAP Choice #2: Yes or no?

Louis nodded.

"Good," said the man. "Then follow me."

Louis followed the man to a castle that appeared out of nowhere. It was the classic haunted castle with creaking wrought iron gates and overgrown vegetation sprouting up the walls. Once in the castle, the man disappeared, his voice booming and bouncing off the stone interior: "Defeat my minions or perish." And the minions came. The further Louis explored the more supernatural beings he faced. He was alone with only the power of choice. Not once did he run toward the door or try to escape. Louis kept choosing the correct options to survive. He didn't backtrack, didn't start over. He walked down to the dungeons and defeated the mummies by unraveling their ratty bandages until they were dust. He defeated the werewolf by poking him in the eyes. Louis plugged his ears when the banshee of the castle began to scream. Then he threw an orange into her operatic mouth and watched her explode. He was fearless.

Finally, he was in the master bedroom of the castle, a room of red satin. Candles flickered in every corner. His eyes darted to the shadows. Then a rustle. From the bed. What he saw made him lose his breath. She was draped across the four-poster bed. She said his name, Louis, and it sounded like a pleasant summer breeze. Her hair was a black waterfall cascading down her shoulders; her eyes, her beautiful green eyes, like emeralds.

When she spoke, Louis shivered.

"Hi, Louis," she said. "Why don't you get a little closer?"

PAP Choice #23: Get closer or slowly back out of the room?

Louis edged closer to the bed.

She sat up and patted the spot next to her. "Sit," she said. "You must be tired."

Louis was tired. Beating up monsters was hard work. He sidled up next to her, staring at his hands or the lint on the carpet.

"You are so brave, Louis," she said. "You are capable of so many things."

Louis felt a funny feeling in him. In his chest, his stomach.

PAP Choice #24: Touch her hand or jump off the bed and stab her in the heart with the wooden stake in your back pocket?

He touched her hand. It was cold. The cold made him squeeze it harder, trying to warm it up. The woman smiled, her mouth closed, a red spreading through her cheeks. She looked at Louis, and this time Louis didn't look away. He cupped her face and smelled her breath, roses and chocolate. Then he kissed her. Lightly. The woman pulled away and smiled, and Louis noticed her fangs. She was a vampire, he knew, and she knew he knew.

"Is this a problem?" she said.

PAP Choice #25: Not a problem or run like hell, Louis.

Louis shook his head, her kiss still on his lips.

"Good," she said. She moved closer to him, towards his neck. He knew what she was going to do. He allowed it. Her bite wasn't painful. It felt like emerging for the first time out a small room full of dust and breathing clean air. It felt like change. Louis held on harder to the back of her head, her silky hair, until his fingers lost their strength. His vision blurred into a swirl of colors.

Then a voice. Not hers. Someone familiar. "Would you like to live forever?"

PAP Choice #26: Immortality or death?

"Immortality," Louis whispered. He felt drops of something on his lips. He licked at it, and it tasted sweet, thick like syrup. He lapped for more, grabbed blindly, instinctively, for the open wrist and began sucking, changing.

When he was done, Louis' vision cleared and he saw the woman on the other side of the room smiling at him and he knew the voice, the voice of the man he drank from, the man who had led him to the castle. He pushed himself off the bed with a new energy. He looked at his pale hands. Felt his pale face. Smiled.

"Welcome," said the man, tipping his hat.

"To a better, better world," said the woman.

*

Big Dennis wasn't a bully. He was just big. He never harmed a soul. When the girls in English class freaked out about the bees buzzing around their hair-sprayed heads, Big Dennis gently caught the bees in his meaty hands and released them out the open window. For his knightly duty, Big Dennis never received a thank you, a smile, a look of acknowledgement from the girls. It was as if the bees simply disappeared, and the last few freak-out seconds never existed.

Often, when Louis walked to school, he'd find Big Dennis sitting against the fence, sleeping. He was prone to sleeping spells, drifting off to la-la land during lunches, classes, and always before school. Once, Louis watched with curiosity Big D snooze. Big D's chins quivered. Big D's big legs were splayed across the sidewalk. Big D whistled when he breathed out. Big D looked peaceful with his bottom lip drooping low; he seemed as if he was smiling. The other kids walked over him like a speed bump, but Louis stopped and watched. He wondered what Big D was dreaming of. A school of big kids? A dancing ice cream cone? Big Dennis appeared so much more content in sleep that Louis hated to wake him up. Softly, he kicked Big Dennis' feet and then walked off without a word.

Big Dennis bothered no one; no one bothered Big Dennis. Except Mr. Hinkel, who, for no good reason, detested Big D. Mr. Hinkel was a spaz. A comb over, pocket-protector spaz. When Big Dennis fell asleep in Biology, Mr. Hinkel screamed into Big Dennis' ear. "Wake up! Wake up, Dennis! This is not your bedroom. Does your bedroom have a dancing skeleton? Does it, Dennis?" Mr. Hinkel made the skeleton spaz like him, bones clunking together like hollow wind chimes. Big Dennis jolted awake, looked at his open textbook, hid his face with his hands.

The day Louis chose Big Dennis to be his first victim, Big

D nodded off in Biology again. Louis wished he could kick Big Dennis awake, but he was across the room. Big Dennis started snoring, a gusty breath in 5.8-second intervals. Mr. Hinkel tried to ignore it, speaking about plants and what gave them color. When he lectured, his hands spazzed around, illustrating how the plant leaned toward the light like this—arms moving and leaning—and the light is what makes chlorophyll work. As he continued, however, as Big Dennis snored, Mr. Hinkel began to get color in his cheeks. At one point, Louis thought red was going to come out of his ears.

"I can't believe it," said Mr. Hinkel finally.

Big Dennis went one snore too far.

"I can't believe he's asleep again." He paced from one end of the room to the other. He gazed at the class. Some were barely awake themselves, others unfazed. "If there is one thing I will have taught you this semester, let it be this. Take note. Do not become like him." He pointed at Big Dennis, his finger like a knife. "He is the best example of a body gone wrong. A boy gone wrong. No self-control. Not one ounce. Just look at him. Fat everywhere. The body cannot take that much fat. Just look at him. Look at him real good because you are looking at death. Death. He will die in two years. Perish. Be no more!"

Louis wanted to bite Mr. Hinkel. Not in the good vampire way, but in that ruthless, murderous way. A few of the students started laughing. Louis wanted to bite them too. Some mocked the way Big Dennis snored. He wanted to bite them too. And through this, Big Dennis was oblivious. The picture of contentment, a smile on his sleeping face. Somewhere in Big D's dream, Louis hoped he was getting his revenge on them all. Something gruesome. And when Mr. Hinkel calmed down and began lecturing again, Louis decided Big Dennis would be the first person he'd bite for three simple reasons.

1. Let's face it, Big Dennis was *BIG*. Twelve Louis-es. Louis could run away if Big Dennis didn't go down. If Big Dennis came out swinging, if he didn't realize what Louis was doing was helpful, Louis could zoom out of there without risking serious injury.

2. Louis wanted his first victim to be someone of mammoth proportions. Someone that mattered, someone people couldn't forget, couldn't ignore. The strange thing was people did ignore Big D, like they ignored Louis. Perhaps the two of them together, the sight of Louis on Big Dennis' neck, would somehow jolt them out of invisibility.

3. He wanted to help Big Dennis. This reason mattered more than the two above. Perhaps Louis would be able to drink death away. Give Big Dennis immortality. Prove Mr. Hinkel wrong. Big Dennis wouldn't die in two years, not in five, not in ten or ten thousand. Big Dennis would live forever. This was his gift, a taste of a better world.

*

The Bite happened at 12:28 pm in a playground in Hyde Park on April 22, 1994. It was a Friday. A nice reasonable day. It had rained the night before, and there were puddles left on the black top. Some of the boys shot hoops. The girls gathered in a corner and gossiped and pointed at the boys shooting hoops. A few swung on swings. Louis leaned against the monkey bars, watching Big Dennis mill around from one bench to another.

Louis had been contemplating for over a month when to bite Big Dennis. He waited for the perfect moment. Any time before 12:28, Louis wasn't capable. But at 12:28, as Big Dennis headed for the bench nearest the playground horses, Louis became capable.

Louis took off. Straight toward Big Dennis, who didn't seem to care or notice that a skeletal, bookworm Asian was darting right at him. And when he did notice, Louis was in the air, and Big Dennis opened his eyes and saw teeth coming straight for his neck. Big Dennis waved his hands, but it did no good. Louis Wangchakorn had a mouthful of him, and Big Dennis began—oddly enough—to fall asleep right there and then. Louis bit hard enough to break skin. He sucked hard enough to get a little taste of blood. It wasn't what he expected, not like how *PAP 117* described it. It tasted like the one time he put his tongue on a frozen rain gutter to see if it would stick and it did. Big Dennis' blood tasted like that, which wasn't too bad, except he expected syrup. Sweet divine syrup.

And through all this, Louis thought about lightning bugs, beautiful lightning bugs. He imagined them rising all around him and Big Dennis, mini spotlights on this momentous occasion. And he thought of all the people he wanted to bite—his mother, Mr. Hinkel, all the kids that mocked and laughed at Big Dennis. He held on. He didn't let go.

Big Dennis started his descent. He stumbled back and forth, until one knee went down, then another. He tottered and swayed. Then went still. He looked as if he was asking God why there was an Asian kid attached to his neck. Finally, Big Dennis collapsed, belly first, Louis following.

Once down, Louis leapt off Big D, wiped his mouth, and ran. He didn't notice the kids standing around Big Dennis. He didn't notice the piece of Big Dennis' skin in between his teeth. Louis didn't notice anything. He ran straight out of the playground, across Halsted, across Laurence, between parked cars on the curb, running toward nowhere, but he had gotten somewhere that day, that special place in his mind that began roaring with song, roaring with voices, roaring with the one thing Louis had been wanting to say since *PAP 117*, since he decided to become a vampire: "I did it! I did it! I did it!"

ENDING NUMBER ONE

Nothing changed.

Big Dennis continued to be Big Dennis. Louis continued to be Louis. They did not become the people they wanted to become because the world is cruel that way. The world gives you these paths and all of them lead nowhere. Especially for people like Big Dennis and Louis Wangchakorn. It is a sadness we know too well, but not a sadness they know. To them, this is their life. To them, sadness is how they live day-to-day. Sadness is a label they do not comprehend, but they feel it. Big Dennis feels it every time he wakes from an unplanned slumber. Louis feels it when he finishes another book.

And so Big Dennis became what Big Dennis-es become and Louis became what Louis-es become. And they went about their lives without thought of each other or The Bite those many years ago that joined them briefly.

Except that one time.

They saw each other. Big Dennis was still big. Louis was still small. Age had grayed them. Age made them slouch. They walked on a city sidewalk, each thinking the same thought.

Big Dennis: *I want to change.*

Louis: *I want to change.*

The two of them thought about transformation, thought it was not too late to be someone, thought tomorrow would be the beginning of another life. A better life. And then they passed each other, accidently grazing shoulders. "Sorry," they said at the same time, without stopping, without turning a head. They kept their eyes aimed ahead of them, at the gray evening blossoming before them, with a hope that would expire when night came.

ENDING NUMBER TWO

In years to come, The Bite became a Chicago playground legend. *Let me tell you about a skinny kid who wanted to be a vampire,* they would say, *and the fatty he chose as his first victim.* The story ended the same way it had concluded—Big Dennis on the ground and Louis running.

What happened next? Louis came to school the following day a different Louis, a confident, no-nonsense Louis. He faced the music and was suspended for a week, a week he spent reading *Pick a Path Adventures.* When kids called him a biter, he clicked his teeth and barked. Crazy, they said, they didn't want any part of crazy. Big Dennis said he didn't remember The Bite. When he woke up, he said he dreamt of monkeys and lions and anteaters and even lightning bugs. It was a strange dream, he said, but exhilarating. A week after The Bite, Big Dennis still had a pinecone-sized hickey on his neck.

Almost instantly, Big Dennis began to lose the nickname Big Dennis. He didn't die in two years or in five. He didn't fall asleep in front of school or during classes anymore. It was as if Louis had, in fact, sucked death out of him, as if this bite saved Big Dennis. He lost ten and a half Louis-es in two years and became Dennis. Dennis the semi-popular. Dennis the grocery store worker. And eventually, Dennis the PhD. Louis, on the other hand, continued to pursue his career as a vampire. He took to wearing sunglasses throughout the day and a long black trench coat. His skin became pale—so pale you could see thin veins on his face—and he never showed his teeth. He met others like him, and at midnight they traveled the Chicago streets on rollerblades. Beyond this, we don't know what happened to Louis.

In their junior year of high school, on April 22 four years after The Bite, Louis stopped at a grocery store to buy birthday candles for his mother. Dennis worked the register at Cub Foods, and Louis was in his line. They knew each other immediately. Dennis scanned the packs and packs of candles, never taking his eyes off Louis, who looked back at Dennis behind his sunglasses.

"Louis, right?" Dennis said.

"Yeah," Louis said.

"I'm Dennis," Dennis said.

"I know," said Louis.

"I know you know," said Dennis.

"Right," said Louis.

"Well," said Dennis.

"Yeah," said Louis.

"Thanks," said Dennis.

"Thanks," said Louis.

Dennis handed Louis the candles and change. Louis grabbed them and turned to leave, his trench coat trailing behind him in a strange wind. At the exit, Louis turned once more and smiled, baring his teeth, and if you looked at him just right, you would have seen something sparkling at the corners of his mouth.

2

The only real stumbling block is fear of failure. In cooking you've got to have a what-the-hell attitude.

–Julia Child

Forecast

When I get back from work, my little brother Pauly runs out the front door and tells me our mom is crying. He pulls at my blouse and tugs me to the door. His cheeks are red from the cold. He looks like someone trying not to cry, trying to be older like his sister.

"Pauly," I say, "What's wrong?"

"I told you," he says. "Mom's crying."

"Why?"

He tugs harder, but I stop and turn him around.

"Why is mom crying?"

He chews at his cheek. He does this until it starts bleeding.

"Stop that," I say. "Look at me. Why is Mom crying?"

"Because she's sad," he says.

"I know, buddy, but why is she sad?"

"Because Dad left and Dad is a fuck-wit and Dad is sleeping with a slutty hoe."

"Did Mom say those things?"

He nods.

I shake my head. "You shouldn't say those words again, OK? Those are bad words. Remember when we talked about good and bad words. Fuck-wit and slutty hoe are bad words. You won't say them again, right?"

Pauly nods.

I move to open the door, but I can hear my mom's wails on the other side. She's always freaking out in front of Pauly, who is sensitive, who is standing at my side, with the tail end of my shirt bunched up in his fist. He seems to be staring through the wooden door, staring so intently I think he believes if he

24

concentrates hard enough, he'll be able to transport his nine-year-old will onto our mom and make her stop crying, make her smile and take care of us.

I take his hand and walk the other way, toward the station wagon.

"Are you hungry?" I ask. "Do you want an egg roll?"

"Can we get one for Mom, too?"

"Sure." I put him in the car and he buckles himself in, immediately playing with the radio dials before I even start the engine.

Pauly's eight years younger than me. There's something wrong with him. He's not too bright, but he's not stupid either, not like what the kids call him at school: Palsy Pauly. I tried to make them stop once when I picked him up and he got it even worse, got it for having his big sister fight his battles. Still, he's inquisitive beyond his years. My high school English teacher says a kid who asks a lot of questions is a kid who wants to figure out the world. If that's the case, Pauly is already uncovering secrets we don't know about.

"Why is everything dark?" Pauly asks.

I point to the car clock. "It's getting late in the day."

"But remember when it was sunny 'til nine? Remember when we swam at the lake when the sun was out and it was nine?"

I nod and make the turn into Wan's Asian Cuisine.

"Now it's always dark," Pauly says.

I want to tell him it has something to do with the sun and the earth's tilt and rotation. I want to tell him that a place in the southern hemisphere, a place in South America, is getting our summer light right now and in a few months it will be our turn again. But how do you explain astronomy and stars?

"It won't be dark for long, buddy. Just a couple months more."

Pauly looks down at his fingers. "When the sun comes back, can we go swimming again?"

"Sure," I say, patting his head. "Let's get some food."

I've worked at Wan's since they opened. It's the only Asian place in this town, the only Asian place in twenty miles. There's little call for ethnic cuisine at the very tiptop of New York. The Wans aren't really the Wans but the Somchais, a Thai family who emigrated here ten years ago. The restaurant name means "sweet" in Thai, but most people mispronounce it, saying "wane" instead. They opened the restaurant their third year in the country, and at first, they cooked up what people thought was weird. They had to change the way they prepared their food. Put a few American appetizers on the menu like chicken wings and fries and mozzarella sticks. Deep-fry more than half the menu. Cut down on vegetables. Cut down on the stuff of their native country. They hate to do it—I sometimes see Mrs. Somchai shake her head at the sweet and sour chicken she just got out of the fryer—but they have to keep afloat.

"Back again," Mr. Somchai says. His hair is white with a few streaks of black. He smiles and waves. "Hello, Pauly."

"*Sawasdee*, Mr. Somchai," says Pauly. He puts his hands together and bows his blonde head in the traditional Thai greeting that Mr. Somchai taught him months ago. For a while, he went around bowing his head at everything—the tree, the rose bush, the creek down the street.

"We were wondering if we can stay here a bit," I say. "Can we bother you for something to eat?"

"Bother?" says Mr. Somchai. "Me and Mrs. will cook real Thai food if Pauly can help."

Pauly looks at me eagerly, his eyes wide, his lips in a pleading smile.

"Will you be good, Pauly?"

He nods.

"Do whatever Mr. Somchai tells you, OK?"

He nods again. Mr. Somchai takes his hand and they go into the kitchen.

There is a table of customers in the back of the restaurant, a couple. Ron, the Somchais' son, waits on them. He's back briefly for winter break from a college in Pennsylvania. I've missed working with him. We often played silly games: switching orders on each other, stealing each other's tips and replacing it with a penny. When we closed up at ten, he and I stayed in the parking lot and talked until midnight. There's nothing he doesn't know about me. On his last day before heading off to college, he kissed me. It wasn't a romantic movie kiss, but it was long enough to make me breathless for just a moment, enough to make me think of him the three months he's been gone. Since he's been back he hasn't mentioned anything about the kiss. Mrs. Somchai told me he has a girlfriend at college, a nice Thai girl.

Ron carries half-eaten dishes in his hand and dumps them into a cart of other dirty dishes. When he sees me, he smiles. "Don't you have a home, Lily?"

"Not right now," I tell him. "I like it here better."

"Right," he says. He goes back to the customers, water pitcher in hand. I stare at his back, through his white button down, then down to the frayed edges of his jeans. His hair is growing out. I can almost tie it into a ponytail. I've already heard Mr. Somchai complain about the length of his son's hair and how it might dangle in the food.

The customers stand and leave. Ron tells them to come again, tells them it was an honor to serve them tonight. They wave, but say nothing.

"You're such a brownnoser," I say.

"Yellownoser," he says. He flashes me the ten the customers left him.

I shake my head, rolling up my sleeves and clearing off the rest of the dishes.

"You're not getting paid for this," he says, wiping the table clean.

"It's called helping," I say.

"You're doing a better job now than when you were clocked in."

"Shut up."

When we finish up, we sit at an empty table and look outside. A few people trickle into the bar next door. It looks like it's going to snow.

"It's slow today," I say.

"No one wants to come out in the winter," he says. "Not that I can blame them. The weather's real shitty. Do you know we get the craziest weather here because the jet stream swoops up over where we are?"

"Mr. Science."

"I'm taking a meteorology class. It's cool. I didn't think it would be. It's one those dumb requirements I had finish off, but man, I really dig it. I—" he stops short, then shakes his head. "Forget it."

"What?"

"You're gonna think I'm a loser."

"Too late for that."

He softly punches me in the arm and I fake how much it didn't hurt. "No, seriously, tell me," I say.

"I want to be a meteorologist."

"Like on TV?"

"Sorta," he says.

"I've never seen a Thai weatherman before. Maybe you'll

do a better job than some of the people here. Tell us the correct weather for once."

"That's the thing," he says. "There's a science to weather. It's all numbers and equations, but sometimes nature does what it wants to do, and when that happens it's a guessing game."

Ron sits on the edge of his seat, eyes wide. There's a child-like excitement in his face, like when Pauly gets a scoop of peppermint ice cream from Buster's. I notice a patch of hair growing under his bottom lip. It's like a button I want to press.

"I hear you have a girlfriend," I say.

He stares at his shoes. "We're not serious."

"You don't have to say that for me."

"I'm not," he says.

I chew on my cheek. Ron stares at the red carpet. I hear Pauly squealing in the kitchen, squealing and clapping. I know my face is red. I fix my eyes on a wooden carving of an elephant. One of its tusks was missing so I replaced it with a toothpick. Ron said it was ingenious. He said I was pretty smart for a white girl.

Now he says nothing, and his mouth is tightly shut. It looks so small, his mouth. I have an urge to shove a peanut between his lips. I tell him so.

He bursts out laughing. "God, Lily, how do you come up with that?"

I shrug and laugh with him.

Pauly runs out of the kitchen, smiling. Ron picks him up and places him on his knee.

"You're getting big," Ron says. "I don't know if my knee can take it." He rocks Pauly dramatically up and down. Pauly laughs again, throwing his arms to the side, as if he was on a rollercoaster.

Then he looks at me and says, "I want to be a chef, Lily."

"Sounds good, buddy," I say.

"I really helped in there. I rolled up some egg rolls. I put some of the shrimp stuff on bread. I put sticks through chicken. I wasn't allowed to put stuff in the fryer though."

"You're still too little for that," I say.

"But I really helped," Pauly says again.

Ron ruffles his hair and says, "If you become a chef then you'll put my family out of business. Then we'd be poor and live in boxes."

"Why would you live in a box?"

"Because that's where poor people live," Ron says.

"Living in a box sounds fun," Pauly says.

"Nice," I say. "Now he'll want me to find a box so he can live in it."

Mr. Somchai comes through the kitchen door with a steaming platter of appetizers. "Pauly's Pu Pu Platter," he announces. He puts the plate on the table. Heat rises from the food. It smells wonderful, like what I imagine Thailand smells like. Then I notice the misshapen egg rolls, the lumps of shrimp on the toast, and chicken barely hanging on skewers. Pauly's creation. Mr. Somchai laughs. Ron laughs. I laugh. Pauly, who doesn't know why we are laughing, laughs. Each of us grabs an egg roll. I take a bite and close my eyes and start nodding like I've just been transported to Food Heaven. "This is the best, buddy. The best."

*

For three days, Mom locks herself up in her room and cries. For those three days, Pauly comes with me to work, where he plays sous chef for the Somchais. At night, he stays in my room and we blast the radio to cover up Mom's wails until we fall asleep. Sometimes Pauly asks why Mom's still crying, why she can't stop. Is she broken, he wants to know, like the CD player that skips all the time? He worries she'll drown in her room, her tears filling and filling the space. Maybe we should leave a floating tube outside her door. In gym class, he tells me, he has to wear floating tubes around his arms and it makes him rise to the surface of the water. There's nothing to worry about, I say, she won't drown. I tell Pauly that not everyone in the world is like our mom and dad. Look at the Somchais, for instance. They're happy, normal people. That's what we are. Happy and normal.

And then Mom stops crying and there's this strange silence in the house. We grew so accustomed to her sobs that when they finally stop there is an absence as if someone has kidnapped our mother and she hasn't stopped crying at all, but now is crying elsewhere.

I'm called in to work. Ron says he has to help his dad pick up a shipment of vegetables. He needs someone to cover for him during the lunch rush. I tell him OK, I'll be there. I try to make my voice sexy and deep and he asks if I'm sick. Since I'm not going to be gone long, I tell Pauly to stay home.

Lunch is the busiest time of the day. People come in from the strip mall across the street and from the bottling plant a few miles down the road. Most of the time it's the same customers who order the same meals, or senior citizens who want to take advantage of Wan's incredibly priced lunch specials. "In Thailand," Mr. Somchai says, "old people are revered. Not so much here. That's why we cook cheap for them. We cook good." I like that philosophy. I like all of Mr. Somchai's philosophies. I like the Somchais. They are everything I want from a family. Not like mine. Not the endlessly crying mother. Not the missing father. Sometimes I wish I were Thai. Sometimes I

31

wish my skin weren't so pale, my eyes weren't so blue, my legs weren't so long, my body weren't so thick. Sometimes I wish I can just live with them, or a family like them, and never return home.

On the rare occasion, someone Thai walks in, like this afternoon. Three Thais, in fact, looking as if they've wandered into a surreal world of Asian cuisine, their mouths slightly parted. They are a family, and the parents take in every detail of the restaurant—the Thai angels adorning the walls, the weird poster of a white baby holding chopsticks, the Buddha that presides over the door of the kitchen. The parents speak and whisper in Thai. I've been with the Somchais for a while now, and though I don't understand Thai, I know the sound of it. It's nothing like Japanese or Chinese. It's not harsh, but it isn't soothing either. To be honest, sometimes it sounds like whining, like Pauly wanting a toy from the grocery store he can't have.

The three of them look out of place, wearing classy clothing, classier than the flannel and jeans uniform of this town, especially the young girl who looks to be my age. She is pretty and small, her eyes big on her petite head. So big, I think she looks like a character in those Japanese cartoons. She wears a pink day dress that exposes the thinnest and tannest legs I've ever seen, so thin I think I can snap them. I have an urge to poke her thighs to see if they are able to do the duty of legs or crumple like a house of cards.

"Is it the three of you?" I say.

The girl smiles, a nice smile with big white teeth to go with her big wide eyes. "Is Ronnie here?"

"Ronnie?" It takes me a bit, Ronnie = Ron. It takes me a bit to realize this big teeth, big-eyed girl is Ronnie's girlfriend. It takes me a bit longer to comprehend what's stirring inside of me—a mixture of rage and sadness—because now I think this pretty girl needs one of her pretty white teeth knocked out.

"Excuse me," the girl says.

"I'm sorry," I say. "Ronnie is out at the moment. Ronnie will be back soon. Would you like to wait for Ronnie? Perhaps order food in preparation for Ronnie." I'm all smiles, too. Big crooked teeth in the big mouth I have.

"That would be wonderful," says the girl.

Her parents smile. They have big beautiful teeth.

The girl turns to her parents and speaks Thai and the parents speak back and the girl nods and says OK, OK in clear English. "I would like to inquire if Ronnie's parents are in?"

"Yes," I say. "Ronnie's mom is in the kitchen. Ronnie's dad is with Ronnie. But I'm sure they will return quickly."

"Wonderful," says the girl. "Can you please tell Ronnie's mom that Cecilia and her parents are here?"

"I can definitely tell Ronnie's mom that."

"Thank you so much," the girl says.

"You're welcome so much," I say.

I take them to a round table at the corner of the restaurant and give them menus to peruse. Before I go to the kitchen, I check in with the other customers, refilling drinks and bringing checks. I can't help it. I take sneak peeks at Cecilia and a little bit of me dies.

When I tell Mrs. Somchai about Cecilia and her parents she makes an O with her mouth and her eyes brows perk up. She hurries out in her hairnet and apron to say hello and other things I don't understand.

When Ron comes back, I say, "Ronnie, someone is here to see you."

"Ronnie?"

I point to the table at the corner.

"Ronnie," Cecilia says and rushes to him. She hugs him so tight his eyes bug. Or his eyes were bugged already. Or his eyes were in the process of being bugged. "I've missed you. Have you missed me?"

"Ronnie, have you missed her?" I say.

"Yeah," he says, and Cecilia pulls him towards the table.

Mrs. Somchai comes and goes from the kitchen. She finishes cooking the lunch rush, and starts working on other dishes for Cecilia and her family. She talks to herself when she cooks. She's frantic, more frantic than usual. I ask her if she needs help, and she says, "No thank you, Lily. Can you check if they want anything other than water?"

I do. And they don't.

Mrs. Somchai brings out appetizers and salads, items not on the menu. The round table fills with food. It smells like cilantro and citrus.

The four parents look already like best friends—the way they laugh, the way they move. Mr. Somchai's voice is loud and full of pride. When he talks it's a mix of Thai and English, like "blah blah blah blah delicious blah blah blah so very good." Cecilia is attached to Ron's arm, smug with her big white teeth, and Ron looks like he sees a herd of elephants rushing towards him. Or a herd of me.

When there are no more customers, Mr. Somchai calls me over. "Ron and Lily are like brother and sister. She is family."

Cecilia smiles. She does not blink. It freaks me out.

"She looks very nice," the father says.

"Very pretty," says the mother.

"I really like your T-shirt, Lily," Cecilia says.

I look at myself. I don't know what I'm wearing. It's nothing special. A band I semi-like with a sauce stain on my right boob. "Thank you very much."

"You're welcome very much," Cecilia says.

"And her brother Pauly," says Mr. Somchai. "Very cute boy."

"How old?" the mother asks.

"Ten," I say. "He wants to be a chef, like Mr. Somchai."

The parents laugh and speak in Thai, and Cecilia says something to Ron in Thai and Ron shakes his head and sips his water. I look at him, and he seems to cower from my gaze.

"Sit," Mrs. Somchai says from behind me, bringing out a fried whole fish with sweet red curry and a silver tub of white jasmine rice. "Eat with us," she says.

I shake my head. "Pauly's at home."

"The weather," Ron says. His voice cracks. "The weather. The weather is not good. Or not going to be good. Or it's going to bad. Low-pressure system. A blizzard. The whole east side. And it's stuck because of another low-pressure system. The roads aren't ready for it, but it's coming. The radar looks bad."

"Ronnie, my little weatherman," says Cecilia and kisses his cheek.

"Ronnie, he loves weather," I say.

"The weather," Ron says.

"I have to go then," I say.

"The weather," Ron says again.

*

When I enter the house again, Mom is crying and Dad's clothes are scattered in large mounds. She color-coordinated the mounds. A green mound lies by the front door. Black in the kitchen. Red and blues in the living room. I don't see Pauly anywhere. I call out to him, but no one answers. I call out again. A mound of whites trembles. Amidst Dad's T-shirts and button downs is Pauly. A pair of briefs dangles off his left ear. Socks and others white articles of clothing are topped heavily on his head. His hands cup his ears. I crouch on my knees and gently move his hands away, but he jolts them back up and shakes his head.

"It's OK, buddy."

"No it isn't."

"I'm sorry," I say. "I'm sorry I left you. I won't do it again, OK?"

I offer him my hand and he looks at it. I tell him we're going on a trip. "Do you want to go on a trip?" I say. He nods, his hands still over his ears. I tell him to go in the car, I'll be there in a second. He does.

I pack a suitcase with some clothes. I don't choose, but grab handfuls and cram them in the suitcase. I go to Pauly's room and do the same. I throw in a few of Pauly's favorite action figures and comics.

When I'm done, I stand outside Mom's door. I want to kick it down. I want to shake her until she sees what she has done to Pauly. I want to tell her she can't do that to a nine-year-old. You can't just stop being his mother. You can't cry all day and leave me to clean up after you.

I can't say these things. I run my hand over the door.

In the car, Pauly still has his hands over his ears.

"You can put your hands down now," I say.

He shakes his head. "I can still hear her."

"Buddy, please, take your hands down."

He shakes his head.

"God dammit," I say, "take your hands off your ears."

He does. "You said bad words." His mouth is shaped like an O.

"I know, buddy," I say. "I'm sorry." I grab the wheel hard.

I don't want to cry. I can't. Not in front of Pauly.

I wipe at my face and start the car. I head over to Wan's, though I don't want to go. I don't want to see the Somchais and Cecilia and Ronnie, but I need to tell them I can't work today. I need to tell them I won't be able to work for a while. Outside the restaurant, Ron throws salt on the ground by the entrance. The sun is out for once. He waves when we pull in. I don't get out of the car, but roll down the window.

"I can't come to work today," I say. "Can you tell your mom and dad? Can you tell them I won't be able to work tomorrow either?"

"Sure," he says.

I don't look at him.

Pauly says, "We're going on a trip."

I can feel Ron's stare.

"Where?" says Ron.

"Where?" Pauly asks me.

I shrug.

"The weather," he says.

"Girlfriend gone?" I say.

He shrugs.

"She has nice teeth."

He shrugs.

"I know why she likes you."

He looks at me.

"You're like an anchor. She'll blow away on those legs of hers."

He smiles. "They are staying at a hotel down the street."

"Is it hard to see sometimes with teeth that bright?"

He shakes his head. "Be nice."

Pauly says, "My mom is crying again."

"I'm sorry to hear that," Ron says more to me than to Pauly. I know he sees the suitcase in the back of the car. "It's not safe to travel today. The weather."

I shrug.

"Listen," says Ron. "Let's get a freeze." He ruffles Pauly's hair. "You want a freeze?"

"Can we, Lily?" says Pauly.

"Can we?" says Ron.

I shake my head. I can't say no.

Ron goes back inside to tell his parents he'll be right back. He hops in the back seat and I pull out of Wan's and head for the convenient store a mile away.

We drive in silence, but I keep looking at Ron in the rearview mirror. Ron looks at me, too. And I think he's trying to tell me something with his eyes but I don't read eyes. I don't understand eyes.

Pauly asks, "What is a cunt?"

Ron snorts into his hand.

"When did you hear that word?" I say.

"Mom kept saying it over and over."

I look in the rearview mirror and Ron shrugs.

"Can you tell him what a...?" I try to say the C-word to his reflection.

"Out of my territory," he says.

"Out of mine, too."

"What is a cunt?" says Pauly again.

"Don't say that anymore," I say.

"Is it a bad word?"

"Don't say it anymore."

"Pauly," Ron says, "Did you know snow and rain are the same?"

Pauly's eyes widen. He loves information. I love that he loves information. I want him to keep on loving information. I want so many things for him. I want him to have a better life, so he can find someone like Cecelia, someone with big bright teeth and skinny legs, even though people like Cecelia take things from you. Even though people like Cecelia make people happy. I want someone to make him happy.

Here, he's not happy. Here, happiness fades.

When we pull into the convenient store, I tell Pauly to stay in the car.

Ron and I get out.

"Do me a favor," I whisper.

"OK," he says.

"Buy me a nude magazine."

"What?"

"Just buy me a nude magazine."

"Why?"

"Please."

"Which one?"

"Doesn't matter."

"Anything else?"

"A root beer freeze. Mix it with some orange and strawberry, too. It's Pauly's favorite."

Ron moves like he wants to hug me, but he places a hand on my shoulder and says, "What size freeze?"

"The biggest one."

He nods and enters the store. I go back in the car.

"Is he getting me a freeze?" Pauly says.

"Listen, Pauly," I say, "where do you want to go?"

He thinks hard, putting his hand on his chin. "I want to go to the beach so I can swim."

"OK," I say, "we'll go to a beach."

"For real?"

"For real."

"What about Mom?" Pauly says. "Will Mom come with us?"

"Not this time," I say.

"But maybe swimming will make her happy."

"I don't think so."

"Beaches make people happy."

"Sometimes."

"And Mom can be at the beach and we can swim and she can stop crying."

"That's a good thought," I say. "You're so smart."

When Ron gets in the back seat, he hands Pauly the freeze and puts a flat paper bag next to him. "I better get back," he says. "Cecelia and her parents are coming over again."

"Is this a marriage meeting?"

"No," Ron says too quickly.

"Are you going to be Mr. Cecelia?"

He ignores me and aims his eyes at the sky.

I pull the car out of the lot and drive the few blocks to Wan's, Pauly slurping his freeze.

"You can live with my family," Ron says. "Until it's better to travel in. I'm serious. The roads are going to be bad." He points out the window, at the clouds darkening from the north.

"Can we?" says Pauly.

"Can you?" says Ron.

"Thank you," I say. "We need to go as soon as we can."

Ron gets out and says think about it. He tells me his mom and dad loves us and wouldn't mind taking us in.

"Thank you," I say again. "Tell them thank you for everything."

Ron leans into the window and kisses my cheek. His lips hover over my face for a bit before he turns to go.

I don't pull out of the parking lot. I sit in the car, trying to feel the warmth of his lips a bit longer.

"Brain freeze," Pauly says. He grabs the side of his head.

"Slow down," I say.

"It hurts," he says and laughs.

"You still want to know what a cunt is?" I say absently.

Pauly nods.

I take the magazine from the bag, *Asian Beauties*. I blink and blink. Pauly blinks and blinks. I almost laugh and cry all at once.

For the next hour, I teach Pauly the things he wants to learn, passing the freeze back and forth in the parking lot of Wan's. When the sun disappears, I turn on the interior light. A few customers go in and out of the restaurant; none take notice of two kids flipping through a nude magazine. I point at a cunt and say that's a cunt. Pauly points to a picture of a man's penis, and asks if his pee-pee will get that big. I tell him that someday real soon his will grow, don't worry. I answer all my little brother's questions. Even the ones I don't know the answers to. Even the ones about our mom and dad and whether the two-page spread in front of us is the thing that's making our mom cry, this spongy-looking UFO Pauly says it looks like. And I take a long hard swig of the freeze, my head, my brain, so cold, and I keep drinking, sucking all I can from the straw before I tell my little brother that this UFO has carried our parents so far away, through millions of time zones and planets and stars and that when they come back they won't recognize us, and we won't recognize them.

Ordinary World

Her name is April Sherwood. She looks like a maiden in a far off world where there would be an actual Sherwood Forest. There is something medieval and rustic about her: pink cheeks, a little mouth she keeps red and moist, and breasts that would look magnificent in a corset. When she talks, it's a pleasant breeze in the ear, and you have to lean in a bit to catch every tickling word.

I have seventh period creative writing with April. I sit behind her because my last name is Sulawong, the only Asian boy in the entire school. Mr. Pittman arranges us in rows in alphabetical order. During class, I lose myself in the tangles of April's hair. I imagine us together in a place that isn't the Southside of Chicago in the middle of winter, not in high school where they sell crappy corn dogs and stale pretzels. No, in April's hair, we are someplace warm, exotic, a faraway island like the one we read about the other day. *Robinson Crusoe*. Stranded, the two of us, wearing only leaves like Adam and Eve, we cuddle close at night by a booming fire I made with coconut rind. Often, during my reveries, I catch myself gently stroking the curly strands of her hair, hoping she won't notice.

Jaime "Fists" Moony sits in the row next to me. She's as pretty as April, but blonde and has recently acquired her good looks. I remember when she had metal in her mouth, when her hair was in the shape of a bowl like grade school boys. Once, she got in a fight and knocked Rob Scapperdeen's two front teeth out. I've been calling her Fists ever since.

Today, Fists quickly slides a note over with her foot, while Mr. Pittman explains how all good fiction must have memora-

42

ble characters like Darcy in *Pride and Prejudice* and Ahab in *Moby Dick*. I drop a pen to pick up the note.

You're kinda weird, Fists writes. *It's creepy when you touch her hair like that.*

Jealous, are we? Is it your hair you wish I were stroking?

Freak. Have you started your story yet?

Can pigs fly?

Seriously. What are you going to write about?

Everything and nothing.

FUCK YOU.

Doesn't April look tastalicious today?

I don't swing that way, Fists writes.

And here I thought my best friend is a lesbian. That would've been so hot.

Are you in love, Thai Boy?

I am in love with the idea of being in love.

Fists hates bullshit. *That's the dumbest thing I've ever heard. Write me when you're not being stupid.*

But she doesn't understand. I *am* in love. I *am* in love with idea of being in love. Oh, April, how I want to say the things lodged in my throat. How I want to write verse after verse about the nature of my yearning. How I want my poetry to seethe with melodrama. How I want it to resemble my beating heart.

Mr. Pittman writes on the chalk board in big letters: CLICHÉ.

*

My mother is at the sewing machine. She's been sewing every day for six months, every day since my father disappeared. She has sewn pillowcases, nurses' uniforms, fancy Thai dresses that she will never wear. She has sewn the dishtowel we hang on the refrigerator door handle, the cover to put over our tissue box, a cooking apron for my aunt across town. Now she works on a vest for me—the fifth one this week. I don't ask for them.

I stand next to her and look out the bay windows. April Sherwood is a fence hop away. I see her brown shingle roof and part of what I imagine is her bedroom window. *But soft! What light through yonder window breaks?* We read *Romeo and Juliet* a couple of weeks ago. Mr. Pittman asked me to read Romeo's part out loud and April to be Juliet, and for that moment we were in love, despite the dangers that lay ahead of us. I bought Mr. Pittman a doughnut the next day, but didn't tell him why.

April lives on Meade by the McDonalds. I have been forgoing home cooked meals to eat a Big Mac and walk past her house, hoping to catch a glimpse of—of what? April combing that luscious hair? April in only a bathrobe? April looking out the window waiting for me? Maybe she will sing like the sirens in *Odysseus*. Maybe she will have an epiphany like when Jane Eyre impossibly hears the voice of Mr. Rochester calling for her.

My mother's sewing machine jags through red and pink fabric. She looks down her nose and through her glasses perched at the tip. I don't think my mother is happy. I don't know how to ask her if she is. She sighs a lot and drifts off often, her hand cupped under her chin. She stares out the window, as if out there, among the suburban houses, the tire swings and kids peddling their bikes in endless loops, she will find her happiness. We are alike in this way, looking in the wrong places, denying what really needs to be said.

She works with precision, works intensely to get the pink and red vest done.

"That looks cool," I say.

"Yes," my mother says, her eyes fixed on the chalk lines

she's drawn on the fabric. "Most beautiful color."

"I'm going to go upstairs," I say. "To read."

"Read all the time. You stay here little longer?" There is need in her voice. I know it well. It was the same one I used when my father first left, and all I could muster was to ask, "Why?" over and over again, as if I was the one who chased him away, as if I was to blame for all my family's sorrow. I still feel like that, like I am the cause of something that was inevitable, but if I dwell on it too long I begin to suffocate. It's like what Mr. Pittman says about good stories: No matter what a character does, we often find him in a dark room searching for a light. What Fists would say during these moments: *Pick up the pieces of your shattered life and move on.*

"I'll stay," I say. "If you want."

"Yes," she says, but continues to work.

I plant myself on the couch. We don't say anything, and I think about April Sherwood. I think about a Big Mac. I think about how both would be good right now.

A half hour passes and my mother pulls the vest out of the machine. "Done," she says.

"Wow. Better than the last one."

"You wear tomorrow?"

"Sure."

I take the vest upstairs and throw it on the pile of other vests.

*

Mr. Pittman is the cool professor, an ex-60s hippy, who has a poster of a scantily clad Heather Locklear covered up by a poster that reads READING OPEN DOORS TO THE IMAGINATION. During my lunch hour, I spend my time with Mr.

Pittman, telling him about all my teenage woes. We often sit with a waste basket between us, sharing an orange. Other than Fists, Mr. Pittman is the only person who knows most of my secrets. Mr. Pittman knows about my dreams of being lost in some jungle in South America, shouting my father's name, but he never saves me. I tell him since my father left it's been quiet in the house. My mother rarely leaves the sewing machine, and I'm afraid her muscles will stiffen and she won't be able to get up ever again. I don't tell him about April Sherwood.

Today, Mr. Pittman is trying to convince me to be a writer. He says I have talent, my assignments fresh and original. He says I remind him of himself when he was younger—the brooding artist type. He says he even had hair like me—shaggy and unkempt. "Can you believe I had hair?" He points to his balding head.

The truth, which I won't admit to him, is I'm not a writer. I only took his class because I liked him as a teacher. My mother is expecting me to be a doctor or lawyer, not a writer. I love to read though, and I've been devouring books late into the night, reading everything Mr. Pittman has assigned and then some. Reading keeps me focused, keeps my mind centered, so it doesn't stray into places I don't want it to.

"You ready to workshop that story today?" he says.

"It's not that good," I say. "I rushed it." The truth: I've worked on it night and day, despite what I wrote to Fists. It's a simple story. Nothing too fancy. No UFOs or vampires. No deaths or fatal automobile collisions. It's my life on the page.

"What's it about?" Mr. Pittman says. He starts peeling an orange and offers me a sliver. I pop it in my mouth and swallow quickly. When he chews, it is long and languid, as if he is mulling over some deep philosophical theory.

"Nothing too grand. Ordinary things, I guess."

"Some of the best pieces of literature came from ordinary life."

"This isn't literature. This is crap. Plus, the story about the bug was far from ordinary."

"*The Metamorphosis?*" Mr. Pittman drops a peel into the garbage. "That was about a man whose ordinary life as a salesman transformed him into a bug. It was, in a way, Kafka's criticism of the ordinary working life. A peon of society. A slave to the unappreciative higher class."

"Dude, he was a bug."

"It's not the literal Kafka is presenting to us. It's what the literal represents. And that representation is ordinary. That in itself is the criticism." Mr. Pittman is getting more and more excited. More and more deep. Fists and I call these moments "Getting Pitted." I try to stick with him, fascinated by how his mind works. I've often wondered why he wasn't teaching in Harvard and wearing a tweed sports coat with leather patches. The orange is still in his hand, and his wrist is cocked like he's about to deliver a fastball. I am worried that it will slip out and strike me on the nose. "*The Old Man and the Sea* wasn't about catching the fish. It was about disappointment. A good writer, you see, finds something in the world no one else does. And it is the ordinary world he explores. It is most often the world we live in. And this ordinary world is filled with disappointment, dissatisfaction, hate, shit, heartbreak, and everything else. Take a step back. Look at all the drama around our ordinary lives. And what are we really? I'm a high school teacher. You're a teenager, and between the both of us, we have problems up our asses."

"Amen," I say and smile.

Mr. Pittman catches himself. He realizes it probably isn't OK to say 'shit' and 'asses' to a high school student, even though that student uses these words numerous times daily.

Still, he turns a shade of red—from embarrassment, from adrenaline—and notices the orange is flat in his hand and his arm is wet with juice. "Well, you get my point, right?"

"It's still crap."

"You see," Mr. Pittman says, dropping the deflated orange in the garbage. "You already sound like a writer."

*

Later in the day, red soda splatters all over me in Biology. Our teacher, Ms. Sulek, was trying to explain the intricate superhighway of veins and arteries via clear rubber hoses and carbonated red soda. "The heart controls everything," she says. "The veins you hold in your hands all go to the heart." My heart exploded. Blood everywhere.

The school secretary tells me I can call home to get new clothes. Because the high school is practically my backyard, my mother walks over and brings a change of outfits. Her pink and red vest, a white t-shirt, and black jeans. She smiles when she hands it to me. I want to tell her to go back and get the Abercrombie and Fitch sweater. I want to say I will be the laughingstock in the high school because no one wears pink unless you want to get beat up. But the sight of my mother out of the house, the sight of her smiling, makes me take the clothes.

I change quickly. I look at myself in the bathroom mirror, surprised at how well the vest fits, how my mother knew where to cinch the sides to accentuate my waist, how the slight vertical strips make me look taller, how the buttons are like polished river stones.

My mother waits, so she can take my stained clothes. I hand them to her, and before she leaves for home, I tell her thank you.

"You look like superstar," she says.

"I feel like one," I say.

*

In creative writing, Fists passes me a note. She's unusually bouncy today, and for a second, I thought she was actually acting like a girl. I've been seeing her talk to the cool jock outside her locker. I don't know his name, but I imagine it to be something like Todd or Brandon or maybe a two-parter like Jay-dog. Mr. Pittman would say that people like Jay-dog make horrific characters because they lack unique characteristics. You can't do much with them. They exist only to suffocate American fiction.

Nice vest, Fists writes. *HA HA HA.*

You take extra estrogen today? I haven't seen shameless boob flirting since that god awful Spice Girls video.

She writes a big *W* in reply. It means whatever. *At least I got the balls to flirt. What do you do but creepily touch April's hair? By the way, that's kinda serial killer like.*

Shut up.

Thai boy, do something about it. I heard from a friend of a friend she thinks you're cute.

I didn't know you had other friends besides me.

Ask her out.

Screw you.

Trust me.

I turn to look at Fists, and she makes her eyes wider and mouths *do it*, in the way that makes me see the old Fists, the one that knocked Robert Scaperdeen's teeth out, the one who I'm sure could take me down in one swift swing.

I shrug. Maybe Fists is right. Maybe April does like me. We can be like all great literary couples: Jane and Mr. Rochester, Emma and Mr. Knightly, Tess and Angel.

Mr. Pittman breaks us up into small groups to workshop each other's stories. I am in a group with April. She smiles at me. I smile back and then look down at my hands. We sit in threes, reading and then silently commenting on a separate sheet of paper. I don't read the other person's piece in my group all that thoroughly. I write: *Good story. Maybe too many people die in it. Maybe not. I like your use of the word* precipice. *But does she really need to jump off it? Keep writing.*

When I get to April Sherwood's story, I read and read again. It is about a possum that talks, a princess in a castle, a dragon that protects and guards the princess, and a prince sent to rescue her. It's deep. Real deep. I tell her in my critique that the possum is the voice of reason, an older generation, like our parents but wiser and not so anal. And the princess is the representation of a world still stuck in a masculine construct, as if all women should remain in the kitchen doing housework. And the prince, the prince is freedom, liberation.

What a fine piece of work, April. You are such a good writer. This is the best thing I ever read. Really, I got chills. Go ahead look at my arm. Anyway, I think you are pretty. I mean really pretty. And I was wondering, you know, maybe we can go on a date. Maybe see a movie. As friends if you want, but maybe more than friends, too. That'd be cool. All right. Talk to you soon.

The next day, Mr. Pittman hands back our stories with the critiques. He gives me a look that says I know what you did. I shrug, and he smiles. Fists is getting into it already with one of her workshop members, telling him he's stupid for not getting the story. "Dude," she says. "The character is not a transsexual dyke. She just likes to kick ass. Especially scrawny kids like you." The kid cowers and says he's sorry. It's him, not her story at all. Mr. Pittman tells Fists to chill. Read the comments silently and sit on it.

I don't waste time. I go straight to April's comments. She writes like she's from Bubble World. She makes circles over her I's.

I think you are really good. I'm not kidding. I don't know what else I can say. I felt something when I read your piece. Please don't make me explain what that something is because it's more complex then telling you it's sadness or happiness or anger. It's everything and nothing. Ha! That abstraction would drive Mr. Pittman nutty! Anyway, I felt like you brought me there, and I was secretly looking in on these people's lives as they lose touch with one another. In a way, it was like I was a ghost, you know?, watching quietly from the outside, like that Dickens book. In short, I liked it. 'Like' is not the right word though. That's the thing. You are really good with words, so much so that I'm embarrassed about what I wrote because really it was meaningless fluff. I mean, I get what Pittman talks about now, about characters and how they can be complex and simple at the same time. How they possess these extremes. Your characters do that. In one moment they love and in the next…well. I guess I have only one thing to say. I don't understand why the characters don't try harder, why they give up so easily. I don't understand why they can't seem to forgive each other. But what do they need to forgive each other for? That confuses me. They seem to really love each other. I mean really love each other. Like Romeo and Juliet. That kind of love. But wait—didn't they die at the end? Maybe that's a bad example. I don't know. If you love someone that much, it only seems natural they would make it. Why can't they?

I'm a girl who likes happy endings, I guess. Regardless, thank you for sharing this. Please think about the happy ending. April.

I look down at my desk.

What is this I feel, this sudden numbness, this unexpected turn? There is such care, such attention in her critique. If this were a story, then this would be the moment I took her hand and kissed it, or perhaps tapped her on the shoulder, thanked her for her generosity, and revealed to her my love. But those are predictable endings. Expected. What I don't expect is this hollowness in my chest, this feeling like I have been stripped down to nothing. It feels like the day my father disappeared. It feels like my nightmares, when I shout for him and he never comes. I don't understand this. Any of this. I don't believe anymore in happy endings. How can I?

I want to stop April from reading my comments. But it's too late. I know she knows I think she's pretty. I know she knows I like her. I know she sees through my bullshit. I see it in the back of her head, the stiffness in her neck. She keeps her eyes forward.

Mr. Pittman lectures about revision. He says it's the most important tool in writing. Revising is like revisiting a place with a new set of eyes. I'm not ready. There's nothing that can be done. He's not coming back. My mother and I need to understand that. Maybe that's the happy ending for us.

When the bell rings, April bolts out the door.

I move to leave for my next class, French.

Mr. Pittman says, "How are you?"

"Feeling kinda sick."

"Love sick?" He smiles.

"I'm tired of love stories."

"My dear boy," Mr. Pittman says, "Every story is about love."

*

Two weeks and April doesn't talk to me. I can't look her in the eye. I can't look anyone in the eye. I spend my days reading. Mr. Pittman asks me what's wrong. He says I've been turning in crap, and where's that revision of the story I wrote? I tell him I'll get it to him, but I won't. I won't touch it.

Fists writes: *You let her slip out of your fingers. She's dating a dick.*

She was never in my fingers.

You guys could've been the perfect couple.

Love sucks, I write.

You suck.

In my closet, there are fifteen vests. Every two days, my mother finishes another one. She sews them exclusively now. I stopped wearing them a while ago.

One afternoon, when I arrive home, I catch my mother in a private moment of thought. The lights are off, and the outside sun is covered by clouds. My mother stares at the gold fabric in the machine. She doesn't blink. Her eyes are wet.

"Take a break," I say.

"Almost done."

"You don't need to make them anymore. I don't wear them."

"OK," she says.

"I like them, but…"

"OK," she says and raises her face to meet my eyes.

In every story, Mr. Pittman says, there is a point of no return. This point is where a character needs to make a decision that will change the course of the story. Once the decision is made, you can't go back. A good writer knows how to call attention to this point. A good writer knows how to slow down the dramatic tension. A good writer knows that the point of no return is a point in which a character must act. The action will have its consequences; it may take us into the light or lead us deeper into the dark. But it is a moment, Mr. Pittman would say, a moment where everything is at stake.

I turn away.

I tell my mother I'm going upstairs to read. I tell her I'm tired. I don't tell her the thing both of us need to hear.

The Man with the Buddha Heads

My mom spends most of her evenings at Ameri-Thai, balancing numbers and budgets, going from table to table with an extra large smile asking patrons about the quality of their meal, instructing her hired chefs on the correct and most efficient way to carve up a mango for the chutney. So I'm surprised to see her cooking in *our* kitchen and not at the restaurant's. She chops an onion rapidly, without tears, then swishes a finger along the sides of the blade, knocking off the pieces that cling to it.

"Where's Bobby?" my mom says.

"Don't know, don't care," I say. I dip my finger into the bubbling spaghetti sauce, and my mom swats my hand away. "I saw a new Buddha head today. This one was freaky—red eyes and really sunken-in cheeks like those starving people in Ethiopia. It was in the third window on the second floor. I swear its eyes were following me."

My mom says some rich white people think Buddha heads are art. She says it's a sin to have just the head of Buddha and not the rest of him. She shivers. One of her blouse straps slips off her shoulders.

I look away.

My mom's sporting a new look I can't get used to. She used to have beautiful black hair, long and straight that went well past her waist like an Asian Rapunzel. It was what my dad loved most about her. Sometimes he stroked her head as she lay asleep on his lap. After he moved out, she curled it, cut it in half, and dyed her bangs blonde. Now she wears tight-fitting outfits—revealing mini-skirts, butt-hugging leather pants, belly button blouses—clothes that moms should never wear. My brother's creepy friends—the blonde twins—call her their "Asian Wet Dream." Whenever they talk about her they make everything sound sexual. *Oh, she can cook for me any day.*

My mom checks on the noodles rapidly boiling in a pot. She's preparing my favorite meal, one of the house specialties at the restaurant, Thai spaghetti, a blend of puréed Roma tomatoes, coconut milk, a tablespoon of red curry, and one Thai pepper that when I eat it, makes my head itch and sweat.

"Isn't Esteban going to miss you?" I say a little too sarcastically.

"He can handle the dinner rush," she says. "You should treat him better. He likes you, wants to bond."

Esteban's my mom's new beau and the newly appointed head chef at Ameri-Thai. He thinks he's all that like Ricky Martin—a Latin loving machine. He talks with a thick Spanish accent—I swear it's fake—and calls my mom his *cielo.* He says he's been around the world, traveling from country to country, a drifter, and now he's looking to settle down. Yeah, I think, you want to settle down with my mom's money. When he's with her, he sticks his chest out and makes sure she notices his biceps. When she leaves the room, he takes a deep breath and lets his stomach collapse over his waistline.

My mom readies a colander in the sink. I can tell that the noodles are about right. "It has to bite back," my mother would say. "Not too soft, not too hard. That in-between stage." She works effortlessly, moving from pot to pot, sticking the tip of the wooden spoon in the sauce for a taste.

"When's dinner gonna be ready?" I say. "I'm hungry."

"Soon," she says. "Everything is just about right."

*

The man with the Buddha heads lives at the end of our lane, in a run-down white Colonial, paint chipping and turning an ugly shade of yellow. Weeds tangle and weave around the rusted gate and into the lion's mouth at the front opening. The house creaks when it gets windy, which it sometimes does during hurricane season in Rhode Island. The columns in front of the house lean like that tower in Italy, like they're going to fall at any time, taking the whole house with it. Off to the right is an old fountain—one of those mythological guys blowing his reed at a naked woman whose breasts are beginning to crumble. In the spring, birds get together on the house and electric lines—sparrows, finches, robins—like a symphony of tweets. There are bird feeders at every corner of the property, always filled.

Outside the gate is a large oak that must've been there since the beginning of time, so huge its branches extend deep into the man's property. The oak looks strange because the electric company cut a big U through the middle of the tree so the power lines could stretch to the house without getting tangled. If you squint, the tree looks like a bald man with tufts of hair growing out of the sides.

At certain angles, through certain windows, you can see a Buddha head, sometimes two or three, lined up on pedestals. That's the eerie part. Everyone seems to know about it. The Buddha heads move around week to week, never the same head at the same window. Sometimes a head might be staring right at you, as you stare right at it.

The man has lived there for over thirty years, I think. At least my mom says he's been there her whole life. He must be around eighty. When my mom was little he used to go all out during Christmas. The house was the brightest thing in Rhode

Island—so bright that neighbors complained and the nearby airport told him to shut it down because the lights running along the driveway were confusing the pilots. My mom doesn't know what happened between now and then, but she, too, has heard strange stories. He was accused of murdering his wife with a pitchfork. He keeps dead bodies in the basement like John Gacy. He's a dangerous schizophrenic. He fought in wars and still hears bombs and bullets. His daughter drowned in the fountain and he can't forgive himself. He's a Satanist and does sacrifices, which explains the Rogers' missing poodle.

I've never seen him, not once. He's a big mystery like the other things I keep wondering about: where Dad is, what my mom sees in Esteban, why my brother disappears into the bathroom for long durations, whether there's life on other planets, how baby birds know when to spread their wings and leave the nest. Because the Buddha House is on the way home from school, every day I stop outside the gates and peer in, hoping to see the man. Sometimes, Bobby comes with and makes up stories to scare me; it's his right for being three years older, a junior in high school.

"I've seen him once and nearly pissed myself," he said. "He had this eye patch, walked with a cane. I was just looking inside the gate, and thought I saw something moving by the ugly fountain. He came after me, for real, burst out of the bushes like a tiger. Called me gook. Growled something serious. 'Fuckin' gook, fuckin' gook,' he kept saying. 'Die, die, die.' The dude thinks he's still in Hiroshima or some shit like that."

Bobby's hands moved in every direction; his voice slowed for dramatic effect. I swallowed hard. I believed that inside the house lurked a man with one eye, waiting to kill any Asian—even Thai halfies like we were—who crossed his path.

"You scared?" said Bobby, looking proud of himself.

"No," I said.

"Yes you are," he said. "Don't lie."

"Shut up."

He hunched over and said, "Die, die," in a croaking voice.

I flinched and he laughed, jogging ahead of me toward home, his arms waving above his head, screaming, "The gutless gullible geek falls for another one."

*

Things have changed since our dad moved out. We used to hang out all the time, the three of us—dad, Bobby, and me. Bobby's real name is Bhudipone, but when he started high school, the kids picked on him, called him booby or booty, so he simplified it: Bobby. He was my best friend. We did everything together—play laser tag, pretend to be knights and rescue a porcelain doll that was our princess. We'd stay up all night and make shadow puppets on the bedroom walls—our favorite, "ET go pee." But Bobby isn't fun anymore, a real jerk in fact. He has new friends—jocks with too much muscle and not enough brain. He's getting stupider too, his grades dropping from what used to be an A average to a C-. Mom has threatened to take him out of Alser High, a public school, and enroll him in St. Vincent's Boys Prep, but her Buddhist pride keeps her from it.

Our dad left last year. He worked for the telephone company, so we'd see him around town on the poles, safely harnessed in. I used to call him Spiderman because he climbed up those poles so fast. He'd take me on certain jobs before I started school. I'd watch him do his thing, working efficiently, as if he was part of the air. Birds would remain on the lines, unbothered. When he was done, he'd push off the top, come down like a feather, landing softly on his feet. I'd clap.

He got jealous of Mom's restaurant; she spent nearly all her time at Ameri-Thai and made Bobby and me help most days. He spent his evenings alone in a big empty house until one day he left. He quit his job at the telephone company and moved out of town. The next week the divorce papers came. My mom signed them like she signed bills for the restaurant, automatic, without a second glance. He promised to take Bobby and me out every weekend—promised to take us paint-balling and disco bowling—but he's been absent the last four months. He hasn't even called. We don't know where he is.

*

After my grandma's death, my mom found a bunch of recipes in an old notebook. My grandma at the age of seventy-four could make anything out of nothing, unique stuff— spicy hot dog salad, holy basil chicken burger on Chinese buns, and deep fried shrimp and imitation crab croquettes slathered in a canned pineapple sweet and sour sauce. My grandma immigrated to America from Thailand when she was twenty, married a Thai man a year later, who passed away when my mom was three. Grandma raised a large family practically by herself—my mom being the youngest child out of six. While the rest of her brothers and sisters traveled far from home, my mom stuck close to the nest.

When my mom met my dad, she was nineteen, he twenty-two; she was interning in a five-star restaurant in downtown Providence; he was washing dishes there. Grandma didn't mind he was white and poor, a high school dropout; she was the rare Asian who believed in love and destiny, consulted the old ancestors in such matters. My mom was in her last year at Johnson and Wales, ready to move to New York and work in the best kitchens, but my brother sidetracked her. It made sense then to stay close to home so grandma could help take care of the baby. When my dad landed the job with telephone company, he liked to brag to his co-workers that his wife was a big shot chef, and she was going to be the one bringing home the bacon, literally. After I was born, my mom began toying with the idea of opening a French restaurant. It was then my dad started being a pain. He questioned her every move. Who's gonna take care of the boys? Are you sure this is what you want? Have you considered working at one of the other restaurants instead of owning one? Do you know how much this is gonna cost us? I remember grandma saying: "White people never understand Asian ambition. Go make restaurant. Cook your heart out. If he love he will understand." The next day, mom bought a commercial lot in downtown Providence, next door to a William Sonoma, and set off to be the top French restaurant in the country.

The food at The Bistro—the restaurant's original name— was great, no doubt, but it was "familiar, no flair" as one critic remarked. Providence was the home of four French restaurants—all established, all packed full every weekend. After six months, The Bistro was spending more than it was making. My dad was saying I told you so. It looked hopeless. But when grandma died, everything changed. The entire family mourned for months, but her recipes were a godsend; they were my mom's way to set her restaurant apart from the others. She changed the name and décor. *The Providence Phoenix* named Ameri-Thai Best Restaurant in Rhode Island six years running and *Gourmet* magazine did an article on my mom—"Asian Beauty Creates New Thai Taste."

*

It's Sunday, a week before Halloween, in the middle of the dinner rush. Bobby and I are supposed to work till closing because a couple of people called in sick at the last moment. We're trained for whatever. Sometimes we wait tables, sometimes we help with the prep, and sometimes—I hate this the most—we wash dishes. Today, Bobby tends the bar, and I make sure the food is plated perfectly before the waiters bring it out to customers.

My brother's in all black, the bartender's garb, but instead of mixing drinks at the bar, he's here, in the kitchen. He's talking to the twins in the back alley—both with short blond hair and blue eyes. They wear combat boots laced to the top and thick bomber jackets with skull patches. Bobby is probably telling them how gullible I am because they laugh and look my way a lot. I try to ignore them. I wipe the edges of the plate clean and nod my approval at a waiter, who takes the dish out the swinging doors. Tonight's special: lemongrass-skewered salmon with a ginger citrus sauce. Everybody's ordering it.

Esteban barks orders to the four chefs working like mad to get the dishes ready. Each chef has a responsibility—one does appetizers, one does desserts, two cook the entrées; Esteban lends a hand here and there, but most of the time he shouts. In the corner, two Johnson and Wales interns are washing dishes, looking miserable.

This kitchen is a well-oiled machine. Everyone does his or her job—no rust here. It sounds like a crazy punk band with no sense of melody—rhythmic chopping, mad clangs, sizzle sizzle, the swishing of the swinging doors, the hurried footsteps of the waiters in their hard heels, click click, the occasional eruption of curses and repeated commands of *Hurry*

hurry! Here, everything shines—the counters, the refrigerator and freezer, the stove, the cabinets, everything chrome. My mom orders special white fluorescents so the chefs can see better, but after a while my eyes get sore, feeling as if I've stared too long at the sun.

Esteban looks over my shoulders as I work on the presentation of the tamarind crab cakes. I center one in the middle of a square plate, and lean the other against it. The chefs work so fast they get sloppy with the sauce. I do a quick touch up and off the plate goes to happy customers. "*Muy bien*, little man," Esteban says. He winks and gives a thumbs up. "You will be successful. I can tell talent when I see it. You are like me. Hard worker. Soon you will be head chef of a restaurant. I know things like this."

I say nothing, but smile at his compliments even though every fiber of my being is screaming, *Phony freak! Fake! You're so full of yourself!*

Esteban goes to the deep fryer and checks on some truffle-infused spring rolls. He shakes the strainers and lets the rolls cool. He turns his attention back on his team of chefs.

"You guys hungry?" Bobby says.

His two friends nod.

Bobby dodges a couple of waiters and takes two spring rolls from the fryer, bobbling them. He gives them to his friends, who eat and suck in air at the same time, the steam rising from the rolls.

I look at Esteban. His eyes are on Bobby, frowning, which looks funny because he's wearing one of those hairnets. Finally, he leaves the kitchen, and I suspect he's telling my mom what's going on.

"Those were for customers," I say.

"So what," Bobby says. "Make new ones."

"You took them out, you do it." I flick him off.

Bobby puts his hand in front of his mouth in mock fright. One of his friends says *tough guy* and the other laughs.

Mom storms through the kitchen, face red, and heads directly for Bobby. She's wearing a black mini-skirt and knee high leather boots, her mid-drift exposed. I shake my head because she looks like a slut. Bobby's friend's eyes bug out. Bobby shakes his head, too, turning the other way.

"Why are you back here, Bobby?" she says, arms crossed in front of her. "There is a mound of drink orders. People are complaining."

"So?" he says. "I'm on break."

"No break during rushes," my mom says. "You know that. Don't be stupid." She glares at Bobby's two friends, and they smile and take steps back. One of them says they'll catch up with him later. Peace. Bobby nods, his temples scrunched together. They walk away, laughing.

"What are you waiting for?"

Bobby starts walking to the doors slowly, mumbling under his breath.

"Hurry," she says.

Before Bobby reaches the swinging doors, Esteban tattles. "The little punk took two spring rolls and gave them to his *vatos*. Thinks he's the big boss man in this kitchen." Esteban lifts his chin and flares his hairy nostrils—his tough guy face. He's not much shorter than Bobby, but a lot thicker. He hates Bobby, doesn't appreciate being called the Latin Loser behind his back.

Bobby turns. "You're such a whiny crybaby," Bobby says.

I laugh into a towel.

Esteban puffs out his chest and takes a step toward Bobby. "What you say?"

"Cry-baby," Bobby says slowly, the syllables distinct. "Understand that, Latin Loser?"

The entire kitchen stops working. It's like a schoolyard before a fight, that quiet anticipation before the first punch. I don't like Bobby, but I don't like Estaban more. I don't like Bobby, but I want Bobby to knock Esteban out. I grab a fork, ready to throw down if my brother gets in trouble.

"Enough," my mom says, walking between them. "This is not a boxing ring. This is my restaurant."

Esteban backs off, lifting up his hands. "For you anything, *mi cielo*," he says.

My insides reel.

"Put two spring rolls in the fryer, Bobby," says my mom.

Bobby pretends to scratch his face with his middle finger toward Esteban then drops two rolls in the fryer; the peanut oil spits and pops.

"This isn't a cheap delivery-in-ten-minutes Chinese restaurant," my mom says. "You don't give anyone anything without asking me first. Do you hear me?"

Bobby shows her his palm and says, "Whatever," pushing through the swinging doors.

Esteban's pleased with himself. He begins to bark orders at the other chefs, real machismo. Work continues. He comes up behind my mom and wraps his arms around her waist. "It's all right, baby," he says. "You got one good boy." He nods at me.

My mom sighs and pulls away from him. She whispers, "Not here," squeezing the bridge of her nose and then massaging her temples. "Don't forget to mop the floor when we close," she says to me. "Everything's so dirty."

*

At the restaurant there are two bronze Buddhas standing at either side of the entranceway, their bodies shapely and effeminate. They hold their right hands up, like Indians saying hello. At the house there is a Buddha in my mom's room, small and gold and meditating. He can fit in the palms of your hand. When my dad first left, my mom used to pray to the Buddha. She would hold him close to her chest, like a talisman against evil. I'd spy on her through the crack of her bedroom door.

Then, her room was a mess and empty. She was a mess and empty.

When my dad took his stuff, I didn't realize what absence meant until I saw the spaces where his things used to occupy, like the framed poster of the '82 Mets that hung in the living room, or his golf clubs in the corner of the garage, or the big-screened TV we used to watch horror movies on.

My mom said it was Buddha that set her straight. It was Buddha that told her to reinvent herself. It was Buddha that told her to move on.

Buddha doesn't say anything to me. I hold my mom's Buddha the way she does and say, "Will everything go back to normal?"

Nothing.

"Will my mom stop dressing like a hoochie mama?"

Nothing.

"Will my brother be my brother again?"

Nothing.

"Where's Dad?"

Nothing.

The Buddha is cold in my hands, his face serene, dreamy. He looks like someone who wants to say something, someone brimming with words and birds. I imagine when he opens his mouth sparrows fly out in rapid song. I imagine a lot of things. My brother calls these moments la-la time, when I'm off somewhere else, detached from the world. I'm in la-la time every time I walk pass the house with the Buddha heads, when I pause at the rusted gates, when I search for any trace of the man who keeps them. I want to know him. I want to know what he sees in Buddha because I don't see anything.

"Yo," my brother says. "Wake up."

I shake awake.

"La-la time," he says.

"Shut up," I say.

We're at Ameri-Thai on a weekend. It's the afternoon and the clouds have gathered, making the day dark and cold. Bobby is not happy about it because it means he can't spend his time with the twins, causing havoc somewhere. It means he has to occupy the same space as Esteban, who sneers at him every chance he gets. Because the restaurant hasn't opened yet, Bobby and I usually spend our times setting tables and dusting and vacuuming. Today, however, someone has vandalized the two Buddhas outside with black marker mustaches. One looks like Hitler Buddha. One looks like Groucho Marx Buddha.

Bobby and I have to deal with it.

"Why do we have to do this?" Bobby says. He soaks a rag with mineral spirits.

"All you do is complain," I say.

"Listen, fat ass," my brother says—though I barely weigh a hundred pounds—"You don't always have to be perfect, all goody-goody."

"You don't have to be a dork."

"Nice comeback."

I scrub Hitler Buddha hard and fast. I dream of giving Bobby a mustache, a curvy one like that weird artist who draws melting clocks. I can sneak in his room at night, and he wouldn't hear a thing. He wouldn't know I was lurking toward him with a sharpie. When he wakes up, there'd be his new mustachioed face.

I smile at the thought.

"Yo," Bobby says. "La-la time."

"Whatever," I say. Blink. Blink again.

I hate Bobby, but what he says about me is right. Since Dad left I've been cautious and obedient. I've tried to stay the same when everyone seems to be morphing into alien beings, and I wonder now whether I should be changing, too, wondering what I want to be and how I want to be it.

"This is kinda funny," Bobby says. He's not cleaning Groucho Marx Buddha. He observes it, the way someone would a piece of art. "Don't you think it's funny?"

I shrug.

"I mean, someone went out of their way to make this happen."

"And we have to clean it up."

"Still," Bobby says. "I like it. It suits this place. What's more American than a vandalized Buddha in front of an Asian restaurant?"

I shrug again.

Bobby starts wiping, slowly, meticulously, as if he can do it forever. "I bet the twins did this."

"Really?"

"Such assholes," he says and laughs.

"Why do you hang out with them?"

"They're all right."

"They're stupid."

"They are," he says.

I turn to look at him. He touches the Buddha's face, scratches the chin of his Groucho Marx Buddha to see if the marker will come off. For a second, I see him—the brother

68

he used to be. The quiet one. The nice one. I was the dreamy one. The talky one. That's how our dad would describe us. I see part of Dad in his face, too, his long nose, his busy brows, his smart-ass grin. I think I hate my brother because he looks more and more like Dad. I hate him because he is nothing like him.

When my brother notices me staring, he says, "What?"

"Nothing," I say.

"Whatever," he says.

We go on working for the next hour. It begins to rain, but we stand under a red awning that shields us from the drops. The mustaches on the Buddhas are disappearing, but slowly. I don't think we'll able to get rid of it all. I think there will always be the faint outline of those mustaches.

"Yo," Bobby says. "I have a proposition."

"What?"

"The twins and I, we want to decorate the Buddha House next Wednesday, on Halloween."

"So?" I say.

Bobby scratches the side of his face. "We need someone to open the gates from the inside."

"I'm not skinny enough to squeeze through."

"But you can climb the tree," Bobby says. "You're light enough the branches won't break." He walks towards me and bends to my level. He's tall, like Dad, almost six five, center for the school basketball team.

I'm waiting for my growth spurt.

"You know you have this obsession," he whispers. "Won't it be cool to see what's going on on the inside?" Bobby stares straight at me.

Every day I stop in front of that house and stare through the rusted bars. Every day I hope to see more.

Bobby's hair is getting longer and it falls into his eyes; he traces the strands around his ears. "You don't have to be good all the time," he says. "It'd be fun."

"OK," I say.

Bobby straightens himself and ruffles my hair.

I pull my head away.

He looks at the Buddhas, sighs, and says, "I'm done. Let's go inside."

*

Once, two years ago, my dad got an emergency call to check out the phone lines at the Buddha House after a lightning storm. He left home near midnight, got in the work truck and headed down the block. I woke up and looked out my bedroom window. In the distance, electrical sparks rained to the ground. A large branch had fallen on the lines. The streetlights were out because they shared the same electrical grid as the Buddha House. The power company was already there, working to untangle the lines and get everything under control. My mom told me to go to bed because I had school the next day.

In the morning, my dad looked exhausted—bags under his eyes, disheveled brown hair, a small scab on his bottom lip. My mom had left for the market to buy the freshest seafood, meats and vegetables for Ameri-Thai. Bobby was still fooling with his hair in the bathroom. At first, my dad answered all my questions in grunts. He spooned cereal into his mouth, the milk running down his chin. He wiped his mouth with the back of his hand. I asked my dad what was it like. Did he see him, the man? Grunt. Did he see any Buddha heads? Grunt. I begged him to tell me more.

"What's with this fixation? You're like your mother and the

damn restaurant."

I shrugged, staring at him unflinchingly.

He was having a bad morning—lack of sleep, probably another fight with mom over something inconsequential. It was nearing the end of their relationship, when she came home after work and slept on the couch, when they bickered about laundry lint.

I didn't say anything, but stared. My dad was a sucker when it came to his youngest son. I tried to look as cute as I could, stuck out my bottom lip, made my eyes droop.

He looked at me and then looked away. He crunched on cereal and looked at me again. He looked away again. He tried to ignore me, but finally, throwing his arms in the air, he shook his head, smiling. "Good god, boy! You can't let your father enjoy his cornflakes." I had won.

After the electricians were done, he climbed up and checked the main phone box. He figured a couple circuits were burned out and he'd have to reconnect the phone line. He cleared away an unused bird's nest, settling on the lip of the box. The lights were back on. A light shone in the second story window nearest him. My dad said he was curious. He took a peek. There was the outline of a man in the window. He squinted and thought it was a statue of a Buddha head. But this Buddha head moved. This Buddha head pushed open the window.

Startled, my dad lost his footing, slamming his face on the telephone pole, which explained the scab. After regaining his balance, my dad said, "Hello?"

"Why did you do that?" said the man.

My dad pointed his flashlight at him, and he shrunk away like he was Nosferatu, shielding his eyes from the artificial sun.

"Sorry, sir." He turned off the flashlight. "You scared me."

"Why did you do that?" the man asked again.

"Do what?"

"Destroy the birdie home?"

As far as my dad could tell, the man was bald. He couldn't make out any features. He wore a robe—not a bathrobe, but a wizard-like robe—long open sleeves, baggy, hanging on his skinny body like an oversized dress. The man looked two stories down at the discarded nest.

"Oh," said my dad, "No birds were using it. In case of another electric storm it could catch on fire and endanger your house."

The man didn't seem to hear what my dad was saying. "I see birdies all the time," he croaked. "All kinds. Some colorful, some not. They sit on the wires. They sing for me. They like the nest." Here, he lifted his face and stared at my dad so accusatorily that my dad looked away. He didn't know what to say. He began working, ignoring the old man. It was two in the morning. It was cold.

The man looked down at the nest again. "Poor birdies," he said. "Poor, poor birdies." He closed the window, and my dad swore he disappeared because when he looked up he wasn't there anymore.

It's my dad's story I remember as Bobby gives me a boost up the old oak. His two blonde friends hide at the side of the house, shaving cream in both hands. Bobby has eight rolls of TP in his backpack.

"Be careful," Bobby says. "The power lines. Don't touch them."

"That's the first thing I'd like to do," I mumble. I make it over to the other side of the gate and drop down, stumbling, falling forward onto my hands.

Bobby throws the backpack over. "Go open the gate," he says.

I walk to the front, but I don't see a handle or anything.

"Come on," says one of the blondes.

"You're so slow," says the other.

"Give him time," says Bobby. He points to either side of the front gate. "Look at the stone posts—on the sides."

Dead vines climb up and down the stone posts. Nothing on the left. The sun begins to sink under the horizon, the sky orange. I take out a slim flashlight and shine it on the other post. A lever sticks out from under the foliage. I move to it quickly and push it up, grunting. Slowly, the gates open, creaking on rusted wheels, and the boys burst through and go to work. One of the blondes attacks the fountain with the shaving cream, circling the woman's breasts. The other quietly shave creams the front steps, writing FREAK but misspelling it FREEK in messy letters. Bobby throws TP from tree to tree. The white TP flutters like ribbons, drooping on limbs and branches.

I've done my part. I walk to the side of the house away from my brother and the blondes. I try to make my steps quiet, but the leaves crunch. The house is immense; it seems to go on forever. In one of the windows, a Buddha looks at the setting sun, his eyes wide open, a shadow creeping across his golden face.

I look through every ground level window, but see nothing. Not one Buddha head. Not one sign of the man. There's a screened-in porch I never knew existed in the back of the house, and a few wind chimes hanging on the limbs of a tree. In the corner of the yard, a few sparrows fight over a bird feeder, nipping each other's tails. Because of the sunset, a long shadow of the house looms across the yard. I begin to think the man doesn't exist.

Once in history class, Mr. Brony made us watch a video about an excavation of some Egyptian tomb. The guy on TV kept saying: "Here it is, the moment we've been waiting for. After blowing up this layer we might possibly have the biggest find in archaeological history." And when the dynamite blew and the dust cleared, they found nothing. No tomb. No treasure. No dead king. Just a few cracked pots. The entire class started booing. I thought about the disappointment of the scientists, about how hard they worked, how they waited for this moment for nothing.

I sigh, turn the corner, and make my way up the other side of the house.

The twins continue to shave cream, jumping up and down, laughing. Then one of them abruptly stops and drops his can. He waves the other over. Both of them crouch down, looking through a lighted window. I run to it, bumping into one of the blondes.

Buddha heads. Fifty of them, in a circle, leaving the middle empty like a stage. So many types. Chubby heads. Ones with pointy hats. Ones with buns on top. Heads with abnormally long earlobes. One with puckered red lips like a drag queen. Buddha heads with open eyes, some shut, some waking from a deep sleep. Some obese, their chins overflowing. Some anorexic. Some with long faces. Some with block chins. Different colors—gold, stone gray, silver, white, green. One head looks like the serious Buddha my mom keeps in restaurant's kitchen, sitting on a small throne over everyone, our critical inspector—tarnished and stern.

"No way," one of the twins says.

"How 'bout it?" says another.

"Freaky," they both say.

The heads mesmerize us—our mouths open, fogging up the window. One of the twins swipes his hand across the glass.

"Look at that one." He points to a pudgy stone Buddha.

74

We don't see him at first. The man. But he's there. He emerges from the Buddha heads, pink duster in hand. He goes from Buddha to Buddha. He doesn't use a cane, but walks upright, strong, shoulders thrown back like a soldier, a slight skip to his step. He isn't bald, but has a full head of hair—silver, floating above his shoulders. Round glasses cling to the tip of his nose. Brown spots dot his face. No magician's robe, but plain navy slacks and a tightly tucked-in dress shirt that makes the man look rail thin. I can hear him humming through the window. He stops at a fat Buddha head. Dusts it. Talks to it. He's so deliberate I wonder if he's seen us.

"Oh my god," says one of them.

"Shut up," I say, trying to hear.

"You shut up," one of them says, pushing me. I catch my balance, my palm hitting the window.

The man turns towards the thud. He tilts his head. He doesn't look angry, but surprised, bewildered. He takes a step closer to the window. Then, quite suddenly, he smiles. Not like a crazy man.

"Hi," he says, pushing open the window.

The twins bolt, tripping and falling on their knees a few times.

My eyes don't leave his face. I'm rooted to the ground.

"I wasn't expecting any guests today," says the man. He watches the twins burst through the front gates. "I don't expect guests most days." He turns back to me. "Just doing some cleaning, though. Got so many of these guys." He waves his duster behind him. "If I don't dust, they'd be covered."

The old man leans out the window and takes a look at the shaving cream smiley faces on the outside of his house.

"Pretty," he says. "They do good work, your friends." His voice has a strange lilt to it, soothing. He chuckles to himself,

75

then says, "Do you like my heads? I have over three hundred in this house, not one alike. But these are my favorites, my precious ones. You see this one? It's from old Burma, Myanmar now. It's about four hundred years old. You can tell it comes from Burma because of the big lips. When I first got him— maybe twenty years ago—his lips were vivid red like someone put lipstick on him. Now the color's fading." He pats the Buddha head, like a father would a son, smiling. "I have so many."

He begins spinning, arms outstretched in the center of all the Buddhas, a joyous dance like little kids sometimes do in the rain. He stops. "I like Buddha heads. Each one is like a different friend. I like to sit in the center here. They listen to me. They tell me they're doing fine. They say, you are a good man."

I unclench my hands, letting my shoulders drop. I want to ask him about his secrets. Tell me some, I want to say. I won't tell. Promise. But what comes out my mouth is the last thing I want to say.

"You're weird."

"Yes," he says. "Yes."

We stare at each other, and I see the loneliest man in the world. That's his biggest secret. He looks small, standing in the middle of the Buddha heads. I want to step inside the house and hold him, tell him to come to Ameri-Thai and I will treat him like a king, bringing him only the best dishes. He won't have to pay because I'll tell my mom he's an important food critic, ranking restaurants around the world like the famous Zagats. I want to tell him that I get lonely too, so lonely that I think of nothing but him. This is my secret.

"Would you like to come in?" he finally says. "I can show you more."

Before I reply, Bobby grabs the back of my neck from behind. "No you're not, retard." He pushes me away from the window. "Don't touch my little brother," he says to the man. He pulls a can of shaving cream out of his back pocket and points it like a gun. In the dark, Bobby seems even taller.

The man doesn't flinch.

"We were just talking," I say.

The man stares above his glasses, the smile back on his lips.

"Just go," says Bobby, "I've got you covered." His eyes never leave the man.

I shake my head, sigh, look at the man one last time, and say sorry with my eyes.

When I get through the front gate, Bobby catches up with me. He smacks the back of my head. "I saved your life," he says.

"He's not like everyone thinks."

"Right," says Bobby. "You would've gone into his house and that would've been the last of you. *Hasta la vista, baby.*"

"Whatever," I say.

"Whatever nothing. The guy's a weirdo. He collects Buddha heads."

"So?"

He puts his arm around my shoulder, and even though I want to shrug it off, I don't. "Where'd the Barbie twins head off to?" he asks.

"Morons went running as soon as the dude came out."

"Big tough guys."

"Real tough," I say, smiling.

Bobby chuckles. "We got samurai blood in our veins, isn't that right?" He pulls me closer.

I push away from him, patting down my head, smiling.

"Come on," he says, "Mom will freak if we're late."

Tonight, we have to go to Ameri-Thai and work till closing. Bobby has dish duty for the next month for his stunt early in the week. I'm on the same job, presentation perfectionist. Bobby will probably squirt Esteban with the sprayer, talk trash behind his back. He will mess with my hair and call me retard or dork or something that will make me want to slug him. And I will drift off somewhere. Think about something. Be in some la-la place where a lone finch bobs in someone's yard, pecking for some worm, pecking until it finds something. When it does, it gets into the air quickly, flying into some tree and disappearing in the tangle of branches.

Regardless, the kitchen will be fun tonight.

Bright Land

I work for a blind woman. She's got a guide dog, a black lab that eyes me when I come through the door. I let him sniff my hand, and he gives it a little kiss, but nothing more besides that. He sticks close to the boss, always at her feet. The boss listens to her headphones, hearing something I scanned for her earlier. That's what she does all day, listens to poetry or some book. Sometimes, when I'm scanning poems into the boss's computer, I read them. Some are cool and make me feel like there's more out there in the world, more things we don't know about. Some make no sense. I think it's because I'm not smart. My dad used to say that. He left my mom and me for another woman and then died. Who's not smart now? I say.

I know she's smart, though, the boss, even if she's blind. And I think she's pretty too, for someone older and all. She's real clean and smells fresh. Not overly perfumed like some of the girls at school, who probably mist themselves in the stuff. She smells like she doesn't need to smell like flowers. She just smells the ways she smells.

I like her. She's nice to me. I like the dog, too. His name is Keats.

I'm part of the WeWork program at Central High School, so I get to leave an hour earlier than everyone else. It's a program for dummies—people who aren't going to college or anything, people who will never leave Columbus. The people in charge of WeWork asked what kind of job I was interested in, and I said I didn't care. I said, whatever. I said, nothing with math or anything, nothing with food neither, nothing where I have to build or put anything together. The people at WeWork said, I had to learn to be marketable. They said, jobs aren't easy to come by. They said, beggars can't be choosers, and I said, I'm not begging. Well, they said, how about cleaning, how about helping a blind person clean. I said, whatever.

On the first day, I was late because I got off at the wrong stop and had to walk a mile to her apartment. The boss lives near Franklin Conservatory. It's a big garden with an outdoor theater on the west side of the city. It's pretty if you like flowers.

I knocked on the door and someone said, "Who is it?"

I told her I was from WeWork and the door opened and out came this black dog. The dog inspected me from all angles, like I had a bag with me or something. Then it looked at me and sniffed real loud.

"Is he safe, Keats?" she said. "Are you?"

I shooed the dog with my hands. "Is he?"

"Most definitely." She turned and walked into the apartment, the dog by her side, but he kept looking back at me.

"Are you coming in?" she said. "Charles. That's your name, right? Charles Wo-jow-cho-wicz."

"That's me," I said.

"Did I say your last name correctly?"

"No," I said, "but it don't matter."

"It does matter," she said. "Names matter to me." She was wearing dark glasses, and her red hair was combed back and kept in place by a rubber band. Her socks matched. Nothing seemed out of place with this woman. Like she was normal.

"I don't mean to make you mad or anything," I said, "but you can't say my name. Not many can. You don't have the right stuff to say it."

"I don't have a mouth?" she said. "I don't have a voice?"

"No, it's not like that. It's just, we say it in a different language. Like the sound is hard for people to get right, you know?"

"Say it for me," she said.

I said it to her, the way my mom says it.

"You know what I hear," she said, tilting her head and leaning her ear toward me. "The first part of your name sounds like a whoosh of wind and the last part is like the sizzle of bacon. Do you like bacon?"

"I guess," I said.

"In France," she said, "I ate the most exquisite piece of bacon in a café outside the Cathédrale Notre Dame de Paris. Can you say that?" she said.

I shook my head and then caught myself. "I mean, no," I said. I never heard of a blind person who traveled. I mean, what would you see? The same things you saw anywhere you went, right? Dark, dark and more dark.

I took a look at her apartment. Everything was neat, in order. There was a TV and record player beside it and hundreds of records in a milk crate. There were paintings of weird colors on the walls, like all someone did was splash paint onto the canvas. There were plants, and above the plants a skylight that lit them up. And then there were books, lots and lots of books, a whole wall's worth.

Really, the place was spotless. The only thing that needed cleaning was the mud I brought in from the outside.

"We will have things to learn from each other, Charles," she said. Keats sat at her feet. "Things and things."

*

The boss, her name is Samantha Lambert. She said her last name means "bright land" in French. "Ironic, isn't it?" she said, "...*having worshipped for my doom pass ignorantly into sleep's bright land*. Ah, cummings, you do perplex me." She talks like this. She quotes people I've never heard of. My main job is to scan books into her computer, hundreds of pages a day. I also do little things, like taking Keats out for a piss or giving him treats or making sure his bowl is full. Everything in her apartment has a spot. This is important. If I dust her records, they should go back in the same exact way. If I clean Keats's bowl, I have to put the bowl back exactly where it came from. There are taped X's where things should go. I do what I'm told. If the boss needs something, I go out and get it. She hands me money and says I should keep the change. I tell her I don't want to keep the change because WeWork pays OK. She says take it. I don't fight her. She usually wins anyways. Sometimes she gives me a twenty for a roll of toilet paper. I tell her she gave me a twenty. "Are you sure you want me to keep the change?" I say. She says, "What, do you think I'm blind?"

"Charles," she says to me today, "do you like it here?"

I've been working for her for over a month, Monday through Friday, 2:30-6:30. "You mean, do I like working here?"

"Yes," she says.

"I guess," I say.

"You are always guessing," she says.

"I guess," I say again.

Keats sleeps on the floor by her feet. His paws twitch. I wonder if in his dreams he chases rabbits or squirrels or small dogs. Hell, I bet he chases me.

"I'm not working you hard enough," she says.

"I'm scanning a fourteen hundred page book here. Less Miser-ables."

"*The world is full of willing people, some willing to work, the rest willing to let them.* Robert Frost."

"You're weird," I say and laugh again.

"*There is no such thing as a weird human being. It's just that some people require more understanding than others.* Tom Robbins."

Keats groans in his sleep.

"Keats agrees," she says. As soon as the boss says his name, Keats bolts up, ready to serve. "Why don't you read that book? It's quite good. You do know how to read, don't you, Charles?"

"It's fourteen hundred pages," I say. "I'm not a reader or anything."

"This is part of the job. Read it or don't come back."

"For real?" I say.

"For real."

*

Less Miser-ables was way long—took me six days of constant reading—but in the end I liked it. I had to reread stuff because Victor Hugo is tough. He got real deep in some spots and I got lost. Maybe it wasn't lost I felt, but fuzzy, out of touch, like my brain got real light—no—real heavy, and there were so many thoughts whirling in my head. Victor Hugo, he made me feel like I was tripping, only I wasn't seeing colors or anything, just ideas and words.

I was kinda proud afterwards, like I really got through something, like I wasn't as stupid as I thought I was. I liked the part where the dude Jean Valjean steals from the priest and the priest saves him instead of turning him in to the cops and how that totally changed the guy's life.

I tell the boss so. I tell her it was the first book I ever read.

She hands me another book, *The Great Gatsby*, and says for me to read it out loud this time, read it to her and Keats. I don't want to because I'm not the best reader or anything. I'm not an actor or anything. The boss is at her computer. She unplugs her headphones and out comes this robotic voice, reading something I scanned yesterday, a long poem by Alexander Pope.

The voice creeps me out.

"That thing reads to you like that?" I say.

She says, "You learn to hear a different voice. I have a lot of voices in my head."

"I'm no better," I say.

"But you are," she says. She convinces me, and I read out loud to her and Keats, stumbling on words, stumbling on what things mean. Keats makes groaning noises, kinda like the noises I wish I could do in my English class when the teacher goes on, but I don't because even though I'm stupid, I'm not rude or anything. I got manners. The boss helps me, though, helps me more than some of the teachers ever did. She takes her time with me. She tells me to slow down, not to go so fast, to really listen to the words, to let the words get in my head.

When I finish Gatsby, she gives me another book. *The Poems of Rudyard Kipling. Wuthering Heights. Rebecca.* WeWork is paying me to read, paying me to hang out with a blind woman and her dog. It doesn't feel like work. It feels like I am chillin' with two friends, only I've never had friends like this. My other friends, they were getting into it too deep. Severs, he's a big stoner. Every time I'd see him, he'd be trippin' balls. And Danny is like a zombie. I don't want to be like that. It felt OK for a while, and then it got weird, like I wasn't me anymore, like the stuff I was poppin' was becoming this whole other person inside of me and that person was eating me from the inside, taking over. Severs and Danny, those guys are gone. They're not people anymore. I don't know. It got me thinking. It got me scared.

*

I come in today and Keats is wagging at the door. "Hey," I say. "You're a good boy."

Keats is in his harness and he makes loud snuffy sounds and bumps me with his head.

I try to pat him, but he's all dancey, pulling away, shifting from one leg to the other. "Where's the boss?" I say and take his harness. He pulls me through the kitchen and into the boss's office. I hear her before I see her. She's crying hard. Keats looks at me, as if to say, *do something.* I look at him, as if say, *do what?*

I keep still at the door. The boss has her head in her arms and she is wailing away. I've never heard anyone cry so hard. Even my mother wasn't this loud after my dad died. Keats licks the boss's hand, but she ignores him. He looks at me again.

I shrug and mouth, *what do you want me to do?*

The boss raises her head. She isn't wearing her dark glasses. I never see her without her glasses. Her eyes are green, real green, but they're unfocused, a little fuzzy.

"Is someone there?" she says.

I don't know what to do.

She wipes at her nose and says, "Charles, is that you? Are you there, Charles?"

Keats nuzzles my hand. "Um, yeah," I say. "I just got here."

"Keats doesn't like it when I cry."

"Oh," I say.

She wipes her face with her sleeve and finds her glasses on the table. "He's a good boy. My good boy. My special one." She's talking more to Keats than to me. He goes back to her and puts his head under her hand.

"How was school today?" she says, rising from the chair, Keats right by her side.

"OK," I say. "I guess." I move away from the door.

She stops right beside me and turns her head towards me. "Sometimes a girl needs a good cry," she says. "Do you understand?"

I nod.

"Do you?"

"Yes," I say, but I really don't.

She brushes past me and into the kitchen. She knows her whole apartment by feel, reaching for the treat jar without a problem and taking a strip of fake bacon for Keats. He gently grabs it into his mouth and holds it there, watching her, holds it there until they move out of the kitchen and into the living room. She turns on an opera I don't understand, turning it up loud. Some man's voice sounds sad, sounds like he's singing for the boss and for Keats and even for me, who wants to say something nice, something a real man would do, something like the dudes I've read about would say, Gatsby to Daisy, Angel to Tess. But I don't say a word. I watch her. I watch Keats with the treat still in his mouth. When the boss settles into a chair—her body sagging, her hand on her temple—Keats begins to chew.

*

I'm on the 131 heading home, thinking about this story the boss made me read. "The Metamorphosis." It was about this dude who woke up one day and was a bug. I was thinking this guy had to be on a bad ride or something. I was kinda like that six months ago. I didn't turn into a bug or anything, but I was somewhere else, on another plane of existence and by myself. I felt helpless, like there wasn't going be anyone to rescue me, like I was going to be trapped in my head forever. That's when my mom called the hospital because I was drooling and swaying and wasn't responding to anything she said. She freaked. She doesn't talk to me anymore, not really. She only says I'd end up like my dad if I don't shape up.

I'd stopped reading the story to ask the boss, "This dude's

trippin', right? I mean, he isn't really a bug, is he?"

She laughed, throwing her head back. Her hair was up. I looked at her neck and then looked away. "It isn't too hard to imagine," she said. "Have you ever felt like you were a bug, Charles? Like you were so small in a world so big?"

I shrugged. "I guess so," I said.

"Always guessing," she said. "Either you have or you haven't."

"Yeah," I said. "I think I've felt like that."

"*It is loneliness that makes the loudest noise. This is true of men as of dogs. Eric Hoffer.*"

"Who's that?"

"Philosopher. He went mysteriously blind when he was a child and then got his sight back when he was fifteen, which was even more mysterious. After that, he read and read and read, afraid he'd lose his sight again."

"Did he?"

"Nope." The boss went silent. Keats was chewing on a bone. He stopped and looked between us and wagged.

"When my dad left, I guess I felt like that," I said. "When he died, I didn't. I didn't feel anything."

"Do you miss him?" she said. She leaned forward. She was wearing a blouse that kinda V-opened and I could see part of her bra.

I rose up quickly and pretended to get Keats a treat. The sound of my movement made her lean back a bit. "I guess," I said. "I don't know."

"Ah, the language of uncertainty."

Keats followed me to the kitchen and sat pretty for his treat. I gave it to him, and he followed me back into the living room and waited for me to sit before eating. "I don't know if I miss him. I know I think about him a lot."

The boss crossed her legs and looked out the window of her

apartment. "It's sunny today," she said. It was. Warm considering it was February. "I think about the last thing I could see, Charles. I think about that all the time." She raised her right hand and it looked like she was stroking a face in the air. It made me sad, watching her like this, when she goes into her head and it's hard to reach her, hard for even Keats to reach her.

"Do you want me to keep reading?" I said. "If you want, I can scan the rest of the story."

"No," she said, her voice far away. "You have a marvelous voice, Charles."

"It's not that great," I said, feeling heat rise into my cheeks.

"I have this disease called Macular Degeneration. When it started it made everything in the center of vision fuzzy, but things to the sides were clear. One day I went walking in the Conservatory. My eyes had been getting progressively worse, getting fuzzier and then coming back clear again. It was like a TV with bad reception. I had just gotten Keats and I was crying because I knew I was never going to see again. Then there it was. My vision. Perfect. And I was staring at an orchid, white with a pink tongue, hanging from a tree. It was beautiful, Charles. I looked at it for a long time, afraid to take my eyes off it. Afraid if I turned away it would vanish in a haze. Then it did." She got quiet again and smiled. "*Where does discontent start? You are warm enough, but you shiver. You are fed, yet hunger gnaws you. You have been loved, but your yearning wanders in new fields. And to prod all these there's time, the Bastard Time.* John Steinbeck."

"I like you, boss," I blurted out. "You make me feel like I'm worth something."

"You are a good person, Charles. A smart one."

"I'm stupid," I said. "My dad used to say that."

She straightened in her chair and looked right at me. "I will have Keats bite you," she said. "You are the smartest boy

I have ever met."

I nodded, and she leaned back in her chair, and I finished reading the rest of "The Metamorphosis," the bug dying in the end. She listened intently, and I read with everything I had. I didn't stumble as much, and she didn't correct me when I messed up some of the bigger words.

On the bus, I guess I'm not really thinking about the story of Gregor Samsa who woke up one day and realized he was a bug. I'm thinking more about her.

The bus comes to a jolty stop and in walks Severs and Danny, looking trashed. Severs is a big dude. His head would hover near the top of the bus, if he didn't slouch. Danny's wiry. He's trying to find change for the bus guy, who's looking pissed. Danny goes to every pocket of his jean jacket until he finds two quarters. I look out the window, trying to blend. I feel kinda guilty ditchin' them for the last few months, but they were getting too deep and I didn't want any part of it anymore.

"Hey, yo, it's Chucky," says Danny. He's talking in slow mo.

"Yo, Chucky," Severs say. "Where you been?"

"Hey," I say, "Been cool."

"Been straight, I hear," says Severs.

"Hear you're back at school," Danny says. His eyelids are heavy. His lips are dry.

"Yeah," I say. "You know how it is, right? My mom's on me and stuff."

"Moms," says Severs.

"Yo, Chucky," Danny says. "We're about to go get a fix. Why don't you come with us?" Danny's looking me up and down. I don't like it. He's looking at me like I'm a snow cone. He moves his hand to his mouth a lot, wiping away something that isn't there.

Severs sits in the row in front of Danny and me. He turns and says, "Yeah, be cool, you know?"

"Nah," I say. "I'm clean now." I look around the bus. There's only a few people, old ladies, really. I look outside. It's getting dark. "This is my stop." It isn't really. They know it.

Before I can get up, Danny pulls me down and locks my arms behind my back and Severs pounds at my head. I try to scream, but the blows make my voice disappear, and I feel like I'm slipping away. I feel them yank my jacket off, and I feel them go into my pockets and take my wallet. And then I don't feel much of anything.

When I come to, the bus driver is yelling at me to wake up and there's a cop next to him. My head is bleeding and there's a big lump.

"Kid, you OK?" says the cop.

I get up, but my head hurts.

"I'm good," I say.

"You got worked over," says the bus driver. "Those kids took your wallet and jacket and crashed through the door. I knew they were trouble. I knew as soon as I saw them."

"You know those boys?" the cop asks.

I put a hand to my head. "No," I say.

He knows I'm lying. He knows I know them. But what's he going to do? "You sure?" he says.

"I just want to go home," I say. "I just want to get out of here." I stand up, but the world spins, and I sit back down. The cop and bus driver block my way. They both tell me to chill. I don't want to chill. I want to get out of here. I get up again and throw my shoulder into them, breaking through, and I'm running out the door, running fast and into the streets and away. They're not gonna catch me because the truth is they don't care about a stupid kid like me or stupid kids like Severs and Danny. One less of us and no one notices.

*

I don't go see the boss the next day or the next day after that. I'm tired and thinking there's no place in the world for a person like me. No matter how hard I try to dig myself up I feel there's something holding me down.

WeWork calls and says the blind woman is wondering where I am, she's worried about me. *They* are wondering where I am. They tell me to get to work or be fired and expelled. This is my chance in life, they say, and why am I messing it up? Do I want to be stupid all my life? I tell them to shove it.

I get on the bus and walk over to her apartment. Before I knock on the door, she opens it, as if she expected me all along.

"I knew it was you," she says, but she's in her jacket and walks past me. I follow her out the door and across the street to the conservatory. She and Keats are walking fast and I have to take two steps to catch up to her one. Keats keeps looking forward, taking glances to the right and left. His tail is down, his head low, always watching.

"Hey," I say. "I'm here to quit," I say. "I'll be gone," I say. "You'll have to find someone else."

She keeps walking. There's a bump in the sidewalk and Keats slows enough for her to lift her right leg over it. I've never seen anyone move so well.

"Where are we going?" I say.

She pushes ahead. The sky's gray, the clouds ready to pour down rain at any moment.

"Listen," I say. "I'm tired."

She stops. Keats stops. We are in the middle of the park and there is no one around us but a few trees here and there. "I want you to take Keats for a walk," she says. "I want you to take his harness and go for a walk."

91

"What?" I say.

"Close your eyes," she says.

"I don't know," I say.

"Close your eyes," she says again. I close them. I feel her hand brush against mine. I feel her push the leather leash in my right hand. I feel her move the harness handle into my left. "Walk," she says. "Keep your eyes closed and walk. Keats won't let anything hurt you. He won't lead you into traffic or a tree or anything."

I keep my eyes closed and take a step and stop. I feel the ground underneath me, feel Keats beside me, feel his chest expanding against my leg. I take another step and then another. He slows then I slow, my feet feeling a slight dip in the ground. I am listening to everything around me. I hear a bag blowing by. I hear car horns in the distance. I hear someone jog past me. I take another turn and another. I'm on grass then I'm on cement then grass again. Keats slows at a sharp descent and I feel my feet taking me down and down. Then I feel him stop. He moves a little backwards. "Let's go, Keats," I say. No matter how much I coax he doesn't move forward. I reach out. I feel brick.

I open my eyes. I'm at the Conservatory, my hand on a wall. The boss stands where she left me, about a hundred yards away, up a hill. I squint. It's suddenly bright, and my eyes have to adjust. I look at Keats who turns to look at the boss. I can't go any farther. I pat Keats.

"Good boy," I say, and we begin to make our way up.

92

Bridgeview Heights Mall

I

Sam Jeelawong lifts his right hand and raises his middle finger. It's a thoughtless move, a reflex. Sam doesn't hate Ryoko. The meaner he is the more he likes you. And he's mean to Ryoko, meaner than to any girl he has ever had a crush on, which should be an indication to Sam that he not only likes her, but he may be in love.

His family owns Tara Thai and hers Tokyo Soul—two food court stores in the Bridgeview Heights Mall. For the past three years, both stores have been competing for the title of best Asian cuisine. Competition aside, Sam thinks Ryoko is the prettiest girl in Bridgeview Heights, the prettiest girl in the Tri-State area, even when she wears the goofy red and white Tokyo Soul visor, even when her hair that is usually down to her back is smooshed into a bun and hairnet, even when she is scowling at Sam as she's doing right now and mouthing, *you fuckin' asshole.* To Sam, this is Ryoko at her prettiest.

The two of them stand outside their stores, offering free samples to passersby—bits of chicken skewered by toothpicks. Between Tara Thai and Tokyo Soul is Totally Tacos, which makes the most money in the food court, even more than some of the bigger chains. Every Friday, a mariachi band plays, beckoning patrons to their shop. On those days both Tara Thai and Tokyo Soul are invisible.

It's a Sunday and the mall is filled with older folks. The local nursing homes in the area plan early afternoon mall outings. Sam spots two older ladies, arms linked, as they take slow steps in his direction.

"Thai peanut chicken," he says. He thrusts the plate in their faces.

Ryoko takes a step toward the ladies, careful not to cross the invisible boundary they established years ago. "Japanese honey chicken," Ryoko says.

The ladies smile and decline politely, walking slowly toward Totally Tacos.

"It's free," says Sam. "And delicious."

"And probably deadly too," Ryoko says. "At Tokyo Soul, our food is cooked by the half-hour."

"If you eat at Tokyo Soul," Sam says, "you'll risk botulism."

"Tara Thai is using horse meat instead of chicken."

"We do not," says Sam.

"Not what I heard," says Ryoko.

One of the ladies stops. She wears a pink windbreaker with a unicorn patch and a bright red hat that reads *feisty*. Sam thinks she looks like a zombie, like a creature he encounters in his role-playing games on Saturday nights, one that attaches to the face and sucks out your soul. Her mouth droops, as if her entire jaw is ready to drop off. The lady points her finger at Sam and then at Ryoko. "We just want a burrito," she says. "Can we have a burrito?"

Sam nods. Ryoko nods. The two ladies move on like rusty androids.

"You scared away our business," Sam says.

"Whatever." Ryoko makes an L with her right hand. "You freak everyone out, freak."

"You're the freak," says Sam.

"Did you get that from the witty store?"

Sam's cheeks redden. He blushes not from anger or embarrassment, but because he loves these small moments with Ryoko, loves how strong and smart and humbling Ryoko can be. He tries to think of a smart retort, something that will give him equal footing, something perhaps that will make her blush, too. But he can't because the clouds have entered his brain and it's a Ryoko thunderstorm. Ryoko hail. Ryoko lightning. She is the strong wind whipping at his heart. He stands, mouth open wide, looking at her.

"Are you crazy?" Ryoko says. She begins to walk away, turning towards another elderly couple.

Sam takes a peanut chicken from his sample plate and chucks it at the back of Ryoko's head.

II

On break, Ryoko Tanaka walks down to the Piercing Pagoda where her best friend Angel works. The Piercing Pagoda barely gets any business. Usually, Angel spends her time reading, piercing her own ears, lip, and once her bellybutton. Angel's full name is Angelique Martinique. It's not her fault, she often says, her parents are a bunch of free birds. For simplicity's sake she goes by Angel. She's not a cute Hallmark angel, more like a fallen one. She dyes her hair white and wears lots of rings and reads books on sex or new age or witchcraft.

Ryoko leans on the Piercing Pagoda counter and sighs.

Angel puts down *The Kama Sutra* and says, "Did you know there are two kinds of eunuchs? Those disguised as females and those disguised as males."

"What does that mean?" Ryoko says.

"I'm not sure yet," Angel says. "Why the dark aura?"

Ryoko pretends to check out a few of the silver earrings. They're not her style—too big and too Celtic. She looks up and says, "I think my family is going to move. I've heard them talking about going to Ohio and starting a real restaurant in Akron."

"Akron is the tenth level of Hell," Angel says, doing the sign of the cross even though she's far from being a Christian.

The silver bracelets around her wrist jangle when she moves.

"Tell me about it," says Ryoko.

"Let's do a Tarot card reading." Angel says.

Ryoko shakes her head. "That stuff scares me."

Angel digs into her silver backpack and pulls out a thick deck of cards. She hands them to Ryoko and tells her to shuffle them and think about a question she wants answered. "Concentrate hard," Angel says.

Ryoko shuffles and repeats the question in her head. *Will we move? Will we move?* When she thinks her question has reached some spiritual realm, she hands back the cards. On the glass display case, Angel lines up three cards in a row. She points to each of them and tells Ryoko each of these cards represent a stage in life: the past, present, and future.

Angel flips the first card. "Eight of Wands," she says. "Your past was good. This means you've been feeling pretty content with life."

"I have been until now," says Ryoko.

"It's also a card of hope," says Angel. "The wands are pointing towards the sky."

"I've been hoping for those new shoes," says Ryoko. "The ones with the brown strap."

Angel laughs and then flips the second card. The Lovers. She smiles. "This card means you have to make a decision. Doesn't have to be about love. It just means there are choices for you. It says you're thinking with your heart and not with your head."

"Is that good or bad?"

"Either, I guess," says Angel.

Angel flips the third card over, the one that holds the future. Ryoko hopes that on the other side of that card will be a simple declarative sentence: *You are not going anywhere.* Instead it's the Three of Swords. The card has an image of a heart with three swords piercing it. The card is upside-down.

"The inverted Lord of Sorrow." Angel's brow wrinkles. "It's not that bad."

"Liar," Ryoko says.

"It's not a great card right side up," says Angel. "It's a little worse upside down. Confusion. Loss. Sadness. War. This card's usually associated with mental disorders."

"Great," says Ryoko.

Angel tucks a few of her white strands behind her ears. "Listen, they're just cards. You can interpret them any way you want."

Ryoko feels defeated, feels as if the cards have already given her the answer, and that answer is Akron. She sees smog over the horizon, the sun hiding in the sky. She sees herself in some place with smoke stacks spouting toxins into the air. She sees rivers full of sludge and WD40 cans. She sees a sign that reads *Welcome to Akron, city of the environmentally dead.*

Angel gathers up the cards and returns them to her backpack. "Go buy those shoes," she says. " If the future doesn't look good, at least you'll have some kickin' kicks."

III

Sam is in Tara Thai's kitchen, slicing onions and dicing potatoes. He repeats Stupid Sam, Stupid Sam over and over again. He thinks of all the possible ways of making Ryoko like him. He thinks of flowers and candy. He thinks of diamond rings and teddy bears. He thinks of telling Ryoko, *your smile drives me crazy.* They're not original or inventive ideas, but still, out of all the things Sam thinks about, throwing a piece of chicken at Ryoko's head is not one of them.

Stupid Sam, Stupid Sam.

This is why he's in the kitchen, chopping. When Sam feels down, he does two things: 1) he reads his gamer guides and studies up on how to be the best role-player in the world; or 2) he cooks. Cooking is Sam's hidden talent, something he picked up after watching both his mother and father in the kitchen for so many years. It's a brainless activity and he's good at it. So good that he does most of the cooking at Tara Thai. So good that his parents want him to create new dishes for the store.

Sam goes to the pot of boiling coconut milk and curry paste and drops the onions and potatoes into it. He then takes out a package of beef chunks and sets it aside. He quickly chops up two cloves of garlic and cuts five stalks of lemon grass in half. He throws the garlic and lemon grass into a sizzling frying pan, so they infuse their flavor and scent into the oil, before adding the beef. When he drops the beef in the pan, he wonders why Ryoko didn't turn around and start pelting him with honey chicken. Why she hadn't poked him with toothpicks? That was what he expected. A retaliation. A barrage of insults and physical abuse that would have left Sam smiling. But Ryoko whipped around, glared at him, and went into Tokyo Soul without a word.

Stupid Sam, Stupid Sam.

He thinks he should apologize to Ryoko. He should say, "Ryoko, that was a pretty dick move I did, throwing the chicken at your head and all. I'm really sorry." He should apologize for every single infraction he's done since they've met, listing them in order, hundreds of them. And perhaps, in that long apology he can come clean to her. Tell her what it means to him to see her everyday in the food court, the both of them standing in front of their respective stores handing out free samples. He should tell her that he has loved her—yes, he admits it—he has loved her since the moment she called him a *brainless fucker.* He can do all these things without calling her a bitch, a tramp, a slutty hoe. He can do these things and not pull her earlobes, take her visor and run away, or hit her with his shoe. He can do the right thing for once without a shred of meanness. And perhaps, just perhaps, Ryoko will feel the same way towards him, and perhaps, just perhaps, she will have that strange pull in her chest, and they can become Robin Hood and Maid Marion, Darcy and Elizabeth, Paris and Helen, all those literature book couples his teacher required him to read. There is the possibility for love, right? Because after four years of enduring Sam, wouldn't you just ignore him, swat him away like a mosquito? After four years, wouldn't you get tired of his immaturity? No, Ryoko reacts. She fights back. She gets angry and bothered and her face turns red and her cheeks puff up and her little hands clench and unclench and she's saying words she shouldn't say and she keeps doing it and doing it, every day, every time they see each other. Except today.

Stupid Sam, Stupid Sam.

It's time, Sam thinks, to put this grade school flirting behind him and climb the ranks of men and tell Ryoko how he feels and gather her up in his arms and kiss her like a vampire would. With hunger and desire. He remembers his mother telling him one day that the only reason she married his father was because he cooked for her. She wanted to marry another man, a handsomer man, a richer man, but his father's roast duck was crispy and moist and she knew right then and there that a man who could cook like this was a man she could and would never let go. It dawns on Sam that perhaps the way to Ryoko's heart is to cook her something special, something like a love potion, some secret taste that will make her heart beat faster, make her sweat, make her fall into Sam's arms breathless.

Smart Sam, Smart Sam.

99

IV

Ryoko hates Jake and Tommy even more than she hates Sam. She's come to terms with Sam. If there is a God, then Sam is her test of perseverance. If she believes in the Buddhist philosophy, then their lives must have been intertwined—in a nonsexual way, of course—and she'll have to deal with him life after reincarnated life. These are Angel's theories, which she's telling Ryoko about again as they make their way to the food court.

Ryoko, still thinking of the tarot card reading, spots Jake and Tommy, ogling a blonde by the movie theaters. Jake and Tommy are common variety mallrats. Horny and bored and at the mall from eleven to closing. They're thirteen and their favorite pastime is to "scope out chicks." They have taken a liking to Ryoko and spend most of their time in the food court "checking her out." These are the terms they use. A girl is either a "chick" or "bitch." They don't flirt, they "mack." They don't make out, they "smoosh." Jake has a nasally whine, and Tommy sounds like he's six-five two-thirty instead of five-four one-twenty. They wear oversized clothes, and tilted baseball caps. They think they're "ghetto," but really they're the two whitest boys in Bridgeview Heights. The both of them will be freshman next year, and there is nothing they want more than to "get some play" before the summer ends.

Ryoko slows down and tries to hide behind Angel. "Jake and Tommy at ten o'clock."

"Why don't you just slug them in the nose?" Angel says. "Claw their eyes out." She pulls Ryoko towards Tara Thai. "I want Thai today. No offense."

Before Ryoko can object, they're standing at the counter.

Sam's working in the front. He straightens when he sees them.

"Samuel," Angel says.

"Angelique," Sam says. Then he looks at Ryoko and says, "Ryoko."

"I hear you like throwing chicken at my friend," says Angel, hands on her hips.

Ryoko glowers at Sam. "It took an hour to get that shit out."

Sam opens his mouth and then closes it abruptly. For a second, Ryoko thinks Sam is choking, but then he says, "I'm really sorry, Ryoko. I'm an asshole." He sounds soft. The words mumble out of his mouth.

Ryoko tilts her head. "What did you say?"

"I," he stammers again, but then clears his throat. "I'm sorry," he says.

Ryoko stares at him. He fidgets with the ties on his Tara Thai apron.

Angel says, "Don't do it again or I swear I'll castrate you." She makes a snipping motion with two fingers.

Sam nods.

"Are you a Buddhist, Sam?" Angel says.

"I guess," he says.

"Maybe you know more about this than me. Buddhists believe in reincarnation, right?"

Sam nods again.

"Can you get reincarnated with the same people?"

"I guess so," Sam says.

Angel claps. "This proves my theory. You guys have been together in other lives. You almost have the same aura. Seriously. Usually auras are similar for family members, but you guys are close."

"What color's my aura?" Sam says.

"Green normally. But when you're mad or deep in thought it's dark green. Almost black. Like now."

Sam starts stirring the fried rice, warming under the heat lamps.

Ryoko watches him. She waits for him to say, "you're ugly" or "nice zit," which she's been trying to cover up. She's waiting for him to whip soy sauce and hot mustard packets at her. She's waiting for Sam to be Sam.

Angel continues to talk and point at the food she wants. She says she thinks that Ryoko and Sam were prince and peasant. No. Princess and peasant boy, but in a past life, Sam was the princess and Ryoko was the peasant boy. Ryoko was in love with the princess. "You know, the same old story. But the princess was a real bitch. A real ice queen. Oops, I mean ice princess. Can I have two spring rolls? Anyway, the princess led the peasant boy on. She let him hold her hand. Then he shit on her. I mean him. Broke his poor little peasant heart. That's why you're still having this feud. There're unresolved issues here. I mean, seriously, this could be your fifth time doing this. Maybe you two should talk and hatch this out. Maybe when that happens you won't have to deal with each other again. Can I have extra soy sauce, please?"

Ryoko shakes her head and says, "Whatever."

Sam piles on packets of soy sauce. He makes another plate of rice and peanut chicken. "I think that'd be cool," he says. "I mean, I'd like to talk, I guess."

"I think you should," says Angel. "Because if she has to deal with you again and I have to hear about her dealing with you again in my next life I'm going to be pissed off. How much for all that?"

"It's on me," Sam says.

"Did you spit in it?" Ryoko says.

"No," Sam says. "I made it."

"The food?" says Angel.

"Yeah," says Sam. "I like to cook."

"Well, thanks," Angel says and picks up the overflowing tray. "You've been cool and I don't know why and I don't care."

Ryoko stares at Sam. Sam looks like something is hurting him. His teeth are clenched awkwardly. Can it be a smile?

"Do you want anything else, Ryoko? A coke? Sprite? Ice tea?"

Ryoko wants to ask: *Who are you?* She wants to reach out and grab the sides of his face and tug. Perhaps it's a mask. Perhaps it isn't Sam at all, but some deformed but gentle kid in a Sam mask. Ryoko looks around. She's waiting for the real Sam to come out and do stupid Sam things. But she sees no one, not even Angel, who has found a table in the middle of the food court. She realizes she's alone and Sam is staring at her with that smile.

"I can get my own pop," she says, "at my own store."

"Right," he says.

"Right," she says, backing away slowly, looking in both directions to see whether Jake and Tommy are still in the area, to see whether she's still on planet Earth, not some alternate reality where people take on their opposite characteristics. The good become the evil. The sluts become the chaste, and brats become somewhat sweet.

V

As Sam closes up, he thinks about his past lives and auras. As he's pouring the leftovers into the trashcan, he wonders whether Ryoko ate the peanut chicken, whether she liked it. As he walks the garbage to the dumpster, he imagines holding Ryoko's hand, imagines kissing her. As he throws the steel containers into the sink for washing, he wonders what Ryoko is doing right now.

Sam is elsewhere. When he role-plays on Saturdays, he allows the game to take over and transport him into that fictional world. It becomes more than a game. It becomes survival. It is his hand bringing down the sword onto a goblin's head. It is his body leaping from a three-story building onto a banshee's stomach. He plays as if it is his life at risk. That's why the Bridgeview Heights Gaming Association named him Gaming God of the Year.

Even now, as Sam begins washing the steel containers, the steam from the faucet rising from the sink, Sam is in a world of *maybes* and *perhaps*, a world of possibility, not unlike the fictional landscapes he often traverses.

Maybe Angel is right. Perhaps he and Ryoko are living out life after life, unable to reconcile their problems. Maybe in another time Ryoko was a magician, able to control the four elements, and he was a warrior, who wielded a broadsword like a third arm. And maybe in this life, they were on a mission to rescue a jeweled tiara from the clutches of a mad queen. The tiara was cursed; it made the wearer evil. The mad queen ruled the countryside and forced her people into becoming slaves. It was up to Ryoko the magician and Sam the warrior to restore order.

But on their journey they fell in love. They couldn't help themselves. When they camped out at night, Sam the warrior watched the curve of the magician's hip. When the warrior cut firewood, Ryoko the magician peeked at his pulsating muscles. They laughed and bumped shoulders on their journey toward the mad queen's kingdom. Nothing could disrupt their love. An army of monkey demons? Decapitated in a few swings of the sword. Fire dragons? Left soaked by a tidal wave. Their love was the most powerful weapon they possessed.

But it blinded them, too.

"I don't think this is a good idea," Sam the warrior said. "We have people to save."

Ryoko the magician flicked her wrist, and in her hand appeared a strawberry-flavored snow cone. How could Sam the warrior not love that?

But this story doesn't end well, does it?

The queen will win, won't she?

She must for Sam and Ryoko to try again in the next life and the life after that. Their lives have become like role-playing games. You fail, you try again. You die, you re-roll the dice. But then an unpleasant thought enters his mind. What if they accomplish their mission? What if they connect in this life? When they are reborn, will they stand on opposite ends of the world, never to meet?

Sam scrubs the container clean and puts it on the drying rack when he hears his name from the front of the store. He goes out, hands dirty with chicken slime. It's Ryoko.

"Hey," he says.

"Yeah," she says.

Sam looks at a strand of hair that falls into her eyes. She pushes it away.

"I heard someone still here," she says.

"I was closing up."

"Cool." She seems to be talking to the napkin dispenser. "I just wanted to say thanks for the food. It was good."

They both stand there saying nothing. Sam's finger twitches. He has the urge to pinch Ryoko, but Ryoko starts walking toward the exit before he can act. She turns one last time and says, "It was really good though. I wanted you to know."

Sam nods, watching her go.

There are things in this world, he thinks, in this life, that are too good to do over and over again.

VI

Ryoko stands in the food court, plate of crispy chicken in hand. She says nothing as people pass. She holds out the plate and stares ahead. She spent the last five days fighting with her parents. When she confronted them about whether or not they were moving, they didn't deny it. Yes, they are. Yes, to Akron. Yes, they're opening a new restaurant. At the end of the month, Ryoko will head to Ohio. At the end of the day, Tokyo Soul will close up. Next week, the Cajun Corral will replace it.

Now, she's thinking of the tarot card reading and how she feels the Three of Swords piercing *her* heart. She's even thinking of Sam—despite herself—who she's rarely seen except for a quick wave here and there. Ryoko closes her eyes and shakes her head. She hates thinking about him. She hates to admit that she has grown fond of Sam, perhaps more than fond.

One night when Ryoko escaped her house, she spent a few hours at Angel's. To get Ryoko's mind off the move, Angel told her about another one of Ryoko's past lives, one more outrageous than the princess and peasant boy story. Angel was convinced that Ryoko and Sam were lovers.

"Where do you get this from?" Ryoko asked.

"Hear me out."

Angel described London in 1665. She said Ryoko met Sam at one of those fancy balls, where the women wore enormous dresses. Ryoko's name was Victoria. Sam's name was Dylan. It was love at first sight. Dylan bowed. Victoria curtsied. They spent the entire night dancing around the enormous ballroom, Victoria's dress trailing behind her. That night, Dylan kissed

Victoria on the cheek and she knew right then and there she was in love. For the next few months, Dylan courted Victoria, picking her up in a carriage and riding her off into a meadow where they had picnics and he read poetry to her. Then sometime in 1666, they were to marry. On the evening of the wedding, someone screamed fire. All of London was ablaze. Victoria and Dylan struggled against the church doors. They were trapped in the burning church. They died in each other's arms.

"I did some research on your birthday," Angel said, "and found out that Venus was really close when you were born. Then I consulted an astrology chart and it said those who are born when Venus is nearest died tragically in their former lives. Something beyond your control. A disaster. I filled in the blanks."

"First off," said Ryoko, "I find it funny that in our past lives you've made two Asians white. Second, I was in love with silly, stupid Sam? Get real."

"Sexy, sensual Sam," Angel said.

Ryoko scrunched up her face and said, ewww, but an image of kissing Sam in front of Tara Thai flashed through her mind. It was quick and it happened again. It kept recurring.

She had felt nothing but irritation for Sam from the very day they met and he squirted her with a water gun. But now, she can't shake him out of her thoughts and she can't understand why he's there when she closes her eyes at night, why he's there when she dazes off, why he's there now, smiling and winking at her.

Maybe it was his food. Maybe it was the peanut chicken. She told Angel she would take one bite. It looked disgusting. But that one bite stirred something in her. She felt like the food court was spinning. Not in a bad way, not like vomit inducing spinning, but pleasant revolutions. She closed her eyes as she ate more, savoring each bite. She ate until there was nothing left. Not one grain of rice, not one streak of peanut sauce. The

Styrofoam plate was clean. Throughout the rest of that day she thought of Sam. She wondered what went through his mind when he cooked. She thought of him so much that when she walked past Tara Thai after closing up Tokyo Soul, she called out for him, hoping and not hoping he was there. When he came out, looking as if he just woke up from a pleasant dream, she told him she liked his food.

Since then, Sam has ducked away from her. He's not the same Sam anymore. He's changed and she can't explain his transformation. It's like one of those dramatic before and after photos of fat people. Before Sam was fat with insults and energy. Now he seems to be the embodiment of the word *nice*. Part of Ryoko misses the old Sam. It was easy to tell him off, to outwit him. The old Sam brought out the unabashed Ryoko, the Ryoko who wasn't embarrassed to curse and retaliate in public, the Ryoko people rarely see. It felt good sometimes to hit Sam. It felt good to call him inventive names. Part of her also wants to know the new Sam, to understand what makes him tick, to eat his cooking day after day, to possibly feel his lips against hers.

Ryoko looks over at Tara Thai but see nothing but the Totally Tacos' mariachi band beginning to tune up for their performance. She hopes for a glimpse of Sam. She thinks they should talk like Angel said. She wants him to tell him about the move, about the new restaurant. She wants to tell him about how she feels. She keeps staring at Tara Thai, but Sam never emerges. Instead, Jake and Tommy strut towards her. They make curves with their hands. They blow her kisses.

VII

Sam scoops jasmine rice into a tupperware container and

pours the hot chicken stir-fry on top of it. He finely chops cilantro and sprinkles it over the rice. When everything is to his liking, he places a lid over the container and heads out into the food court.

For the last week, he's been obsessed. He has had two thoughts: cooking and Ryoko. He spent most of his time in the kitchen, perfecting his dish. When he wasn't satisfied, he threw out what was in the frying pan and started over. He tinkered with the flavor of his dish endlessly, adding a squirt of fish sauce, a tablespoon of sugar, squeezing a lime for a drop or two of juice. By the end of the fourth day, he had it: Siam Sam's Satisfying Chicken Stir-Fry.

Sam has consciously avoided Ryoko. He feared doing something stupid, something that would make her hate him, which he knew he was more than capable of. While he tried to be nice, to be the man she dreamed of, a part of him wanted to revert to the way he was. When he saw her briefly yesterday, he wanted to poke her with a chopstick. When she was across the mall earlier today, he had an urge to send spitballs in her direction. Better to hide than to risk messing up another life.

In the food court, people have started to gather around Totally Tacos. The lead man—Paolo, another gamer—is dressed in black with silver sequins. He wears a large sombrero. He attaches a fake mustache that runs down his chin. He picks at his guitar and tinkers with the tuning knobs.

Around the crowd, Sam finds Ryoko. She grimaces at two boys, who are showing her something in their hands. It's Jake and Tommy. They're in the gaming club and think they're bad asses; they think Sam is a hack. Sam remembers in one adventure an axe-wielding troll decapitating both their characters in one hit. They bitched about how the game was rigged, that a level 23 troll shouldn't have that much power. But these two fools forgot that a troll's strength is multiplied by two in swampy areas, and they were in a swamp, the Swamp of Forgetfulness.

Sam gets close enough to hear Ryoko. "Gross," she says. "Go away."

"Don't be like that," says Jake.

"Touch 'em," says Tommy.

Sam walks behind the two kids. He is nearly a foot taller. Jake and Tommy don't notice him until Ryoko looks up. She smiles desperately and mouths, please help.

"Yo," Sam says.

The boys jolt around. They look annoyed, their lips tight. Sam knows he has interrupted their "mack" time. He knows, to them, he's a "downer."

"What you got there?" Sam says, noticing that in their hands are poop and vomit. He bursts out laughing, not because he finds the scene absurd—two thirteen-year-old punks, trying to flirt with a beautiful girl by showing her poop and vomit—but because he has thought of it before and never had the nerve to do it. "You get these at the joke shop?" Sam says.

"Yeah," says Tommy. He puffs out his chest and tries to look tough.

"Two for five," says Jake, who doesn't look at Sam, but keeps his eyes on Ryoko.

Ryoko stares off to the side, toward the Totally Tacos crowd, at anything but the lump of poop and the spread of vomit in Jake and Tommy's hands.

"Nice," says Sam. "Can I touch it?"

Jake and Tommy shrug.

Sam takes the poop and palms it. It's heavier than it looks. He squeezes it. It gives under his touch. He bends down to take a closer look at the fake vomit in Jake's hand. It's rubbery and slick. It has corn chunks in it. He laughs at the details.

"This is cool," says Sam.

"Isn't it?" says Jake, suddenly excited. "This chick don't think so."

"We just want her to touch 'em," says Tommy.

"It won't hurt, Ryoko," Sam says. He holds the piece of poop out. "Just a little touch."

Ryoko narrows her eyes. When Sam role-plays he knows the instant he has made a wrong move. He knows out all the infinite options he has at his disposal he has chosen the wrong one, acted too quickly, acted without thought or consideration, and this decision would lead him to doom. He knows now, standing in front of Tokyo Soul, the mariachi band starting up, that he has done just that. Sam should apologize to Ryoko and tell Jake and Tommy to scram and take their poop and vomit with them. The right words build in his throat, but something holds them back, something he doesn't understand. This is the same something that tells him to pull Ryoko's hair despite the outcome, the same something that makes him mock her even though his brain is telling him to stop. He holds the piece of poop in his hand, extending it at Ryoko's face. He's smiling when he shouldn't.

Ryoko grabs the poop and whips it across the mall. It bounces high up and continues to roll until it comes to a stop in front of Pizza Palace. People walk around it, their faces twist in disgusted. Jake and Tommy take off after it.

"What's up with that?" Tommy says.

"The bitch is crazy," says Jake.

"Nice throw," says Sam. "That thing was like a rubber ball."

"I hate you," Ryoko says to Sam.

Sam keeps smiling. He can't stop.

"You're an asshole. A stupid asshole." Ryoko's body heaves heavy breaths.

Sam extends the tupperware container to her. "I made this for you."

She looks at it. She takes it and then opens it up. She smells it and smiles. Sam thinks his food has saved their relationship. But then, with a smile, Ryoko dumps Siam Sam's Satisfying Chicken Stir-Fry all over Sam's head, and then turns to Tokyo Soul as Paolo goes into his solo.

Brown sauce drips from his hair, chicken chunks cling to his shoulders. Sam smells delectable. A few people in the mall stare at him and laugh. Others ignore him. And in spite of all of this, Sam still smiles, looking at where Ryoko used be, oblivious to the fact that he will never see her at the mall after today, oblivious to her move to Akron, oblivious to the possibilities of their relationship had he done the right thing. He knows none of this, only that he has failed once again and this time what he has done is irreparable. The thought doesn't bring him down. Instead, he finds himself giddy with pleasure, his head moving to the music, his foot tapping to the rhythm of the guitars and the drums and the cha-chas. He will get another chance, in another life. He will start preparing for it now, so when they meet again, he will say the right things and do the right things. In the next life, he will be all that she needs and wants, not immature or foolish. He will get it right. There'll be nothing to keep them apart.

Threatlessness

So you're walking home from the library with a bunch of books in your backpack—the new Clive Barker, Stephen King, Dean Koontz, Peter Straub, the horror masters—and it's night, new moon. The country roads are darker than usual, the cornfields around you ominous, predatory. Nights like this you'd expect a monster to jump out and drag you into the cornfields and that'd be it. You'd be front-page news, another unsolved murder in rural Illinois, another addition to the growing tall tales of children lost in the corn. It doesn't help that someone goes missing every few summers or so and the body isn't found until the fields are mowed. The newspaper article would describe the claw marks across your torso as inhuman. The article would mention the zoologist, who could not identify what type of animal would be able to inflict such grotesque damage in the middle of nowhere Illinois. No fox could do this. Too small. There were certainly no bears. The zoos—the nearest one about three hours away—have not reported a missing lion. Your murder would keep experts scratching their heads. You'd be famous for it. You'd be on one those paranormal investigative shows you obsess about, and they'd do a reenactment of what might of happened that night, and the boy playing you would not look like you at all. He'd be taller and stronger, and he would put up a fight, and that monster would be called the Cornfield Canine. Legends and lore would grow from your death, and generation after generation, people would still remember your name—Barry Annan Kriegel.

This would be a good story.

But the truth: I got beat up. Plain and simple.

The worst part: I lived.

*

I find myself in a bed that's not my bed, and in a room that's not my room. The sun hurts my eyes. I'm hooked up and beeping. I try to move but can't; my body feels encased because it is encased. In bandages. In casts. In slings. My legs are elevated. My neck is in a brace. I can't turn my head. I'm staring at a ceiling that is not my ceiling.

My mother says, "Hi, Peanut." She peers over me.

"I hate being called Peanut."

"I know." She smiles and then she starts to cry. Tears drip on my face, and I can't dodge them because I can't move. What comes out of her eyes goes into mine. "I'm sorry," she says. I can't talk either because her tears are torrenting—a word I made up—into my mouth.

"Woman, you're blubbering on our son."

It's my father. He would say blubber. He would address my mother as woman. His voice—a low rumble—shakes walls.

Someone towels me off and I see both of them now, and understand why everyone thinks they're an odd couple with an odd son. My mother's small like me, like most Thai women, not like the Scandinavian stock my father comes from. Kriegel men are raised to wrestle bulls. My father's brothers are rodeo clowns, and my father, for a few years when he was younger, worked at a circus as the Strongest Man in the Universe. You would think some of his genes would pass down to me—those mountain man arms, those legs like Redwoods. But no. When your father runs away from the circus and spends a year overseas and falls for a petite woman from a petite country, you roll the dice when it comes to genetics. I got my mother's frame—

four feet five inches and arms like twigs—and my father's features—big mouth, big eyes, big nose. A science experiment
gone wrong.

"You been out for a while," my father says. "Two days." I
notice how thick his blonde beard is. Jungle-face, I like to call
him. For the life of me I can't grow facial hair of any sort.

"Don't say that," says my mother.

"What then?" my father says.

"We're glad you're awake or something like that."

"It's implied, don't you think?"

"Or I love you, or, Hey, there, champ, or—"

"Champ?" He looks down at me. "Want me to call you
champ?"

I can't shake my head.

"Be better to Peanut." My mother chokes on her words.
She is about to rain on me again.

"I hate being called Peanut," I say.

"She knows," my father says and pulls my mother close to
him, and it's as if she disappears into his enormous chest. And
from this vantage, they seem to meld into one creature, like the
Chimera or the Centaur. He rocks her until she's done and then
he says to me, "You got anything to say?"

"You should see the other guy." I try to smile, but my jaw
hurts. Neither of my parents find humor in the situation.

*

This was how I was discovered: In the morning, right as
the sun was coming up, a Jack Russell sniffed at my hands and
began barking. Its owner, a girl, parted the corn and found the
rest of me. At first, she thought I was dead, but she heard me
breathing or trying to breathe. By then, blood had nearly filled

my lungs. The girl and dog were on their routine morning walk. She ran home and called an ambulance.

Her name: Florence. Her dog's name: Oliver.

I go to school with Florence. She's five desks to the right of me in English, and two desks in front of me in Geography. At Festival of the Countries—a yearly high school event—she was the Netherlands and had tulips and Dutch chocolates at her booth. She wore wooden clogs, too, and put her hair in braided pigtails. I was Thailand and my mother made fried rice no one ate. Florence is pretty, but not overly pretty. A girl like her usually lives at the end of a horror movie. The prettiest and sluttiest ones go first, but the semi-pretty smart ones live, and at times, save the day.

"Call her," my mother says. "You need to thank her."

"Can't I just send a card?"

"I already have, Peanut."

"I hate being called Peanut."

"I send a card and call her everyday."

"Really?"

"I call her and say thank you for rescuing my one and only baby boy."

I want to shake my head.

My mother points to a bouquet of blue carnations. "These are from her." She picks up a little card and reads it. "'Get well. Your friend, Florence.' Isn't that nice?"

I suddenly feel nauseous and room spins and I get sick on myself. I have these bouts. My mother calls the nurse and they begin cleaning me up. I'm not used to it, this attention, the flipping and turning, the fact that I'm naked in front of a stranger and my mother, but this time I'm not thinking about that. I'm thinking about Florence and her flowers and her card. I'm thinking of a love story for once, not a horror one, where two people meet and both of them survive until the end.

*

On the fifth day, my parents allow me to speak to the authorities. No one saw the other guy. My injuries—an endless
list of brokens—made the police think it could have been
more than one person.

When Sheriff Parker comes by, he winces at my appear-
ance. "I know, I know," I say, "I have to quit that modeling
job." He asks the standard questions, and I keep repeating *I
don't remember*. "You don't remember one thing from that night?
Not his face, not his voice? A snippet of anything that could
help?"

"You're assuming it's a he?" I say. "You ever seen She-ra?
Or Xena Warrior Princess?"

Not a chuckle. "You didn't provoke anybody at school?" he
says.

"Provoke?" I say.

"Talk to somebody's girl you shouldn't have?"

I laugh and my chest and throat hurts. "Oh, yeah," I say.
"I'm rolling with the girls."

"You don't know what could set off a hooligan nowadays."

Yep, he says hooligan.

"And there are lots of hooligans around here."

Yep, he says it again.

"I try not to consort with hooligans."

"Peanut," my mother says, and I can tell by her tone she
means, be serious.

"Son," Sheriff Parker says, "I want to find the person who
did this to you."

He is a nice cop; nice cops always get killed. They're usually

117

the first one in, the first one dead.

I skate around the truth. I do remember something. It isn't a sound or a face. The something I remember isn't going to help Sheriff Parker find who or whatever did this to me. It is a feeling, an impression, of suddenly being weightless, of losing control of my body, of not having a body at all. I remember this. I felt my face planted into the earth, and I thought, as silly as this may sound, that I was a seed, and come a few weeks me-flowers would begin blooming all over the place because I was an invasive species like the honeysuckle my mother tries to get rid of even though it smells so good. I remember this.

"I don't remember anything," I say. "I don't want to."

*

My mother gives me Florence updates. "We're buddies," she says. She tells me Oliver has a new collar, pink with spikes, and Florence is travelling to a university a couple hours away to compete in the Regional High School Mathalete Competition. "She's really nervous, but she thinks the team can win it all." My mother tells me Florence says the whole school wants me to get well and come back, and Sheriff Parker has been around talking to students, though she can't imagine anyone at school being capable of doing that. "The school is telling everyone to be careful when walking alone. They're asking people to go out in pairs." My mother tells me Florence doesn't walk the same route anymore. "She's not scared, but she gets sad thinking about that day." My mother tells me Florence is coming to visit soon. "She wants to bring Oliver, too, but the hospital probably won't allow that."

I like these daily updates; I pretend not to. I pretend to be nonchalant. But most of my time, I spend thinking about Florence. What's she doing? How much of the time does she think about me? I do nothing but lie in bed, so I create other worlds: Florence and me escaping Hitchcock's birds, Florence and me fleeing a haunted house, Florence and me fighting off a coven of vampires, Florence and me.

The thing about horror is this: If you remain together, nothing can defeat you.

＊

Ten days pass. The doctor orders more brain scans. The way he describes it: the brain is like a peach in a jar. Shake the jar too hard and significant damage occurs. "I'm a fruit," I say. He doesn't laugh.

The nurses come in and out. They give me painkillers. They replace the bedpan. They ask me how I'm feeling. "It's like I'm on a cruise," I tell them, and they giggle and giggle. One of them says I have the gift of gab, and my father says he doesn't think it's a gift.

I like these interruptions. It keeps my mind occupied. Left alone too long, I drift. I overwhelm myself with hopelessness. How do I describe it? Like this is all there is to the world. Like I'm trapped. Like every time I turn there's a wall. This feeling makes me fold into myself. I was experiencing this before the accident. I don't remember when it started, only it started, and the only way to control it is to I lose myself in twisted and horrific stories, stories of places and people not of this realm, stories that can't possibly happen in real life. Afterwards, I feel better about where I am. I can finish a book and say, *well at least I'm not being chased by a demon who wants to disembowel me and devour my soul.*

Still, the nights are longest. The hospital is quiet. My parents are home. Most of the time I can't sleep. I'm stuck, staring at the dark ceiling wishing it were a sky. Sometimes, I imagine myself in a coffin and dirt is piled on me until my sight is blocked, until the only sound I hear is the wheeze of my lonely breath.

*

My parents take turns at the hospital. My mother enjoys these mothering moments. She misses them, and I recognize I'm not an easy kid to mother. At home, before all of this, I'd disappear into my cave and read. I'd get straight A's, except gym. I did my chores. Her mom job has been a breeze. I think she's been waiting for something like this.

My father, however, is not equipped for this, especially feeding me. I don't make it easy.

"Can you do a choo choo train?" I say.

He grumbles.

"How about a jet engine?"

I open my mouth wide and he shoves a spoonful of potato mush into it. His hand is enormous, like an asteroid coming at my face. He grimaces at the teeth missing in my mouth. I like poking the spaces with my tongue.

"Daddy," I say in a sugary sweet voice. "I have an itch."

"Where?" he says.

"You don't want to know."

"Deal with it."

This is how I pass my time, making my giant father squirm.

Those books from the library—they were beside me when Florence found me, my hand clutching my backpack tight. They weren't stolen, weren't lost. Nothing was taken. Not my wallet, not anything. This, again, has thrown Sheriff Parker for

120

a loop. "Why would someone do this if they didn't have a reason?" I want to tell him a boy like me is an easy target because I exude threatlessness. It's a word I made up. But it seems apropos in this situation. Threatlessness: the inability to pose a threat. Because of that, no one needs a reason. I am reason enough.

But those books. Despite his inadequacies as a caretaker, my father reads to me. My mother couldn't get past the first decapitation in Clive Barker's novel, but my father relishes the violent moments. He has a great reading voice, and I find it easy to imagine him as the Strongest Man in the Universe those many years ago, flexing and tipping cars. I can imagine him in silly spandex, saying silly lines like, "Strength has no limits for I am the Strongest Man in the Universe." When I was even smaller than I am now, my father launched me in the air like I was a basketball and caught me.

I'm thinking about those moments today, the feeling of flight, of invincibility. Today's not a good day. My head hurts over my right eye, like an ice pick is stabbing at it, and my body seems extra heavy, tied with concrete blocks.

"You ever drop me?" I ask. I interrupt my father mid-paragraph. He is reading about an insane woman keeping her favorite author hostage, but my mind can't keep focused.

"What do you mean?" he says.

"When you threw me up in the air. When I was a kid."

"Not once." He shuts the book.

"I thought maybe that would explain me."

He doesn't say anything. I can tell that he is thinking hard about the right thing to say. I can tell that he wishes my mother were here for these moments because she's good at stuff like this.

"It's cool, Dad," I say. "Don't stress about it."

He nods.

"I would beat me up," I say.

He listens.

"If I saw me walking and I had nothing better to do, I would do it. I would beat the crap out of me. It would be fun."

Then I say nothing. I don't want to be here. I mean, anywhere. I close my eyes. I hear nothing but the machines beside me and my father's metronomic breathing and the TV of another patient a room over.

Then, like an alien abduction, the bottom of the bed rises. I open my eyes.

"You're too mouthy," my father says. He lifts the bed. Curling it like a dumbbell. I'm on a merry-go round. Up. Down. Up. Down.

"I have a big mouth," I say. "Literally."

"Someday you'll grow into that big mouth of yours."

"Maybe not," I say.

"Maybe not," he says.

"Maybe I'll always be a big mouth, small-headed kid forever."

"Maybe. That's OK, too." The bed squeaks with each repetition.

"Is it?" I say.

"Sure." His shoulders are as wide as the bed, his arms about to burst out of his sleeves. I used to run my matchbox cars over his muscles. When it went over a bulging vein, he said, "Speed bump." Now he holds the bed under his chin, and I feel my body slide toward the headboard.

"Mom would be pissed if she saw you doing this."

"She's not here."

"The nurses, too."

"They're not here."

"Are we having a father son moment?"

My father smiles and all the grooves in his forehead bend up. He puts the bed down. "That mouth of yours, I swear."

*

Cards from my classmates are stacked on my bedside. Get Well balloons float a few inches from the ceiling. Flower arrangements are stacked at every corner. I'm getting all this love, when no one gave me the time of day. Now, they write things like: *Stay strong, buddy*, or, *God is watching over you*, or, *You're a beast*. My mother reads everything to me and says, "Peanut, you have lots and lots of friends."

"You know what they say," I tell her. "A friend in need is a friend indeed."

"Are you being sarcastic again?"

"Whatever do you mean?"

The fact remains: I have become a presence in my absence.

*

Florence sends white roses and another card. It's a picture of a Jack Russell with one of those silly megaphone cones around its neck. She writes a longer message on the inside, and I tell my mother I can read it myself. She understands and tapes the card on my elevated arm and leaves the room.

Dear Barry, I hope you're getting better. Your mom is super cool. She calls everyday and keeps thanking me, though I tell her I did what someone else would have done. She talks about you a lot. I mean, she's a mother after all. Not just updates, though. She tells stories about when you were younger. Did you really chopstick a

dead fly and eat it? I guess we do weird things when we're little.
I also like the one where you helped the ants take the cracker to
their home. These stories make me feel l like I know you already.
I've been busy with school. At the yearbook meeting, I suggested
we do a page dedicated to you. Everyone liked the idea. I hope
you don't mind. I know we haven't talked, but we've had an in-
teresting introduction. (Haha). Each day goes by and you're not
in your seat. And I notice. Everyone notices. So get better, you
know. I'll come soon. Your Friend, Florence

I stare at the card, at the wave of her handwriting, how the
F in Florence flourishes. I don't want to leave this moment.
Because in my mind I see her at her desk writing this, Oliver at
her feet. Because I believe everything she says, not like the other cards, not like the balloons and flowers. Because my body,
for the first time, doesn't hurt. Because someone out there is
thinking about me.

*

Numbers don't make sense. And because numbers don't
make sense I don't know how long I've been here. When the
doctor comes in, he tests my vision and asks me how many fingers he's holding up. I don't know. I mean, they're fingers, but
the concept of numbers have escaped me. It's like a wall has
been built in my brain, and I can't access certain information.
Sometimes, it's temporary; sometimes not. The doctor doesn't
like what he sees. I can tell. I can tell when my father is extra
nice, or my mother continues to call me Peanut, even though
I hate it.

I think I will never leave the hospital. At times, I'm OK
with this. Out there are hidden dangers. In here is predictable

routine. Think about apocalyptic movies or when zombies attack. The survivors are always searching for shelter, a place
to guard them from the perils of the outside world. The hospital is that shelter. I understand its sounds. I understand its
rhythms. I wake up. I eat. I get washed. Bandages are replaced.
Temperature is checked. The same nurses come in and out.
The same doctor. The same parents. The same shows on the
same TV.

But even here, I realize, you can't escape for long. Eventually, the zombies will come. Eventually, you're reminded of the
things you don't want to be reminded of.

*

Today an orderly wheeled out a body and parked it in
front of my door for a few seconds. I heard him say "Finis"
to a passing nurse. From my bed, I was able to turn my head
slightly and catch a glimpse of a blurry hand. I don't know if
the hand belonged to a man or a woman. I don't know how
the person died. I don't know whether the person was young
or old, whether it was an illness or an accident or old age. I
don't know who cried for the body. I don't know what the
body has left behind. I am haunted by this lack of knowledge.
I shouldn't be. I've read hundreds of books where bodies are
mutated, dissected, mauled, books where at least five people
die gruesomely. But real death—I don't know. Real death—
well it's real. It's scarier than anything I've ever read.

This thought invades my bruised brain: You are here and
then you aren't.

*

I can't talk. When I open my mouth out come these sounds. More scans. More blood work. The doctor says, the brain is a complicated organ. He says answers are not black and white. He says this might be temporary. He says things are misfiring.

But it isn't temporary. I'm without a voice for days. Me without a voice equals uselessness.

I nod or shake my head at yes or no questions.

"Are you doing OK, Peanut?" my mother says.

I shake my head.

"He hates being called Peanut," my father says.

I nod.

Most days, my head feels like its in a vise and someone is turning and turning it until eventually my eyes will pop out and my brain will ooze out of my ear. I write the doctor this and he says, "Hm."

Will my head explode?

The doctor doesn't laugh. "No," he says, "but we're monitoring it."

Darn. I really want my head to explode.

Humorless, he says, "Biologically impossible."

*

Each day there is something else wrong, and each day I'm subjected to more tests. Each day, the cards and good wishes come less and less. Each day, my mother breaks a little more. Each day, my father seems weaker. Each day, Florence doesn't come.

I sleep most of the time or pretend to. It hurts to have my eyes open. My father reads to me, but I don't hear him. I'm some place else. I'm far. I'm not in this world. Where am I? I don't know.

Sheriff Parker visits one afternoon. My father shakes his hand and I notice how Sheriff Parker winces. My mother remains by my side.

What's up, Stranger? I write.

He doesn't look at me. He keeps his eyes on my father. "I've learned a few things."

There's a monster in our town. I knew it.

He shakes his head. "Nothing thrilling like that."

"Sorry," my father says. "Can't shut him up even when he can't speak."

The sheriff offers a small smile and then continues. "Couple of city boys came down and caused a ruckus at the bar that day."

Yep, he said ruckus.

"Riled people up. Said not so nice things about our town."

Like what?

"I don't want to use that type of language," Sheriff Parker says.

"I appreciate it," my mother says.

Pretty please.

"Peanut." My mother squeezes my hand.

"They got tossed out a little before you were walking home that night," the sheriff said. "Witnesses said they were headed to the fields."

Took two of them to take me down, huh?

"I think the boys were drunk and nasty and you just happened to be there at the wrong time."

It's always the wrong time for me.

Nobody laughs.

"No one took down a license plate?" my mother says.

"Or a name," says my father.

The sheriff shakes his head.

127

"I don't understand it," says my mother. She begins to cry. My father puts his hand on her shoulder. I hate the sound. It's not a silent cry. It's hard and it's loud and draws the attention of the nurses outside. My mother, though small, possesses the cry of beasts.

I want to tell my mother I understand it. I understand everything. I understand that we live in an ugly place. I expect this. There is nothing right or just that happens here. Evil exists. It does and it needs no explanation. It needs no cause. It just happens. In a cornfield. In a graveyard. In a home, haunted or not. I understand that we don't ask for this, but sometimes this is what we receive.

Sheriff Parker says, "I'm sorry."

My mother gathers herself. She uses my father's shirt to dry her face. There are wet spots and streaks on his blue shirt. "Thank you," she says.

"If they come to the bar again," the sheriff says, "the bartender says he'll call me ASAP."

Unsolved Mysteries, I write.

"Afraid so," Sheriff Parker says.

Have you considered the Cornfield Canine?

*

You fell asleep in the corn. You didn't get beat up. You were walking home, and the night got to you so you stopped at the side of the road and ventured into the corn. Who knew that you would discover a circle of flat land in there? Just the ideal place to lie down and look at the sky. The ground was soft, and the earth plush like a pillow. It seemed inviting, the ground, and when you lay on it, the sky opened up. This was a vantage rarely seen. Everyone is too busy looking forward. But there are other parts of this life. You know that now. The birds know it, too. So you lay there and the stars were too numerous to count, but you tried anyway. One, two, three…four hundred, eight hundred, one thousand. You counted and you fell asleep, only for a moment, only until you were awakened by a dog, the Cornfield Canine, and he wasn't as big as you imagined him. In fact, he was your size, small with a black spot at the tip of his tail and he lay next to you, and you could feel his breathing and his short snorts through his short nose. And then came this girl, and she lay next to you, too. She didn't say anything. You didn't say anything, and this was how it should be, just the sky, a dog, and galaxies above. Eventually, she asked whether you were afraid, and you told her no. She said there were dangers in the corn. Not here, you said. She said people often lose their way. Not if you stay still, you said. Sometimes people find you. Oh, she said. Oh, you said. And then you felt yourself sink into the earth, just you. Not the girl. Not the dog. You didn't think it was possible, but you were even further away from the stars. And sleep weighed heavy on your eyes again. You closed them and waited for whatever dream to come.

Tip

The Mothership came through the door, tripping on clothes and cans, and told me in that voice I knew she used with her second graders that I should get my shit together. (She didn't say shit.) She said I shouldn't be such a lazy ass. (She didn't say ass either.) She said it broke her heart when I dropped out of school. She said she never thought her life would turn out like this. A philandering husband. A socially inept son. What has she done to deserve this? Fuck. (She most definitely didn't say fuck.)

"You're getting a job," she said. "This…," she waved a sharp finger around the room, "…has lasted long enough. Do you hear me, young man?"

Of course I heard her. Of course I knew what she meant by "this." This = empty cans of Mountain Dew, bags and bags of junk food, AC/DC rocking on the dusty CD player, comic book action figures enshrined on a bookcase of comic books, posters of naked anime characters on black walls, and a life size cardboard cutout of Spock looming above the bed.

Of course I heard her. But how could I respond? There were dire circumstances to attend to. I, Savage Rose, was surrounded by a coven of vampires who were avenging the death of their leader beheaded by my magical katana. And here I was, back against the cold, gray stone of a mausoleum. I rapidly tapped on buttons. *Jump, run, duck, Savage. Get the hell out of there! Cemeteries aren't good places to be at night.*

And then the screen went black.

My mom held the unplugged computer cord in her hand. "Get a fucking job." She said fucking. She said it the way she would teach her students a new vocabulary word, enunciating every letter, pausing at every syllable. "Do you fucking hear me?"

*

Two things the Mothership got out of the settlement: me and my dad's '72 VW Beetle. She spews smoke into Florida's environmentally conscious air; she backfires occasionally like a gunshot. I love her because of that. When I drive her I feel like we are one, like those mech-tech animes I watch where the hero and his robotic armor share the same soul. That's what I feel about Betsy. That's her name.

I didn't give it to her. It's not a name I would have chosen. But as long as I could remember that's what she went by. My dad called her that every time she gave him a hard time. "Come on, Betsy. You know you want to." He rubbed her dash gently, and it was like a magic spell that woke her.

I fell out of Betsy once. My dad and the Mothership had a fight—it seemed my whole life they were fighting—and my dad stormed out of the house with me in hand and said he needed donuts. I was five and donuts sounded good.

I don't remember much except for the accident. We bought a dozen and I climbed into the passenger seat with a Boston Cream and my father whipped Betsy out of the lot before I closed the door. Momentum sent me soaring. My back hit the pavement first. Then my head. But I held onto that donut. Clenched between my teeth.

I had a bump on my noggin' but nothing too serious. "You're like a tank," my dad said. Then he started laughing and shaking his head. "Don't tell your mother. This is between me, you, and Betsy. A secret. How's that sound?"

Betsy and I get on the road. We go from strip mall to strip mall, scanning store front windows for help wanted signs. Things are bleak here. Not like the game world where there is always something to do. A new quest. A new villain to destroy. Here, you pass guys in the middle of the median with *Please Help* signs begging for pennies. Here, you have little control over your outcome, your destiny. It's a shit word, destiny, but when you're a gamer it's the one thing you keep in your mind because, really, prolonging your destiny is your main objective. If you win, you go on. If you lose, you create another character and you go on.

Here, you lose and you lose. There's a lot of losing. I'm losing.

Betsy stalls out at a light.

"Betsy," I say, "don't be a bitch."

"Betsy," I say, "turn the fuck on."

Betsy is being a bitch. Betsy is not turning the fuck on.

Cars swerve around me. Some honk. After the fifth unsuccessful turn of the key, I get out. I start pushing. It's June and it's Florida. It's June and it's Florida and it's hot. A car stops next to me, one of those fancy low riders with neon streaks on the sides. The car window lowers. Bass thumps and rattles from the interior.

"Hey, fuck face."

I know who it is immediately. Douche Bag.

"I like your ride."

I keep pushing.

"You home school now? In mommy's second grade class?"

I don't turn to look.

"Listen, want some help, man? For real."

I hear his buddies chuckling in the back.

"Did you hear what I said, fuck face?"

132

I turn the wheel with my right hand and guide Betsy into another strip mall.

"I guess you're like some He-Man, right? Fuck you then."

He spits and misses but it lands on the car seat. It's green and yellow, like the blobs I fight in the game for cheap points. The car screeches away.

When I get Betsy up the incline and into a parking spot, I'm clutching my knees, chugging for air. I'm not in the best shape. I'm not like Douche Bag and his douche bag friends, who are probably heading towards some beach so they can go shirtless and flex for bimbos. No, I've got a gut like an inner tube, and I've got to find a job or the Mothership is going to flip.

I look up.

Simply Thai Take Out & Delivery. Driver Wanted.

Betsy, you sneaky minx, you.

*

A real gamer knows his territory. He studies maps and figures out short cuts. For high experience points, he knows where to hunt the big game and where to safely rest after a battle. The dimensions of the game world become second nature for him. He needs to know he is not wandering into the marshland of a Manticore or into the underground dwelling of an Otyugh, or worse yet, into the frosted hills where the Ettin roam.

There are no monsters in the subdivisions I deliver to. Once in a while an alligator snaps up a Pomeranian or a python swallows a cat or a cottonmouth bites the boy poking it with a stick. Wrong place, wrong time, I say. Shit happens.

It's been a few weeks since I've been working for the Boon-liang family. I can't say their name right. Every time I try they laugh and smile and say white people can't say it; it's not in our genes. They're cool enough and all. I mean, the way I came into the store that day, shirt damp, hair damp, so red, I imagined, like I was about to pop and they still gave me the job. I pointed to the sign and Mr. Boonliang left his station by the stove and cleaned his hands on his apron. Behind him were his wife Tanya and his seven-year-old son. Further behind him, hiding and scowling, was Grandma Boonliang.

"You drive?" Mr. Boonliang said.

"Yes," I said.

"Have car?"

I pointed at Betsy.

He glanced outside. Betsy rusted in the sun.

"Car work?"

"When she wants to."

"Need car to work."

"She's fine."

He nodded. "You like Thai food?"

"Is it like Chinese? I like sweet and sour chicken without the sweet and sour."

Mr. Boonliang made a face like I had stepped in shit and the smell of it was overpowering.

He called back to his son in a language that didn't sound like anime talk. His son ran off into a room and came back with a map. Mr. Boonliang lifted the boy up and slapped the world map onto the counter. "Boy, tell man here where China is."

The boy pointed to the north.

"Boy, tell man where Thailand is.

The boy pointed to a small country on the equator.

"Boy, tell man what country make better food."

The boy screamed, "Thailand."

"Cool," I said. "Sounds good to me."

The boy smiled and ran back to his mother, giggling all the way.

"What is your name?" Mr. Boonliang said.

I hesitated. I could have given him my real name, but the thought of that suddenly depressed me. In the game world, naming your character is an important moment. Some idiots are crass with their names: Cockface, Jizzman, VaGina. Those hackers are quick to go. So are the common names like Todd, Tom, or Tim. But the legends, they have names that when uttered people shrink in fear. Sometimes their names last longer than the lives of their characters. They are talked about even after they have been slain.

I said, "My name is Savage."

Mr. Boonliang tilted his head.

"Savage Rose." I stuck out my chest, the exhaustion from pushing the car into the lot evaporated out of me.

"Savage," Mr. Boonliang said. "Sound like cabbage. You like?"

I stuck out my tongue. "There is nothing worse."

Mr. Boonliang laughed and said something behind him to his wife and she smiled. Grandma Boonliang hadn't changed her expression, hadn't even blinked.

"You know area, Savage?"

"Lived here all my life."

"Tomorrow then. 3:30. OK?"

"How much will I get paid?"

"Four dollar an hour. Keep tip."

*

The Boonliangs spend most of their days at Simply Thai. If I didn't know they had a house, I would assume they slept there, spreading sleeping bags on the floors Grandma Boon-liang keeps immaculate. Everyone at Simply Thai has a responsibility; it's like a role-playing game where there's always a fighter who thrives at hand-to-hand combat, a mage who cast spells from a distance, a cleric whose sole responsibility is to heal the party, and a thief of some sort to detect and set traps. Tanya works the register and answers the phone. She insists she speaks perfect English—like Audrey Hepburn, she says—and she does if Audrey Hepburn were Thai. "They say they no understand. How can they no understand? I speak like actress." I don't disagree with her. She's too cute, small and thin like a halfling, and appearing a lot younger than some of the skanks at school. I like watching her move because it's as if she's gliding on ice, as if she possesses the gift of levitation. Mr. Boonliang mans the rest of the kitchen. He's wicked with the wok, agile like a ranger, lightning quick, flipping three things at once, all the while never breaking a sweat. When customers come in, he makes a show for them, playing the drums on the three large pots of boiling curry, singing old Sinatra or Nat King Cole tunes, talking to them like they were his best friends. When he boxes up their meals, he says, "There is special magic in here. Magic that will make you come back." Then there's Grandma Boonliang, whose only existence is to sweep the floor, wash the dishes, bitch at her son and grandson and glower at me. She reminds me of a Night Hag I battled once, except she isn't blue or covered with warts and boils. Her teeth are yellow and crooked, which is the reason she keeps her mouth clamped shut when she's not complaining, which is seldom. Even in another language you know the sound of a complaint; that's universal.

The boy's name is actually Boy. He's as tall as my legs, as thin as my left arm. There's not a shy bone in him. Not like when I was a kid and all I did was stand behind the Mothership wherever we went. I'm not good with kids or anything. There's something about them, their smell, not like I'm one to complain. But this kid is all right. More than all right. He zooms around the restaurant in a cape. He picks his nose often, and when he thinks no one is looking he either pastes it on his clothes or wipes it on the leaves of the fake fichus. Every day, when I arrive for work, he flies up to me and says he's a new superhero. Monday: "I'm Wonder-Boy." Tuesday: "I'm Super-Boy." Wednesday: "I'm Bat-Boy."

Today he meets me at the door. "Guess who I am?"

"I don't know."

"Guess."

"I'm not like a guess master or anything."

"Guess."

"You guess," I say.

"I already know who I am."

"So do I."

"Tell me then."

"Thai-Boy."

"Nope."

"Obnoxious-Boy."

He laughs. "No."

"Crazy-Boy."

He shakes his head.

"Annoying-Boy."

"Am not."

"Brat-Boy."

"Uh-uh."

I mumble, "Retard-Boy," but the kid is like Super Hearing-Boy and he puts his hands over his mouth.

"We're not supposed to say that word," he whispers. "My teacher said so."

I bend down so only he can hear me. I tell him I have a secret. I tell him secrets between guys like us are sacred. It's a badge of honor, an unbreakable bond. If he tells the secret to anyone then bad things will happen. Fire dragons will burn his favorite toy. Ice giants will freeze his room. Trolls will steal the TV.

Boy's mouth is an O.

"You still want to know the secret?"

He nods.

"Your teacher doesn't want you to say retard because she's retarded."

Boy sputters in giggles. I like the sound.

"Between me and you?" I say.

"You want to know who I am today?"

"Tell me."

"I'm Awesome-Boy."

"That sounds about right."

Because Simply Thai just opened, business is sometimes slow. At the dinner time rush, Betsy and I deliver about five meals. Most of the time I sit and wait for the next delivery or I sit and think about what I need to accomplish in my next quest or I sit and chill with Boy.

The kitchen, however, never seems to have a slow moment. There's always something to do, always something to cook, always something to clean. The old lady washes pots and pans. Tanya glides back and forth between the fryers and the register. Mr. Boonliang chops vegetables and meats. I want to help, but feel like my big oafy body will get in the way.

Boy says, "You're big, Savage."

We're playing tac-tac-toe on one of the take-out menus.

"Yep," I say.

"Why are you so big?"

"Why are you so small?"

"Because I'm seven."

"I'm seventeen."

"My dad's like a hundred, but he's not big like you."

Mr. Boonliang hits a pot and laughs from the back.

"You're like one and half of him," says Boy. "Maybe two."

"Drink milk," I say. "Exercise." I do neither, but I think this is what a good person should say to a kid. Being here makes me want to be a good person. Go figure. "Eat vegetables, too."

"Like cabbage," Mr. Boonliang says. He bangs on a pot.

Tanya laughs. She shakes a fryer basket.

Grandma Boonliang scowls from the sink.

"Yuck," I say.

"You're really big," says Boy.

"Your point?"

"I drink milk. I exercise at school. I eat vegetables. I'm not big."

"It doesn't happen overnight or anything."

Boy sticks his bottom lip out. He thins his eyes. He crosses his arms.

"What's the matter?" I say.

"I want to be big," Boy says. "I want to be like you."

In battle, you don't have the time to stop and think about the consequences of your actions. You work on instincts. You dodge the dwarf axe. You pluck the silver bow. You drive the poison tipped dagger into the heart. It feels like that now. Something sharp in the heart. Something gnawing away at my chest. This Asian boy, whose name is Boy, who just blocked my Xes with an O, just said out loud, he wants to be like me. No one should be like me. I'm the guy parents tell their kids to avoid. I'm the poster child for what excessive gaming could do to you. I'm the one kids pick on mercilessly at school. Steal his lunch. Book check him in the hallways. Trip him when he walks

139

by. I'm the easy target, the obvious choice. The other boys will find people like me after lunch, in the school bathroom, and they will push and punch and beat people like me down, until all a person like me can do is curl into a fat ball. Then they will whip out their dicks and piss on a person like me. They will scream, "Golden shower, golden shower," and one of them, their leader will take a dump and push it in people like me's mouth. He will do it, their leader, who is nothing like people like me. He will shit and force feed it. And then what choice do we have? What possible choice? Can you blame us for not going back? Can you blame us for not telling anyone about what happened? Can you blame us for shutting ourselves up in our rooms, escaping through cyber world adventures? Can you blame us for not wanting to hear our real name anymore because our real name reminds us of our real troubles? Better to be the creation, the fiction. Better to have a modicum of self-worth, even if it's all projected into a non-entity. Who in their right fuckin' mind wants to be like me?

This boy named Boy. That's who. It's enough to make me cry. And I almost do; shit, I haven't cried in god knows when, not even when the Mothership told me my dad wasn't coming back and who the hell knows if we'd ever see him again.

Tanya says I have a delivery to make. I take the food and rush out the door. Betsy starts cleanly for once and we speed down the road into a gated subdivision, where everyone is kept safe behind a brick wall and the only stranger they expect will be the delivery boy who has their Thai food and extra packets of soy sauce.

*

After every night, Mr. Boonliang gives me a bag of food

to take home. "One last delivery," he says. "For your mom the teacher." When I told the Boonliangs the Mothership taught second grade at Edison Elementary, the entire family beamed. "Really," they said, as if I told them she was the President of the United States or something. Boy said she was the other second grade teacher at his school and was much nicer than the teacher he had who didn't allow anyone to say retard. Mr. Boonliang explained that teachers are revered in Thailand. Tanya said Mother's Day and Teacher's Day is on the same day. Even Grandma Boonliang nodded in approval. It's no big deal here, I told them. How can it be no big deal to be essential in children's lives? they wanted to know. How can it be no big deal to monitor and watch twenty-something kids five days of the week? How can it be no big deal to impart knowledge? I guess they have a point.

The stuff Mr. Boonliang makes for the Mothership isn't on the menu. "This is what real Thai people eat," he says. As opposed to fake Thai people, I want to say, but I've learned to curb myself. "Tell me what she thinks," he says.

The Mothership thinks she is in heaven. She thinks this job is possibly the best thing to happen in my life and hers. When I arrive home, she is still up, grading simple math problems, putting the last touches on a lesson plan, and cutting and pasting on colored construction paper. I don't know much about my mom's work, but I imagine she's a good teacher, because truthfully, despite all the fighting, she's a good mom, though I would never tell her.

Lately, I have a feeling she isn't sleeping because of the bags underneath her eyes and how she yawns constantly and how she keeps repeating *I'm tired* every three seconds.

"Go to bed, then."

We're sitting down and eating together. We've been eating

together since my job. Before that, we hadn't eaten together in years.

"I wish," she says. "I've got too much to do."

"I'm sure second graders won't notice if you just wing it."

She smiles and yawns.

"Or give them quiet time," I say. "Six hours of quiet time."

"Parents would love that." She spoons more chicken and potato curry over her rice. When she takes a bite, she swoons. "Your boss is a magician."

I've never thought of Mr. Boonliang as a boss. I've never thought of Simply Thai as a job. It's just the place I go to every day. To hang out, drive, and get paid for it.

The Mothership yawns again and says, "I'm tired. So, so tired."

I chew on a spring roll. "Can I borrow some money?" I speak with my mouth full and crumbs drop on my shirt. "I want to buy a cape."

"Oh god," the Mothership says.

"Boy wants me to wear a cape. He says superheroes have capes."

"Why don't you use your own money?"

"Because I have you." I wink. Or I try to wink. I'm not really a winker and don't know what possess me to do it. I don't tell the Mothership my money went into graphic novels and the newest Captain American action figure. I don't tell her I bought Dungeon and Dragon miniatures and I pre-ordered the new zombie shooting game.

"You're going to wear a cape when you deliver people's food?"

"I'm a superhero. Without me, how will people eat?"

"And Mr. Boonliang is OK with this?"

"As long as his food gets to the right people."

"It's weird," she says and sighs.

"What about me isn't?"

She shrugs. She can't say anything to that.

"Boy comes with me on deliveries now."

She takes another bite and then another. Every time she swallows, she closes her eyes and sighs in deep contentment.

"I get bigger tips with him. He usually gets candy."

"His parents don't mind?"

"Not at all," I say. "We're a good team. People open the door and see this Asian boy in a cape, and suddenly I'm a few bucks richer and it's Halloween for him."

The Mothership cleans her plate. I can see in her eyes she's debating whether she wants more, whether to pack the leftovers up for lunch. "Tammy told me Boy never says a word in her class."

"Really," I say. "It's like his whole point in life is to talk."

The Mothership rises from her chair. She begins to clean up, putting our dishes in the sink, leftovers into Tupperware. "I've seen him at recess. He sits by himself."

"Do the kids pick on him?" Something starts to bubble in me. "Little fuckers."

"Language," the Mothership says.

"Do you know?"

"I know he doesn't say anything. I know he looks sad."

"I really need that cape, Mom." I'm talking to the table now. I don't want to imagine the worst, but the worst is all that enters my brain. I've haven't felt like this since the last time Savage faced imminent death at the hands of the Ant Queen and her minion Ant Soldiers. And then, all I could remember was how hard I was chewing on my cheek, how every hit point off Savage's life was a hit point off mine. We were connected then, like my dad was connected to Betsy. Like me to Boy. I imagine a new adventure for us—Savage Rose and Awesome Boy. The dynamic duo. We will take down all who have wronged us with our strength that can move planets. We will launch far into the atmosphere, our capes billowing in the wind, and no one can touch us. We have become untouchable.

*

Before working at Simply Thai, Betsy and I liked going on long drives. Her a/c went out years ago, so I'd keep the windows down, and though it could get unbearably hot, especially in the middle of the day, I enjoyed how the wind whipped through my hair, how it felt on my face. On my drives, there was never a destination. There was never a purpose. I turned when I wanted to. Stopped wherever I pleased. I took country roads, interstates, roads that led to dead ends. I drove in forested areas, among flat fields, through wetland. I got lost on purpose, but I don't think of it as getting lost; to be lost is to be deterred from an end point, a direction, a goal. This I never had. I just drove and eventually, when I was tired, or when Betsy was tired, we headed back.

My dad used to tell me about this show he watched when he was a kid. He didn't remember the title of the show, but he said it was about a samurai who went from village to village to village. The show never addressed why the samurai was wandering, only that it was in his nature to keep walking. At the end of each episode, the samurai would say, "Where will the road take me now?" He would look left then right and then he would be off to a new town with new people and new adventures.

I wonder if that's what my dad is doing right now, walking. I wonder if, at some point, he will head back in my direction.

*

Betsy and I are parked across the street from the elementary school during lunch time. I tried to situate her behind a tree so I'd go unnoticed. I imagine how creepy this might look—a beat up Beetle, an overweight, suspicious looking man, watching kids at recess. I'm here to find Boy. He's easy to locate. He's the one not screaming at the top of his lungs. He's the one not running on the school playground like mad. He sits on a park bench. He looks at his swinging feet.

I notice immediately what is missing. His cape. This is not the boy who zooms everywhere at the restaurant. This is not the boy who can't stop talking. I'm seeing a superhero's other identity, Extremely Shy and Scared-Boy. He sits there the entire recess, and when the lunch monitors blow the whistle, he gets up and walks toward the school.

When I get to work later in the day, Boy is already waiting for me. I'm in a cape, red with silver streaks on it.

"Whoa," says boy. "Totally cool."

Mr. Boonliang laughs. "Looks sharp. Big tip today."

Tanya is on the phone taking an order, but when she sees me she covers her mouth, trying not to laugh.

"What do you think, Grandma?" I stick out my chest. I put my hands on my hips.

Grandma Boonliang scowls from the folding chair. Her mouth is clamped shut, her eyes slits. Then she says in clear English, "Stupid," and turns around. It's the first word she's ever said to me.

Mr. Boonliang mouths, "She likes you."

Tanya covers the phone and says, "First word in English."

Boy says, "What's your name?"

"Isn't it obvious?" I say. "I'm Delivery Boy."

Today, Simply Thai is the busiest it's ever been. I go out and make six stops, come back to find more orders, and go out again. Boy isn't allowed to go with me, not until he finishes his math homework, not until he's eaten some dinner. I've barely seen him at all, but at seven, he's at the door waiting with two large bags in his hands. He struggles with the weight of the food, but I take it from him and we head towards Betsy.

"Hi, Betsy," he says and rubs the dash like I do.

"She's had a busy night," I say.

"My mom and dad are happy." Boy straps himself in. "This one is going to the usual house." He tells me the address and I know what he means by usual. I'm amazed how he retains numbers, how he remembers directions. Often, he tells me where to turn, reminds me of what house it is after being there only once. He would be a good gamer with these skills, the ultimate gamer, but I don't tell him that.

The usual house orders twice a week. The same items: pork fried rice, chicken wings, and soup. Most deliveries are to usual houses. People who order will order again, especially on Mondays, when no one wants to cook at the beginning of a work week. You can tell a lot about the places you deliver to. Single mom. Divorcee. Family of five. Gamers. Especially gamers. The usual's house isn't far from the restaurant. He's a college kid who lives above his parents' garage. Every time he orders, he gives Tanya instructions to go to the garage door. He's seen Boy and his cape before. He said, "Nice cape," then, and when he sees that the both us have capes this time, he says, "Nice capes," and gives us an extra dollar.

The other order is new. We drive into a subdivision—Oakville—with identical houses. Same roof, same colors, same lawns. Even the cars in the driveway are the same. Environment saving hybrids, spotless sedans, loaded mini-vans. Betsy

146

thinks this neighborhood is snobby and backfires. Boy startles then laughs, telling Betsy to behave like I usually do. An older couple walking their dog stare as we pass; two girls stop on their bikes; a few boys pause their game of basketball.

It takes a while to find the right address, and when we do, Boy and I jump out. We are efficient. Our transactions take no more than a few seconds.

Because Boy likes to press buttons, I let him ring the door bell.

The door opens. I almost drop the bag.

"Fuck face." It's Douche Bag.

From the inside, I hear someone asking whether it is the delivery boy. I hear the voice tell Douche Bag the money in on the table. I hear the voice say she's hungry.

Douche Bags says, "I got it, Ma," but his eyes never leave me. Me in a cape. Me in a cape with a little Thai boy named Boy.

"This your little toy," he says. "Fag."

"Here's your food," I say. "Twenty-three forty."

Boy looks up at me. He doesn't know what's going on. "You know him, Savage?"

"Savage?" Douche Bag says. "You told him your name is Savage?"

"Here's your food," I say. "Twenty-three forty."

"Why don't you tell him your real name, fuck face?"

I hear someone asking what's taking so long. I hear someone say Father is hungry.

"In a minute," Douche Bag says. He lowers himself to Boy's height and says, "His name isn't Savage, little guy. We call him Poop Eater. Isn't that right?"

"Here's your food," I say. "Twenty three forty." I'm a skipping CD. A game that just froze.

"Super Poop Eater, that's his name," Douche Bag says and looks at me and my cape with silver streaks on it. "Saving the world by eating one turd at a time. Isn't that right?"

Boy tugs at my leg. I don't look down. I want to press a button on a video game controller over and over again. Press a button until my thumb hurts and he is dead, blood seeping into the earth. It would be that simple to vanquish him from existence, to erase him from memory.

Douche Bag hands Boy twenty-five dollars and rises. "Keep the change, little guy." He takes the food from me and nods. "Fuck face." He closes the door.

I don't know how long I stand there. I don't know how long I stand there when Boy wraps his hand around mine and squeezes. I don't know how many times Boy says my name, Savage, which isn't my name at all, which is a fantasy like everything else in my life. I don't know how long he repeats, "What's wrong? What's wrong?", and how long I stay silent because I don't know what to tell him and because anything I say now will be another lie because I do know one thing: I can't save him; I can't save my mom; I can't save myself. I don't know how long Boy cries, or how long I cry, or the both of us crying into our capes. I don't know how long we sit in Betsy, in front of Douche Bag's suburban house, in this suburban neighborhood. I don't know how long I turn the key, over and over, hoping Betsy will turn on and carry us someplace else, but knowing—really knowing—that she won't.

3

The perfect dressing is essential to the perfect salad, and I see no reason whatsoever for using a bottled dressing, which may have been sitting on the grocery shelf for weeks, even months—even years.

—Julia Child

Happy Ends

My mother went over the deep end when she decided to take our deceased dog, Puddles, to Happy Ends Taxidermy. I didn't want to go with her. I said, "Listen, we can bury Puddles in the back, where he used to jump at the butterflies. He would love that." But my mother, pig-headed as usual, decided with preposterous certainty that Puddles would not like to be buried. "My baby Puddles," she said, "would like to be with me." She said this in a way that creeped me out, the way those terrible twins in the movie *The Shining* said, "*Come play with us forever and ever and ever…*"

Besides, I wanted to tell my mother that Puddles wasn't always her baby. I wanted to tell her that Puddles was Dad's dog, and I wanted to tell her that she was jealous of Puddles for the first few years, giving Puddles the evil eye, because Puddles got all of Dad's attention. This was the hierarchy in Puddles' life: Dad, me, my sister Crystal, and maybe Mom. I say maybe because Puddles gravitated to the adopted Asian boy next door, Henry, giving him licks all over his chubby face.

Puddles liked yellow people. My father was full yellow. My sister and I were half-yellow, and my mom was the brightest white you'd ever seen. White-out white. Born in Indiana.

"Help me get Puddles in the car," Mom said, which really meant, *Put Puddles in the car by yourself because I'm going to pretend I'm busy and disappear.*

I hefted Puddles, who was wrapped in the old Amish comforter he loved, and carried him to the station wagon. He was heavier than he used to be, rigor mortis having set in I imagined, but he didn't have the dead smell yet, even after a day.

He still smelled like Puddles—a mixture of earth and rain and probably rabbit poop, his special cologne, my dad used to say with a laugh.

I didn't want my mother to do this by herself, even though she was out of her mind, so I climbed into the passenger side seat and waited for her. She was by herself a lot now. Crystal was at UCLA, I was managing the restaurant, and Dad was—well—Dad was dead. Most days, my mother would stop by the restaurant to see whether everything was in order, but she'd spend maybe fifteen minutes there before she'd hurry back home to walk Puddles, or to give Puddles his afternoon treat, or to bathe Puddles, or to groom Puddles, or to let Puddles out for a potty, or to feed Puddles his second meal, or to give Puddles his meds, or to take Puddles to vet appointments. Now, because there was no more Puddles, I wonder how'd she spend her day, how she would find happiness.

My mother got into the car and turned on the ignition. "They have to start as soon as possible," she said. "Any longer it'll be too late."

*

Puddles was a good dog, the best dog, though he looked malnourished and mangy. He wasn't though; that's just how he looked. He was gray with uncooperative fur, and all the pigment on his nose went away, leaving it pink like a raw meatball. He wasn't a show dog by any stretch; he was a Thai dog. We had rescued him when we went to visit my father's family in Phrae, a city in Northern Thailand. I was nine at the time, and my sister Crystal was eleven. My father's family was nice, though none of them spoke English. My head got rubbed a lot and my cheeks got pinched, and my grandmother always wanted to see my penis so that she could confirm that I was indeed a boy. She kept grabbing at my shorts, chuckling, trying to yank them down. The rest of the family laughed, even my mother and father and Crystal.

There was no doubt Crystal was a girl because everyone doted on her. They kept saying she was *soi*, beautiful, and she would make a wonderful Thai movie star. Movie stars in Thailand were almost all half Thai, half Caucasian. And I hate to say it, but Crystal was pretty then, movie star pretty, and is pretty now; it was on this trip that Crystal decided to be a movie star for real, to flee the Midwest and go to school in L.A.

This was my first trip to Thailand. Crystal was here once before—when she was one—and didn't remember anything. How could she? I don't remember much myself, except for the temples and the food and Puddles, of course. The Thai food tasted nothing like the food we served at Lotus. It was extraordinarily different, loaded with flavor. It made what my dad cooked up at the restaurant taste bland and unexciting. I told him so.

My dad laughed and it was loud. When he laughed, it shook the walls. "This is the real deal, kiddo."

"Why don't we have the real deal at Lotus?"

"De Forest, Wisconsin, can't handle the real deal."

"I can handle the real deal."

"Because you are the real deal." And my dad lifted me up like I was doll and spun me around. He seemed happier in Thailand, with his family, freer. He smiled every day. He doted on Crystal and me. He made sure Mom was included in everything, though I could tell the trip wore on her—the heat, the humidity, the mosquitoes, her foreignness. There were moments she just sat there, smiling dumbly, listening to my father speak rapid Thai, then asking, "What did you say?" Sometimes he would translate, and other times, he told her it wasn't important.

Near the end of our trip, Dad took us on a temple tour of the north. We had been in a VW van for a couple hours, making our way back to Grandmother's house. My dad had hired a driver for the entire day, and asked the driver to pull over at a fruit stand on the side of the road.

My mother fanned herself with a Thai newspaper and sighed. "More fruit?" she said. "I'm fruited out."

"Father," Crystal said, sounding like a British actress, "I would like to partake in a decadent mango please."

"And you, kiddo?" he asked me.

I loved the fruit called mangosteen. Loved how it made my fingers purple. "The purple ones with the white inside," I said. "Yummy."

My mother sighed again. "Too much fruit, too much poop."

I giggled.

Crystal said, "Oh, Mother," and tilted her nose up.

"I can't wait to get back to apples," my mother said. "And Wisconsin blackberries."

Dad laughed. I covered my ears.

Crystal pointed at four dogs lying in the dust; one was tiny, no bigger than my dad's forearm. Dogs weren't an uncommon sight. They were everywhere, in fact, wandering the streets. They looked sad, which made me sad. Crystal had asked why these dogs didn't have owners, and Dad said this was how things were in Thailand; we would have to get used to it. It wasn't a good enough reason for either of us, but we didn't prod him.

"Look at that one," Crystal said in her normal voice. A puppy lay in the middle of a puddle. It looked like a gray hairball. "I'm going to pat it."

"Dad told us not to touch any of the dogs," I said.

"Don't be a doofus," she said. "It's a puppy."

Before I could tell her I wasn't a doofus, Crystal headed straight for the puppy. The puppy inched toward her in the puddle and began to give sharp little barks. The other dogs ignored Crystal; some were asleep. She knelt beside the puppy and touched its head and snatched her hand away, giggling. The puppy began wagging its tiny tail in the puddle, splashing her. Crystal laughed, which only made the puppy wag faster.

I went to the puppy because now I wanted to touch it, too. We knelt there—Crystal and I—patting the puppy, letting our fingers graze its back. I could feel its ribs. It licked voraciously at our fingers.

"What are you two doing?" Dad said. He had a bag of fruit in his arms.

"Puppy," I said.

"Father," Crystal said in her British accent again, "is he not quite adorable?"

"I told you not to touch any dogs. They're wild here. They don't have homes. They don't have owners, which means they haven't had their shots. They—"

The puppy barked. Barked again. Sat up in the puddle, staring right at Dad.

He clicked his tongue at the puppy and said something in Thai. The puppy rolled over in the puddle to show us its deflated belly.

"What's that, Father?" Crystal said. She pointed to lumpy, squiggly streaks under the puppy's skin. She pointed to hundreds of red dots. She pointed to fat black ones, too.

The puppy was soaked. It didn't care that it was on its back in a puddle. It didn't care about the dirty water. All it cared about was showing us its little tummy with dots and lumpy streaks.

My father shook his head and mumbled something in Thai. "Worms," he said. "And ant bites. And ticks."

"Poor puppy," I said. I wanted to touch it but I was afraid my dad would yell at me.

"Come on, kids," my father said. "Let's get going."

"We cannot abandon this puppy," Crystal said. She didn't move. She knelt close to the puppy, eyes fixed on it.

"Crystal," my father said, his voice stern.

I didn't move either. On this matter, Crystal and I were a united front.

The puppy barked again. On its back. In the puddle.

And then Crystal did what she always did to get her way. She cried. She was an expert at crying, a crying black belt. She had different types of cries, and knew which type would get her desired reaction. She carefully put her hands over her eyes and wept like a widower at a funeral. In fact, this was the same cry she used at Dad's funeral thirteen years later. Back slightly hunched, shoulders shaking, her sobs muffled and intense.

And then I began to cry, too. Not because Crystal was crying. Not because there was a puppy in a puddle with worms and ant bites and ticks, but because after three weeks in Thailand, after seeing strays everywhere, after averting my eyes from every dog roaming the streets without love, I had finally had enough. This was why my dad nicknamed me *Dek Jie Awn*, Sensitive Boy.

It was a cry fest. A cry-tastic cryathon. Our cries forced the other dogs to scramble away. But not the puppy. The puppy sat up again, water dripping off its gray round head, and began to howl. We—me, Crystal, and the puppy—were the ultimate cry choir.

My dad tried to calm us, but we cried over his pleas. I don't remember how long it lasted, but eventually, my father picked up the puppy and put it under his arm.

When we got back into the van, wiping our tears away, my

mother was still fanning herself. She rolled her eyes at the sight of us. "You've come back, I see, with more than fruit."

*

Mrs. Martha waited in the parking lot. She was the owner and proprietor of Happy Ends, and probably the person who came up with the catchy slogan: *Preserving memories for over two decades.* She was a blond, big-boned woman, Scandinavian blood, like most of the citizens of De Forest. She came to Lotus often and ordered the same thing. The Number 3 special: Sweet and Sour Chicken, white rice, and a spring roll. She was married to Mr. Martha, a landscaper in the spring and summer, a hunter come fall. Their older son Luke worked at Lotus and cut our lawn.

Mrs. Martha put Puddles in a Radio Flyer wagon and pulled him into the shop, my mother following close behind.

Outside, I made a call to my sister, who was probably doing something important and didn't have time to talk. I wondered how she would pick up the phone this time.

"Ah, like, hello, man," a wispy voice answered.

"Who are you today?"

"A hippie," Crystal said. "I'm, like, totally busy right now."

"You're always totally busy, " I said. "But your mother is getting Puddles stuffed."

"Ah, like, wow."

I thought this news would break Crystal's character. But she remained vigilant. She sounded stoned. She sounded rock solid stoned. I imagined hippie Crystal on Haight Ashberry in San Francisco in a tie-dyed shirt, passing a double barrel bong around, and talking to her hippie friends about "the man."

"Should I be worried about Mom?" I said.

156

"Ah, you know, Mommy's a free bird, man."

"What are you saying?"

"You gotta let her fly. You just gotta let her fly."

I massaged the bridge of my nose. I leaned hard against the car. In a few hours, I would have to open the restaurant. My patience was thinning. "First, don't repeat lines. It's weird. Second: I need hippie Crystal to bring back my sister Crystal because that Crystal needs to tell me what the fuck to do."

"You're such a buzz kill, twerp."

"Shut up," I said. "You didn't find Puddles yesterday, did you?"

"You didn't," I asked, "have to tell Mom he died, did you?"

Nope, she didn't. She didn't have to hold Mom who was weeping hard on my shoulder, weeping as hard as when Dad passed away. Harder even.

"There are a lot of things you didn't have to do," I said too harshly. I knew Crystal would know what I meant by this. I knew she knew I was talking about Dad. She knew how I found him, at the restaurant after closing, clutching his heart, and how I had to be the one to tell Mom and how I was the one who called Thailand to tell his family and how I was the one who arranged for his body to be shipped back to Grandmother after the funeral, despite my mother's strong resentment. I knew Crystal knew what I meant.

She sighed. "Geez, twerp."

"Sorry," I said.

"Let Mom do what she needs to do."

"Yeah," I said.

"Let her have *this*."

"Yeah," I said.

"Ah, Mommy's a free bird," hippie Crystal said, all flaky and high again.

"Totally, man," I said.

*

The hierarchy of my father's life? That was the problem. I didn't know. He certainly loved his son and daughter. He certainly loved Mom. He certainly loved Lotus, though at times, he didn't. But there were some days he seemed far from us. Some days, when he looked over the golden fields from the backyard, his eyes unblinking, and I could tell he was elsewhere.

If you were to ask my dad if he was happy, he would have told you without hesitation, Yes. Very. He would have listed all the reasons for his happiness, and it would be an exhaustive list that might have included Wisconsin beer and cheese curds, the TV show *No Reservations*, and Mom in black stockings. My dad would have kept listing until there was no doubt that, yes, I. AM. HAPPY. He was never one to unload his problems. He lived to serve others. Always. This was a depressing thought. Just once, I wanted to hear him say, "To hell with De Forest. I'm going to cook real Thai food. I'm going to make their white faces red with authentic Thai heat. I'm going to fragrant the restaurant with herbs and spices no one can pronounce, because this was the food I wanted to cook all along. Not the food you want to eat, not the syrupy, deep-fried gluttonous morsels. This food. *This* food from my country. Eat it or fuck off!"

But he didn't.

He cooked what was expected of him, expected of any Asian establishment in the middle of Nowhere, Wisconsin, and that was sad.

Of course, my dad loved Puddles, too. Puddles was special to him. Puddles was born in Thailand and came over to America just like him. Puddles understood what it meant to make a

158

new home, a new life in a different country. Puddles had access to my father's most intimate secrets because my father talked Thai to him. Often my dad would talk to Puddles, and we'd ask him what he'd said, and he would reply, "It's between me and Puddles," or "Why don't you ask Puddles?" Puddles even came to the restaurant with my dad, sleeping in the corner of the kitchen out of everyone's way. This lasted a year before the health inspector found out and banned Puddles from Lotus.

Before my dad passed away, after I graduated from high school and took classes at the community college, I worked at Lotus. I mean, I've worked at Lotus all my life. Crystal and I were raised in the restaurant. We did the small things, like cleared off tables and refilled the soy sauce and salt and pepper shakers. Most of the time, we ran ragged around the restaurant tormenting each other. But now, I worked. I employed the things I was learning in college to improve the business. I created a database that catalogued numbers and percentages and made fancy charts that illustrated what was Lotus' best-selling dish on a given day, week, month, or year. I searched out cheaper food distributors and designed snazzy newspaper ads and coupons. I made sure Lotus was listed on the website of the National Association of Thai Restaurants in the United States. While Crystal got all the leading roles in the high school plays, while she made a life for herself in Los Angeles, I was planning to take over my father's business.

Once, when the restaurant was slow, my father cooked me a plate of noodles that wasn't on the menu. I didn't look up until I was finished eating, and when I did, I was near tears.

"*Sensitive Boy*," my dad said. "What is it now?"

"Why don't you cook this?" I said. "This is amazing."

He laughed loud. Luke, who was washing dishes, startled.

"I'm not kidding," I said. "People would love this."

My dad threw a dishtowel over his shoulder. "People here don't have that kind of palette."

"How can you be so sure?" I said. "If you gave this to Luke, Luke would tell you this kicked ass. Wouldn't you Luke?"

Luke's hands were suds and he shrugged. "I'm more of a meat and potatoes guy, really," he said.

"You see," my dad said.

I shook my head.

"Before I came to America," my father said, "do you know what I wanted to eat most?"

"I don't know," I said, "a steak?"

"Popcorn," he said.

"Seriously?"

"I wanted popcorn. Someone talked about it once. Said popcorn in American movie theaters was the best popcorn you can get. The popcorn I ate I bought at the mini-mart, and they had flavors like sweet basil and chicken."

Luke said, "Chicken-flavored popcorn?"

My dad chuckled. "During my first semester at cooking school in Madison, I went to a movie with your mom and got American popcorn. Awful. The butter was so greasy and there was really no flavor to it at all. The upside: I got your mother."

Luke chimed in: "Katie Mulligan said Italian food in Italy sucks."

My dad nodded.

I still didn't get it. "Don't you think you should serve customers *real* Thai food if they come to a Thai restaurant?"

"You sacrifice," my father said.

There it was. The one time my father opened up to me. The one time he said something revealing about himself. Two words. My father looked straight at me, as if he were willing his thoughts into my brain. You sacrifice. You sacrifice your old life for your new one. You sacrifice what is familiar for uncertainty. You sacrifice your Thai family for your American family. Every day of my father's life in America had been a sacrifice. Every meal he'd cooked at Lotus had been a sacrifice.

I didn't get it then, not at that moment, not in that kitchen as the steam from the sink heated the room, and I wouldn't get it five months later when I found my father's body, and I wouldn't get it when Crystal spoke eloquently about him—so poised—at his funeral, and I wouldn't get it until his body was far from us, shipped back to his Thai family, and I saw my mom outside with Puddles in the garden she and my father had created, the tiger lilies in bloom, the butterflies fluttering from one cone flower to the next, and my mother holding Puddles hard to her chest and shaking.

*

Happy Ends was filled with dead animals, which I found disconcerting. From any angle in the shop something was always staring at me. To the right, a buck's head. To the left, a coyote. Ahead, a badger. Behind, the black bear. There was also the wide-mouth gator, the bald eagle guarding its nest, and the grazing bison with a cattle egret on its back. And what kind of taxidermist would you be without a jackalope?

Mrs. Martha pointed to the jackalope and said, "That one isn't real."

"I was just thinking what kind of animal that is," my mom said.

I shook my head, and my mom gave me the eye that said, *I'm not stupid, I'm trying to be nice.*

Mrs. Martha was a professional, outlining what would be done, giving us a timeline, and quoting us a fair price, which was unnecessary since my mom's mind was made up.

"We can do just about anything," Mrs. Martha said. "Look over here for instance." She took us to a fat bird in flight. "You see, this bird here is a kiwi. It's not a flying bird. It's like a penguin or ostrich. Grounded. But we damn made it look like a 747."

"Amazing," my mom said.

"What's the point?" I said. I didn't mean to sound snotty.

My mother elbowed me.

Mrs. Martha smiled. "The point is we can do whatever it is you want us to do. This is the most important decision you'll have to make. What would you like Puddles to look like? We can't undo what's already done. So you want to be sure about Puddles' final position."

"What do other people do?" I asked.

"Mostly, they want their dogs lying down, properly, front paws crossed."

"Puddles was never proper," Mom said.

I agreed and remembered how he loved rolling around on his back, his tongue hanging out. He would entertain himself outside, rolling and rolling. Mom said it was indecent. Dad never tired of it.

"What do you think?" my mom asked.

"What you think is what I think."

"I want this to be our decision." My mom stared at me, her eyes soft, her blonde hair unkempt and frazzled. She appeared so vulnerable suddenly, standing among a menagerie of animals, arms crossed tightly over her purse. Mrs. Martha waited patiently, dusting off the sleek backs of stuffed mallards.

"Dad would have liked it if Puddles were doing his trick," I said.

Mom's eyed perked up and she smiled. "*Sawasdee*," she said.

My dad taught Puddles to lift up his paw and wave. He

would say, "*Sawasdee*," and Puddles would wave his left paw. Each morning, before Crystal and I would leave for school, Puddles would wave good-bye, and when we returned he would wave hello.

"What does that mean?" Mrs. Martha said.

"Hello and goodbye in Thai," said my mother.

"How do you know if someone is coming or going?" said Mrs. Martha, laughing at her own joke.

My mother and I smiled. We told Mrs. Martha what we wanted. We told her what paw should be raised and how high. We told her that Puddles should lean just slightly to the left, and his mouth should be parted in a doggy smile.

"And what about his tail?" Mrs. Martha said.

I wanted to tell her to make his tail move back and forth, like the day we found him in the puddle in Thailand, like how he greeted my dad every day, wagging like a metronome. And then I started crying, not because of Puddles, not because of his tail, not because of Dad, but just because.

"Up," my mother said and held my hand. "We would like his tail up."

Tell Us What You Want

I don't tell Maggie about our three-year-old son failing to use the potty again. I don't tell her about the conversation that ensued, the lecture on the necessity of informing me, his parental unit, when he needed to poop and that pooping his pants was not what big boys do. I don't tell my wife what our beautiful boy said in his beautiful boy way: "OK, Dad, I'll poop next week," or how I stood there fuming with his soiled slacks in one hand and sanitary wipes in the other and baby powder lodged in my armpit or how frustration washed over me, building first in the chest, radiating like a tsunami throughout the rest of my body until I was sure my eyeballs would burst out. I don't tell Maggie it wasn't just about our son refusing to use the toilet for the second time that day, but also, it was about the restaurant closing down; it was about this feeling that something was adrift in our lives, something uncomfortable, like food stuck in teeth. I don't tell her what I said to our son about his scheduled poop next week—"No, JJ, you poop every day. You are a pooping machine"—or how I made him go to his room and he asked, "Can I pee in my room?" and I said, "No, JJ, you pee and poop in the potty," only to find later that he did pee in his room.

I don't tell Maggie any of this because she doesn't let me. As soon as she comes home from rehearsal she launches into the narrative of her evening at the community center with the other wannabe thespians. The effects of being on the stage still must have carried over because she projects her voice, as if she's talking to an audience member in the back row of the theater, instead of to her bedraggled husband no more than a few feet away. Maggie talks with a slight French accent, even though she's not French but Thai-American, even though she has been cast as Liat, one of the lovers in the musical *South Pacific*, and Liat is neither French nor Thai but Polynesian.

"Lower your voice," I say, disrupting her. "JJ's in bed."

Maggie whispers *sorry*. "The theater follows you home," she says. "That's what the director tells us." She moves as if she is gliding on a dance floor, the same way she did when she worked the restaurant, effortlessly, floating on the very tip of her toes. "Don't you think that's funny?" she asks.

"What?" I look out the dark window, distracted.

"You weren't listening."

"Long and messy night," I say.

"I was telling you about the new cast member." Her smile widens and I can tell the weekly whitening treatments are working. "You won't believe who it is."

I shrug.

"Bradley Custer," she says.

I don't know the name. I don't know much, only that I want to put my head down on a pillow and drift away, my wife beside me or not.

"My ex-boyfriend."

"Oh," I say. "That Bradley."

That Bradley. The one before me. The one Maggie almost married. The one who skipped town one afternoon and left a note saying he was heading to Hollywood to make it big and to hell with this Podunk town because he wasn't coming back even if they dragged him kicking and screaming. That Bradley.

"He hasn't changed a bit," she says and does a little spin without spilling a drop of wine. It's a dance move, I'm sure, something the director choreographed. I can't help but be irritated with anything she does. Her voice, her stories, her theatrical-ness. It's as if she is playing the role of my wife, as if she is playing the role of JJ's mother, but her real character, the one I fell in love with, is diluted in this act.

"He's gotten pudgier," she says, "but, man, he can sing. That voice of his, I swear." Maggie sits on the sofa next to me and leans back, looking at the ceiling, her wine glass held between two fingers. I wonder what she's thinking, wonder whether she regrets marrying me, having JJ, the restaurant, re- grets the path she has taken in her life. She's Buddhist, and she talks a lot about paths and roads and how everything is predicated on an individual's choice, and I wonder if she were presented with a choice—me or this other life—which would she choose?

"Bradley's taking the role of Cable," she says, "my opposite. Donny Wilson dropped out because his mom died. Couldn't sing to save the world. Now, the show is saved."

"It's community theater, not Broadway," I say though shouldn't.

She narrows her eyes. It's the Shirley Maclaine look, the one from the movie *Terms of Endearment*. She used it a few times in the last play as Lady MacBeth. I hate that look. I hate how her lips purse together like an unwelcomed kiss, hate the consternation etched into her forehead, hate the deepened crows feet around her eyes. "The director says we should nev- er think about what we do as only a community play." Hate her indignant voice. "He says what we do is art for the world."

I look away. Aim my eyes at a photo of us from three years ago. The woman next to me now is someone I do not know. Her bangs are teased blond, her shirts low-cut, her jeans too tight, her face layered in foundation. She talks with her hands, her entire body. She says everything with the tongue of melo- drama. I call this woman The Actress, stressing the slither at

166

the end of the word.

Outside, the autumn breeze blows down more leaves from our hickory, and I know tomorrow I will spend two hours raking, only to have JJ jump into the piles so I'll have to rake again. And I know tomorrow won't be any different from today, and the thought makes me slump further into myself, into the cushions of the couch.

JJ cries in his room, loud and breathy. A bad dream cry. Maggie knows it's her turn, knows this cry will last only minutes before he will drift back to sleep. She saunters to our son's bedroom, The Actress, with the poise and elegance of an Audrey Hepburn, wine sloshing in her glass with each calculated step.

*

Four years ago, I would've woken up at six in the morning, kiss Maggie's forehead and told her I'd see her later, and then drive to Mike and Maggie's on the main strip to prepare for the day. I'd chop vegetables. Knead dough. Start the ovens. I'd get the stock going. Weigh meat and fish into appropriate portions. Devein shrimp. Debone chicken. I'd ground up spices. Refill the salt and pepper shakers. The soy sauce bottles. The sugar containers. I'd wash windows, dust counters, vacuum floors. I'd come up with the daily specials, which I'd write on the chalkboard by the entrance of the restaurant.

Mike and Maggie's was an everything restaurant, which meant it served all types of cuisine—Italian, Mediterranean, Asian Fusion. We catered to the meat and potato conservatives. The eclectic foodies. The meatless vegans. My menu was seven-pages long—descriptions of dishes like erotic poetry. There was even a *Tell Us What You Want* option where our customers can order something off menu and we'd try to prepare it, try with all our power to please. Sometimes, we couldn't; sometimes we failed because we were missing an essential ingredient. But even then, our customers left satisfied.

I spent my days at the restaurant. Maggie, too. She waitressed, bartended, cooked. She played these roles perfectly. It was us and the food and how the food made people feel. We'd end each night in the bedroom—each night!—making love despite our exhaustion, despite our skin smelling of oil and spices. But what was better than the subtle taste of ginger on the nape of the neck, a hint of mint behind the ears, garlic-infused sweat? This was pleasure at its most heightened state. This was, I suppose, how JJ came to us, those passionate nights after work.

The restaurant closed for reasons restaurants close; they just do. Happiness does not pay bills. Happiness does not bring consistent customers. JJ is not the reason for the end of Mike and Maggie's. JJ is not the reason for where Maggie and I are now. He isn't. If anything, he is the product of the happiest time of my life, and because he is, every moment I'm with him is heartbreaking.

Like this morning.

I'm watching him in his room. He doesn't know it. I'm watching him look at his toys, deciding which one he wants to play with: the plastic spatula, the pudgy bunny, the army man. He turns from the toys to look out the bedroom window, where the sun is filtering dust into gold specks. He looks at the gold specks, swiping at his nose. He picks up the spatula and tries to hit the specks. He laughs to himself and then stares at the gold specks again, mouth slightly parted, frozen, his brain computing, memory cataloguing. He smiles and then realizes I've been watching him all this time.

"Daddy," he says.

"JJ," I say.

He points at the gold dust.

I nod.

"Mommy," he says.

"At the bank. Work."

"Me and you again."

"Everyday, buddy."

"Hungry," he says.

"Carrots?"

"No."

"Peas?"

"No."

"What then?"

"Cookie."

"Cookie?"

He nods.

"Of course."

"Daddy," he says and reaches out for me.

And this is what I miss—to be needed. To be wanted. To matter. Because to this beautiful boy, I do, despite what the day will bring—frustration, annoyance, fatigue—this keeps me going.

I pick him up. I kiss his cheek. I get him a cookie.

*

I despise the sound—the ting of Maggie's phone indicating another text message. The ting is sharp and I feel it vibrate in my bones. She's holding JJ in her lap, as he watches Saturday morning cartoons. JJ doesn't like the sound either, and turns and glares at her—that Shirley Maclaine indignation.

169

"Sorry," Maggie says. "Mommy's friend needs help."

Mommy's friend always needs help. Mommy's friend is "depressed." Mommy's friend is "broken-hearted." Mommy's friend's dream came crashing down on him because he failed as an actor. Mommy's friend has been needing help for the last two weeks because Mommy's phone tings every minute, because Mommy is on the computer typing long emails. Sometimes Mommy's friend calls and I listen to Mommy's laughter. I listen to Mommy's side of the conversation that always sounds like she's consoling a baby deer.

JJ points to the phone. "Quiet phone," he says.

Maggie doesn't see or hear him, but is rapidly tapping away at a message.

I pull JJ on my lap and hold him tight. He smells like dirt.

"Poor guy," Maggie says more to her phone than to anyone in particular. "Some floozy ripped his heart out. Just what he needs right now."

"Poor guy," I say.

JJ crawls off my lap to get closer to the TV. He takes the remote and turns the volume up. I don't like how close he is, don't like what it is doing to his eyes, but I let it go this time.

"He tells me he vomits hourly," she says.

"Poor guy," I say.

"The director says to use that sorrow, and Bradley has, and his performances have been phenomenal, but all that sadness. It's hard."

"Poor guy," I say.

"He's come back broken."

"Poor guy," I say.

Maggie looks at me and tilts her head. She opens her mouth to say something, but the phone tings again—that fuckin' ting!—and I've lost her.

I move to the kitchen. I take out the cutting board. I try to imagine myself inside Mike and Maggie's again. That small kitchen. The warmth from the burners. The smell of bread and curry and grilled meat. I work on JJ's afternoon meal. I take out the carrots and chop them into two-inch sticks. I slice cheddar cheese into small squares. I cut a hotdog into four pieces and slice little X's into the ends, so they flower open when cooked. I pour milk and chocolate syrup into a sippy cup. All for JJ. My boy.

I'm retreating, I know. I'm not saying what I need to say, afraid of what I might hear.

Maggie's on the phone now, repeating, "It's OK, it's OK," and I want to say it isn't OK. None of this is OK. I want to say I need you, not JJ, but me, the other poor guy, whose dream came crashing down on him too, who now is unemployed and unhappy, who feels alone and adrift.

"You have every right to feel this way," Maggie says to the phone.

No, I don't. This sadness, this deep, deep well, is not anyone's right.

*

I go on car rides in the middle of the night because I can't still my brain, which whirls and whirls and whirls and I become angry that Maggie is snoring softly beside me, oblivious to everything. I think I can drive off, take the highway out of town and not turn back. It would be that simple, an act of the body without the brain. Press the accelerator. Don't look in the rearview mirror, no matter what. Not even if you see your son back there waiting for you. Not even if you see your wife. Your restaurant. You keep going until you hit someplace and that someplace will provide all the answers you've been searching for and that someplace will love you and need you, and you will know why you exist on this planet. It's a bit existential, I realize. Maggie would evoke the great director. She would say, "The director tells us we should never run from what we fear, but face it head on." The director is a tool. He is a half-balding man who teaches part-time at the community college and drinks too much. And I think this is stupid. She's stupid. Bradley is stupid. The play. Our life. But I always reach a certain point on the drive where I round back, and then I sit inside the car in the driveway, looking at our home, noticing how tall the grass is, noticing JJ's toys scattered in the yard and sometimes I nod off, waking when the suns butters the horizon, and sometimes, like this morning, Maggie finds me before she heads off to work. I think I'm dreaming because there is a cloudy haze around her head and she says something I'm not hearing. I roll down the window, and for a split second I think she's come to me and this is the very moment I wake from this bad dream, like the one JJ often has, the ones that jolts him into tears.

"JJ is hungry," she says. "He peed his pants, too."

"OK," I say.

"I'm late for work," she says. "I would've cleaned him if I wasn't late."

"OK," I say. I get out of the car and close the door.

"I'll call to check on you guys later."

"OK," I say.

"Bye," and Maggie doesn't move to leave but stands there, looking at the ground and I have the urge to hold her, to reach out and touch the back of her neck, but my hands remain deep in my pockets.

*

It's been raining, and JJ wanted to go the park, but I told him it would be muddy. He has Maggie's fastidiousness, so he cringes at the word muddy. He doesn't like wet messes. Ironic.

I take him on a car ride instead, and in the backseat, he stares out the window, naming things. Car. Tree. Sign. Leaves. Clouds. I sneak glances at him and he's content with where he is and what's he doing. Contentment comes easy for him.

I turn down the main strip. I point to the large brick building on the corner. "Library," I say.

"Library," JJ says.

I point to the gas station. "Gas station."

"Gas station," he says.

I point to grocery store. "Grocery store."

"Grocery store," he says.

I know this area well, know it for the 1098 days I had driven these streets, past these places on route to the restaurant, and I know that on the 1098th day I drove away from the restaurant for the last time.

It is up ahead. I can see the red-tiled roof in the distance, the blinking neon sign that says open. It's now a flower shop.

"Mommy," JJ says.

I look to where his finger is pointing and it is Maggie. She's sitting on a bench, outside the bank, a purple sweater wrapped around her shoulders. The rain has eased up, spitting, and she's eating a sandwich.

"Mommy," JJ says.

I slow the car down. Park it in front of the hardware store across the street.

"Mommy," JJ says.

When the restaurant first closed, the two of us did not do anything for a week. We held each other. We sobbed. We lamented. We were a we. After a week, Maggie said she was through with the sad sap mentality. She said it was time to put our lives back together. She wrote a list of rules for herself, and has been following that list ever since. But I was stuck. What were our lives without the restaurant? What were our lives when our dream no longer existed? Perhaps I'm projecting. Perhaps it wasn't her dream at all. That week, Maggie found a job at the bank, tried out for *Grease* and got the lead part of Sandy, and from then on our lives changed.

I remember Maggie telling me about her sadness once, a time before me, before JJ, before even Bradley. "Sometimes you have to look inward," she said, and as hard as I've tried, I see nothing.

Maggie doesn't notice us. She doesn't raise her eyes up from her sandwich, and when she finally does, she turns towards the restaurant and takes another bite. Right now, she's the girl I met five years ago. I thought then, as I do at this moment, that this woman was / is miraculous the way miracles are. I should tell her this. Instead, I watch. JJ watches. Even he knows this is what we are meant to do. Eventually, she rises, brushes the crumbs from the front of her blouse, and returns to work. There is nothing more for us here, so I turn the car around, head back home, the red of the restaurant disappearing in the distance, and JJ, again, begins to name the things he sees along the way.

*

The play opens in two days. *South Pacific* posters have found their way into every open space in town, onto the bulletin boards at the cafes and grocery stores and stapled on the telephone poles. Maggie's in character most of the time, talking with a soft Asian accent that makes JJ laugh and say, "Funny talk." She asks that I make Hawaiian food for the week, so I prepare luau pork, poi, lomi lomi. She asks if it's OK if she sleeps in the other room to mentally prepare. "The director says immersion is what makes successful actresses." And there she emerges, The Actress, who floats across our house, who sings melodic tunes, who brings a guest with her after rehearsal before opening night.

"This is Bradley," The Actress says.

"Brad," I say, sticking out my hand.

"It's Bradley," he says and takes it firmly.

"My apologies," I say.

Brad turns from me. "And this must be the little man," he says.

JJ hides behind my leg. Brad is big and blonde and without a chin. Brad kneels down and his knees pop and he groans. "Can you give me five?" he says, and puts his hand up high. JJ shakes his head. I love him in this instant more than any other time in his life.

"JJ," says The Actress. "Be cordial."

JJ shakes his head.

"He's shy," I say to Brad.

"He normally isn't," says The Actress.

Brad rises and grunts. "That's cool, you know. I'm scary looking."

"Don't be silly," The Actress says and gently puts a hand on his shoulder. "You're wonderful."

Brad *is* kinda scary. He looks like a baby man child. Put a bonnet on him, stick a pacifier in those pouty lips, put him in a diaper and that's what he'd be—baby man child. This thought makes me smile.

JJ tugs on my leg. He wants me to lift him up. I do. He

points at Brad. "Tell man to go."

"JJ," The Actress says. "That's not very nice to say."

"Man go," JJ says.

"You're not being a good boy," The Actress says.

"It's OK," says Brad, smiling his baby man child smile. "I'm not offended."

"You're going to think we've raised a heathen," The Actress says.

"Never," says Brad.

"Our son is not a heathen," I say. "Isn't that right, JJ?"

JJ nods though he doesn't know why.

The Actress stares at me, as if this is my fault, as if I have implanted this behavior into our son. "He's not normally like this," she says. "He's normally a good boy."

"He is a good boy," I say and kiss his cheek. He squirms and giggles.

"Kids, you know," Brad says. "Maybe I should go."

"Sit." The Actress points to the couch. "We need to practice."

"Mommy," JJ says. "Man go home."

"You aren't being hospitable," says The Actress, "He's our guest."

"I want Mommy and Daddy," JJ says.

Brad sits crossed-legged, laughing and holding the bridge of his nose. It's an actor's laugh—fake, controlled.

"JJ," the Mom eyes come out, "you're being disrespectful. You know what happens to disrespectful boys?"

JJ's little forehead crinkles.

"No cookies. Forever."

JJ begins to cry and I start rocking him. The sound of his cries has never sounded so beautiful. It's like the sizzle of garlic, the bubble of boiling broth.

The Actress looks at me. "Can you do something?"

"I can," I say, but I don't. I stand there with my crying son, bouncing him up and down, as he hides his face in the nape of my neck, and I can feel the wetness run down my back, and I'm OK with this. More than OK. This is my exclamation point. This is my message.

"I'll go," I say after a minute. "Nice to meet you Brad." I turn with JJ in my arms to the kitchen for a box of cookies, and for the rest of the day, we will gorge ourselves in crumbly delights until our bellies ache.

*

Later that night, after I put JJ to sleep, I check on The Actress and her friend only to see him crying on her shoulders, the baby man child, and I'm almost tempted to ask if he needs a pacifier. My wife rocks him, her arms around the fleshy parts of him, and I'm left in the silence of the house, watching.

*

On opening night, JJ and I sit in the front of the theater, in a special section reserved for family members of the cast. He is in a shirt and tie, though he's been wiggling the tie around so it's askew. The Actress has been nervous the entire day, pacing the house, reciting her lines over and over to herself. She's like this before every play, a ball of unraveling yarn. She's so frantic I think there's no way she'll get it together, but when the curtain parts and the music begins, she is the most elegant character on stage, the lights kissing her white skin, reflecting off her black hair. JJ claps and points and says, "Mommy," and I shake my head and say, "Liat."

I'm moved, despite off tune singing, despite fumbled lines.

I'm moved by Bradley, and understand how he thought he might make it because he is damn good. I'm moved by this community play because somehow I feel it is singing to me some essential lesson.

When I used to cook at the restaurant, I sometimes started crying during the busiest moments of the day, not because I felt overwhelmed, but because I mattered to people. What I was doing mattered, and I remember Maggie passing me in the kitchen and giving me loving touches before delivering plates or making another drink, and how at the end of the day she would sometimes be crying, too.

"Why are you crying?" I'd ask.

"Because," she'd say. "Sometimes a girl has to cry."

And sometimes a boy does too. Like at this moment, when Bradley's character dies and Liat is left to mourn her lost love, and I'm thinking it isn't Bradley's character, but me, on stage, and I'm thinking I have died, and Liat, Maggie, no matter how hard she sings I won't wake because there is nothing in me to wake.

"Daddy," JJ whispers, "I pooped my pants."

I hear him.

"Daddy," he says again.

It is as if he's at the other end of a tunnel.

"I pooped my pants," he says.

I don't move.

"I pooped my pants," my son says, louder and louder and louder. There are shushes and grumbles, but I remain unstirred.

"I pooped my pants! I pooped my pants! I. Pooped. My. Pants!"

He is so loud the play stops and the ushers are asking me to take care of my son. "Sir," they keep saying, "Sir," and Bradley's man child's face peeks from backstage, and the actors and orchestra are looking at one another, not sure what to do because the director never prepared them for this situation, the one where a three-year-old boy is screaming that he has pooped his pants and the father absolutely does nothing because he has recognized something in himself, his life, his marriage, and that recognition has stopped his heart, his brain, his every extremity. Maggie rushes off the stage to JJ, who is crying, and she is in costume, and her face is layered in makeup and it is smeared because of her very real tears, and she says in a voice that is her own and it is loud and anguished, and worst of all, ashamed: "What's wrong with you? Goddammit, what's wrong with you?"

4

The art of bread making can become a consuming hobby, and no matter how often and how many kinds of bread one has made, there always seems to be something new to learn.

–Julia Child

The Melting Season

In this region of the country, when the snow melts, lost things emerge: dolls, deflated tires, a canoe, a missing sneaker, a hammer, a child's big wheel, the forgotten rake, plush dog toys, lawn mowers, a toilet. And for Kevin and Martha Byington, their fifteen-year-old son, David.

The Byingtons had gone through what might have been expected of grieving parents. At first, they were not concerned. The blizzard had made everyone stir-crazy, and David might have gone out after being cooped up for four days. He was a teenager after all, a good-looking boy, born from a handsome Caucasian father and a petite Thai mother. He possessed their best traits: his father's solid chin and sharp Germanic nose; his mother's dark black hair and soft brown eyes. David was athletic and agile, and his body reflected this. He could climb on top of the house to shovel the roof without the need of a ladder and would jump down without so much as making a sound.

After that first day, however, and the next three days that followed, panic set in. Kevin and Martha went frantically door to door with a picture of their son, asking if anyone had seen him. It wasn't the most accurate picture. But in haste it was all Martha could find. Their boy at twelve. A foot and half shorter and skinny as bamboo. Face in scared elation. Sledding. The town knew of the Byingtons, the interracial couple and their son. They knew about Kevin Byington, or Dr. Byington, the general practitioner at the health clinic. They knew about Martha Byington who operated her own catering business and made the best cannoli this side of the Genesee River. They knew secrets about Kevin and Martha that husband and wife did not know about each other.

The next week, they blamed everyone. Kevin Byington struck an officer for perceived incompetency and spent a night in jail "to cool off." Martha Byington accused the local police department of being racist. It would be another three weeks before tempers simmered. What was left were hope and endless optimism. Kevin Byington called home every hour between patients, expecting David to answer with his usual, "What's up, Doc?" Martha Byington cooked David's favorite meal each and every night: steamed meatballs with garlic jasmine rice. She would set an extra plate at the table, expecting David to jet in the way he always did, apologizing for being late, stuffing his mouth one whole meatball at a time.

Both of them returned to religion, Martha slipping on her Buddha pendants after years of keeping them locked in a drawer and praying to Buddha for her son's swift return, and David attending Sunday morning services, asking God for the same.

Then they grieved. The realization that they might never see David again, their lovely boy who could do no wrong, was too much to bear. In conversation, they referred to David in the past tense. "He was a talented boy, wasn't he?" At the mall, they would say, "David would have loved that sweater. Don't you think we would've looked great in it?"

On the morning of April 20, Martha Byington was looking at the sunrise with a warm cup of tea in her hand, thinking about how it had been so long since she had seen the sun, really seen it, and felt the warmth of it play on her face, thinking about how a spring day like today makes it possible to continue living, when she happened to look at the very end of the driveway, at the very edge of the woods where there once had been a twenty foot mountain of snow pushed higher and higher by the Byingtons' hired plowman, Marcus Flavin, and there she saw the unmistakable shape of David's boots, the pair she had just bought for him so he could go out and shovel people's driveways in the neighborhood for extra cash and then the unmistakable color of his hair, which was the color of hers.

FORECAST

In town, everyone knew Bill Matford, News channel 4's meteorologist. "Matford said we're in for a doozey," town folks said. "Billy was barking about how it ain't going to end any time soon." In the case of the snow that hit the region on November 16 through the 19, Bill Matford was right on the money. The snow wasn't going to end.

In such adverse weather conditions, the world soon looked apocalyptic. The trees sagged and snapped under the weight of the snow, sounding like echoing gunshots. Power lines snapped. There were ten-foot canyon walls along the side of roads. Towns shut down. Police instructed motorists to go home and sit the storm out. Nothing escaped the color white.

THE STORM

When David was younger, snow days were for the family. Kevin Byington would light the fireplace and dim down all of the lights, and Martha would bake her special upside down cake. Then, the family would gather to play hearts. At night, all of them put on their hats and gloves and entered the snow, which was usually waist high, and built a snow family.

During this storm, Kevin Byington remained in his study, and Martha sat on the couch, watching the Food Network.

David could not see the river birch ten feet outside the window. The snow came down thick, a sheet of white. The wind whipped against the house and rattled the doors. Martha's wind chimes sang with the gusts.

When Martha Byington was asked about the last time she saw David, she had told the authorities he was writing in his journal. When the same question was posed to Kevin, he said the same. "It's all he does. That journal." That journal wasn't hard to find. David never hid it. He trusted his parents, a rarity among teenagers. His current journal, a fancy green velvet one he got for his birthday, lay where he had left it. On the kitchen table.

During the time David was missing, the journal was all the Byingtons had of their son. At first, they read the last couple of entries to see whether David had left a clue of where he might have gone.

November 16, 1984. It's snowing. I just started reading Lolita. Why would you name someone Humbert Humbert? I get the feeling something bad is going to happen. Like all of a sudden everything is going to come crashing down.

November 17, 1984. It's still snowing. I'm making good money though. Shoveling. I can get Candice flowers. Girls like that kinda stuff. My dad taught me that. Anyway, Lolita. I was right. Candice's parents would think I'm the anti-Christ for reading this.

November 18, 1984. I'm not going to lie to you. It's still snowing. Finished Lolita. Wow.

It didn't take long for the Byingtons to get in touch with

Candice Chapman. It didn't take long before the authorities questioned her over and over. It didn't take long for Candice to break down and admit to everything she knew. Yes, David called her the day before he disappeared. Yes, they were secretly going out for ten months. Yes, her parents didn't approve. Yes, she loved him. Yes, they planned to meet the day he disappeared despite the storm. No, he didn't show up. No, she didn't know where he was.

LOVE

Candice Chapman could fly, David wrote in this journal. His school basketball team was practicing in the same gym as the cheerleading squad. It was there that he witnessed Candice Chapman being launched into the air—*twenty feet, maybe even thirty*, David wrote, *like a rocket*. She did the splits and fell elegantly into the ready hands of her cheer-mates. *I want to know her.*

And so he went about knowing Candice Chapman. First, he wrote letters to her, slipping them into her gym bag when she wasn't looking. He would find her replies in the inside of his locker. With each passing note, their letters became more flirtatious.

I think you are the prettiest girl in this school, he wrote.

There's only thirty girls in this school, David.

In the universe.

And then there were the secret meetings in secret places. Under the hickory at the back corner of the cemetery. Behind the boarded up gas station. At the Bluffs at dawn.

It didn't take long before the Chapmans heard of their daughter's trysts. The Chapmans were a conservative Christian family, and they forbade their daughter to see David again.

Especially David Byington. Did she not know of the rumors spinning around town? Did she not know Martha Byington, which wasn't really her name, wasn't a Christian, and that Kevin Byington made particular house calls to a particular house a couple of towns over on a regular basis?

The Byingtons were trouble. So was that boy.

Then the boy disappeared. And the Chapmans, though apologetic and sympathetic for the Byingtons' loss, were in some way grateful.

YEATS

The summer before the storm, David skateboarded to the clinic and met his father for lunch. Summers in central New York were too short. It was a three-month hiatus before the clouds congregated again. When the summer came, sprits lifted.

David hadn't done lunch with his father for a while, and in the last few months, he found that he rarely saw his father at all. When he did, Kevin seemed distracted, not himself. That afternoon, David had brought leftovers. Braised beef and carrots and whipped potatoes, something his mother cooked up. His father, however, when presented with the food, made a face that almost looked to David like a grimace, and quickly said he was in the mood for something that could clog his arteries. "Some heart attack meal."

They drove a town over to the diner and ordered two cheesesteaks, an order of cheese fries, fried mushrooms and zucchini spears, and jalapeño poppers with melted cheddar inside. As a joke, the waitress asked if they wanted a salad, and Kevin Byington laughed and said to feed it to the cows outside.

David had never seen his father like this. Not that he minded. Kevin Byington could be fun. He remembered his laugh and smile, the way he flirted with his mother when he thought David wasn't looking. In fact, this was where David learned how to be intimate, how to trace a finger along an arm, how a gentle kiss on the forehead could be more loving and satisfying then one to the lips. When he was younger, he often remarked that this intimacy was gross, but secretly, seeing his parents so in love made him feel safe, made him feel protected.

They ate and made small talk. *How was basketball camp? Any thoughts on college? Have you read any good books?*

"A girl gave me some poetry by YEEts," said David.

"You mean Yeats," said Kevin. "Y-E-A-T-S?"

"That's right. You know him?"

"I read him in college."

"What do you think?"

"I think I can stitch up a cut better than I can read poetry," said Kevin, laughing. His son did not, and for a moment, he noticed how much David had grown, how he was no longer a boy, but a man. Moreover, he appeared much like his mother. Dark hair, light colored skin, small, imploring eyes. It came as a sharp abrupt surprise. If a stranger were to look this way, they would not think this was a father and son. He wondered if David saw the same thing across the table, someone foreign.

Kevin took a sip of cola and then said, "My brain doesn't process poetry all too quickly. Do you like Yeats?"

David nodded. "It makes me think, you know?"

"About?"

"Everything, really. There was this one poem—I don't remember the title—but it was about these two people and they were in love, but it was really sad. And they wanted to be birds, white birds, I think, and fly to a place less—" Here David stammered. Kevin knew he was measuring his words, another similarity to his mother, especially when she was first learning how to speak English. She would stop mid-sentence, look up at the sky, hoping the right words would drop down through her head and out of her mouth. "—a place less confining. Does that make sense?"

"Yes," Kevin said.

"Don't you ever think about that?"

Kevin Byington had been thinking about many things as of late. He could not tell David any of it. Not when David was speaking from a place he had not known, not in his many years as a father. David was smart, brilliant even, but seemed to go about his days the way his mother had—without a care in the world. But this was a different David. Contemplative. Struggling with ideas beyond his own existence. This, Kevin knew, was what drew him to medicine.

He reached over and patted his son's hand. "Seems like Yeats has struck a chord."

"I guess," David said.

"This girl that gave you the book, is she a good friend?"

David nodded.

"A girlfriend?" asked Kevin.

David smiled and looked away. "She's a friend."

"Sure, sure," said Kevin. He checked his watch, and though he wanted to talk more about this friend, he had to get back to the clinic. "Buy this friend flowers. You buy a girl flowers and she's all yours."

THE MARKET

Every Thursday, in the warmer months, Martha Byington shopped at the local farmer's market. She strolled through the market, which was located in the city hall parking lot, with a basket hanging on her arm. She stopped and smelled the strawberries. She tapped a few melons. She tested the firmness of the tomatoes. Then, she bought what she needed for the week, decided by what gatherings she had to cater, what dishes she would make for dinner.

Martha Byington knew every vendor by name. She knew their kids because some of them attended the same school as David. She was casual and cheery in tone and demeanor. "Ronald, how are the potatoes?" "Mitzy, now, you promised me special rusty apples from the orchard last week. I'm here to collect." She was not the only patron, of course. Out came the wives on Thursdays. Out came the eighth graders skateboarding around. Out came the high school girls to be ogled by the high school boys. The Farmer's Market was the town's weekly gathering.

She went about her business. Talked the weather, which was always serious business. Chatted with a few wives about the latest sale or haircut. Bought a bag of kettle popcorn for David, his favorite. And then, she was done.

What was left after her exit was the nodding and whispering that never reached her ears.

SMALL TOWNS

Routine runs your day. Your wife wakes at the same time for work at the nuclear power plant. The school bus waits for your daughter for only two minutes before taking off, and when it does, you rush to get her slow ass to school. You see the same people. You hear the same stories. You know, somewhere, you are being talked about.

The winters stretch endlessly. The gray clouds close in on you. They never go away. You are desperate for color. You order hundreds of bulbs. You plant them in the fall and wait until another winter passes to see them bloom, only the rabbits and squirrels get to them first, destroying more than half of what you put into the ground. You say, this is the life you wanted. You belong here. But here is heavy with sorrow like a snow-weighted branch. Here is always better after a shot of whiskey at the local bar before driving home. Here was where Marcus Flavin lived all his life; his father and his father before him. Here was where Marcus complained to the bartender when sassy pants Bill Matford announced the first snow of the year.

"Goddamn it," Marcus said. "Billy just loves to stick it to us."

"Bill's just doing his job," said the bartender.

"His job makes me miserable." Marcus knew because of the forecast that he had to be up early in the morning, plowing. He would start with the schools, banks, and businesses, and then work his way through all his residential clients.

"At least you'll make good money," the bartender said. "Keeps you busy."

"I'd just wish one year," Marcus said, "God would lift his curse on us."

"Right there, friend, you're asking for a miracle."

RUMOR

September 13, 1984. Candice says I shouldn't believe everything I hear. But I felt like she knew more than I did, like she's keeping a secret. I'm surrounded by secrets.

September 14, 1984. Forget it. Forget it. Forget it. Forgotten.

September 15, 1984. I saw him.

COOL DOWN

The night Kevin spent in jail, he thought only of his son. This wasn't a jail he expected to see. He was raised on westerns and imagined stonewalls and rusted bars. No, he was detained in a sterile room with a bed and sink. White walls, a square window that let light in. He sat on the bed with his hands digging into his eyes. He hit the officer because he thought the police weren't doing enough. He hit the officer because he needed to hit something. Because, that day, every moment, every second, he thought he saw David. When he walked past the open door of David's room, David was on his stomach writing in his journal. When he walked downstairs to living room, David was pressing buttons on his video game controller. When he went outside to shovel the snow off his car, David was on top of the big snow mound at the end of the driveway.

After the last sighting, he called the police. He told them David was somewhere near. The police came quickly and searched the area and house, but found nothing.

"I saw him," Kevin said.

The officers explained to Kevin that they had done all they could. There were no tracks in the snow, no evidence of any change since they last checked.

"My son was here," Kevin said.

They told him he wasn't.

"He was here." He spaced each words through clenched teeth.

Martha put a hand on his shoulder.

It was her touch that sent him over. The slight pull of her fingers. Kevin felt a rush of anger, an uncontrollable urge to hurt. He wanted someone to feel what he was feeling, this incredible darkness that was strangling his entire body.

He let his left fist go.

TEA

When Martha Byington saw her son's boots in the snow, she did not rush outside. When she saw his hair, she turned away and dropped her mug onto the floor. Tea splattered on her bare feet, but she felt no pain, only a numbness that spread to all her extremities. Unsteady, she supported herself on the sofa. She dared not turn back.

RECIPE

Kevin and Martha Byington were once in love. Their story is quick. He was finishing off his residency in Florida, and she was in the country illegally, working at a friend's Thai restaurant. He had lunch there. She served him. He kept coming back. One year later, they were married. Two years later, David was born. In those three years, Kevin and Martha were happy. Kevin helped Martha with her English, paying for language and cooking classes. She quizzed him as best she could on medicine, and prepared all his meals, which he always remarked as tasting like "a little bit of heaven." Soon Martha was no longer a timid Asian girl. Soon her accent was nearly erased.

One thing that always bothered Kevin about Martha, however, was that he knew very little about her. When they first got together, he excused this oversight as a limitation of language and the overflowing passion they shared for one another, but now it was three years later; they were married and had a son, and were quite possibly moving to another part of the world where it was rumored received over two hundred inches of snow a year.

Often, when he wasn't working, he would simply watch her in the kitchen, as she floated from stove to refrigerator, refrigerator to sink, sink back to stove. He was doing this, watching his wife, when he decided to ask her about the life she left behind. The baby was sleeping in the other room.

"Do you miss it," he said, "Thailand?"

The question seemed to catch Martha off guard. She stumbled a bit while dumping vegetable detritus into the garbage disposal. She regained her composure quickly and smiled. "No," she said. "Why do you ask?"

"It was something I was thinking about."

"I don't miss anything."

Kevin detected something in his wife's voice. A hesitation. A stumble. He thought himself good at detecting lies. He knew immediately if his patients said they were taking their medication and they weren't, or whether a patient was sticking to that low-carb diet to keep diabetes in check. On this occasion, Martha's accent, which she tried so hard to eradicate, weighted her words. Martha noticed it also, and quickly cleared her throat. "My life is a dream. Everything is a dream."

"I want to learn more about you." He watched Martha stir something in the pot.

The house smelled of coconut milk and a hint of citrus. Martha was working on a new recipe. She went back to a cookbook and pretended to not hear him. She didn't look up.

"And, I don't know," Kevin said, "maybe when David gets older he might want to know about the other side of him."

Martha snapped the book shut. "There is no other side of David. The past is the past." Martha went back to chopping. Her knife sped through stalks of green onion and celery.

Kevin did not expect this kind of reaction. Immediately, he

regretted asking, regretted ever bringing it up. "I didn't mean to upset you."

"I'm not upset," she said. She stopped chopping and smiled at him. "There are going to be more things in the world for David to worry about than my past. Promise me you will help me protect him from those things."

"I promise," he said. But Kevin Byington couldn't help feel something breaking that day, something that kept breaking, pushing his wife away from him, further and further, until nearly fifteen years later they existed in the same space like strangers.

WOMAN

He was always careful, taking different routes to her house, checking every direction before exiting his car. Eventually, he knew someone would find out. After fifteen years in this town, he knew someone always finds out.

She lived alone, and he knew he was not the only one. This thought came as a comfort to Kevin. He was not the sole object of her desire. They both understood what they were doing was pure act. He did not want to know any more about her than what he already knew. She was a medical chart. A malnourished body, like his.

When he was with this woman, whose skin carried the scent of grass and dust, he was with Martha. It was her back he touched, her mouth he kissed, her body he leaned into. He was quick to finish. He was quick to leave. He never said anything intimate to her, not like those moments with his wife, where he would hold her, and tell her the truth of his heart. With this woman, he reminded her to take her medication. He inquired whether she had made an appointment with her gyno.

He instructed her to stay away from fatty foods.

PREDICTION

The day Martha saw her son at the end of the driveway, Bill Matford predicted the last of the snows. "Melting season is upon us again," he said. "Get your mud kickers on. It's going to be messy." Bill was a reliable meteorologist, more accurate than the big guys at the Rochester and Syracuse stations. The town trusted Bill because he was a local boy. Local boys just don't lie. Yet, they also knew when a weatherman, any weatherman, predicted the last of the snow, there was a good chance that winter had one more surprise for them all, one last good-bye.

CAT

When David Byington learned to walk, he had the habit of roaming out of the range his parent's supervision. Kevin and Martha were not neglectful parents. David was the center of their lives, and they kept close watch of him.

Especially Martha. Routinely, she woke up three times in the middle of the night just to check if he was sleeping soundly. When he started school, she sometimes sat in her car, adjacent to the playground, and made sure he came out each day for recess. Once, when he didn't, she rushed into the school only to find David reading in the classroom because he didn't feel well.

Martha Byington was plagued with nightmares that David would vanish from right under her. Sometimes, she violently kicked her husband in her sleep, mumbling something about David. Sometimes, she grabbed his arm and tugged him close. Each time, Kevin shook his wife awake and gently whispered that everything would be OK, it was only a bad dream. "How's

David?" she would say, half awake, and he would assure her that he was perfectly fine.

That one moment David could be beside her and the next he could vanish was something she couldn't bear. For Martha, her fear was more than a sense of parental protectiveness. David had become the symbol of her new life, and she did not want anything or anyone taking this life away.

It only took a handful of seconds, however, and David would wander off, following some sort of fascination. His parents, when he was learning to walk, leashed him. When he could talk, Martha taught him how to say the word "sunshine." She would call out, "Sun," and he was expected to respond immediately with "Shine." It was their word, she told him, because he was her sunshine.

One day, Martha was in the garden preparing the soil for the spring. Melting season was nearing an end, and there were only splotches of snow here and there among the green grass. David had been beside her playing with worms. He was five, and in a few months, he would be attending the first grade.

No more than thirty seconds—Martha dug up some old roots and pulled out some stubborn weeds—and David was gone. How he slipped past her without a sound had always bothered her. She looked in every direction. The Byingtons lived on three acres, much of it wooded. In the summer, when the hickories grew in, you couldn't see past the dense leaves.

Martha shot up and began walking towards the woods.

"Sun?" she said and then waited for a response.

It was still too early in spring for the leaves on the trees to be thick. In spite of this, in whatever direction she turned, all she saw were trees, a dizzying amount of them.

"Sun," she said again. "David?"

The wind passed through the branches. She picked up her

pace, stepping into the marshy ground of the woods, almost losing her boot. A lot of David's toys were in here, left and neglected, covered in the snow for months before emerging again. An action figure. A glider. A tennis ball.

"Sun? Sun?"

And then she heard him. Faintly. Further up ahead.

"Sun—"

"—shine." His back was to her. He was wearing a dark jacket that made him blend into the trunk of trees. When she reached him, she pulled him towards her.

"You scared it," he said and began crying because she had begun crying.

The neighbor's orange cat that often visited their garden for birds sprinted in the other direction, hiding in a thicket of fallen branches. David must've seen it and followed it into the woods.

"Why didn't you answer me?" his mother said.

"I was only petting it."

"Don't you understand? I could've lost you." She hugged him again, pushing his face into her shoulder. If she could, she wanted to push him into her, so he would always be part of her, so he would never leave, so she would know where he was.

"I knew you would find me," he said, voice muffled.

REWRITE

David tried to write something, but crossed it out several times, starting over. In between the pen scratches, one could decipher a few words like *hate* and *truth* and *love*. Finally, the uncrossed passage, which was short and written in loopy cursive with circles and hearts dotting the "I," read: *Tell me a story where we live happily ever after.* And after that, a quote from a W.B.

Yeats poem "The White Birds": "...*Time would surely forget us, and Sorrow come near us no more...*"

Secrets

After the fifth month of David's disappearance, only two days before Martha saw David's boot at the end of the drive-way, Kevin Byington packed his things and moved out of the house. Kevin said he couldn't stay where everything reminded him of his son. Martha couldn't leave for that same reason.

The day Kevin left, Martha sat at the couch, watching the TV on mute. She did not move or turn to look at him, as he gathered his suitcases by the front door. He gave the house a once over, making sure he had gotten the essentials. The rest he would come back for.

"David knew," Martha said.

Her voice was too soft. He asked her to speak again.

"He knew," she said.

Kevin did not understand what his wife was talking about. He put down his suitcase and sat on the couch next to her. "What are you talking about?"

From behind some pillows, she took out David's journal. Kevin knew Martha had been reading it. She had been reading all his journals—the one he piled in his room from other years—but the year of his disappearance, she returned to the most recent. "Our son knew," she said. She handed him the journal. One section was bookmarked.

Kevin read it, and as soon as he was finished, he dropped the notebook, buried his eyes into his palms, and wept. For minutes there was nothing but the sounds of sobbing. Martha did not move to console him. She sat and watched and waited until he stilled, until he could gather himself.

"I used to tell David stories," she said, "when you were at work, before his afternoon nap."

"I'm sorry," he said. "I—"

She quieted him with a hand. "These were our stories," she said. "Our secrets. Would you like to hear one?"

"Martha," he said. "I didn't mean to—"

"A story," she said. "Would you like to hear one?"

He nodded. Hearing her story was the least he could do.

ACCIDENT

It was mid-afternoon and Marcus Flavin had already plowed twenty driveways and ten parking lots. He had one house left, the Byington's.

Through his years of plowing he had never seen so much snow. This was something of epic proportions. Their little town made national news; his daughter—who had been home the last four days because of school closures—had a friend in Alabama who called and asked whether the pictures she was seeing on the news were real.

Marcus travelled the county roads at ten miles per hour. The snow came down thick. White out conditions. It wasn't the smartest time to plow, but he had one house left and did not want to come back later on.

The Byingtons were long-time clients and had a three hundred foot driveway. In the beginning of the snow season, Marcus would come over and stick red poles in the ground on either side of the driveway, markers. The poles were about eight feet tall, and when he pulled into the driveway that day, only a half a foot was showing on the nearest one. It was all he needed. He lowered the plow and steamed head. He did not look out the front window. He kept his eyes glued to the sides, looking at the tips of those poles. The snow in front of his car kept growing and growing until he reached the very end of the driveway where there was a fifteen-foot mountain of white. Snow like this took five or six passes, so Marcus backed up slowly, and zipped forward again.

Momentarily, he tried to look at the house, which stood twenty feet from the driveway. Sometimes, he saw the Byingtons at dinner. They appeared to be a happy family, despite the talk that went around town. Today, however, Marcus could not see the house, only a hint of a light in what must have been the front windows.

No matter. He was hungry. He was tired. He needed to get home. Marcus Flavin drove faster, piling more and more snow at the end of the driveway. There was so much powder it was impossible to feel anything else but the thrust of the engine, the weight of the snow. And it was impossible to hear anything else but the rumble of his pick-up and the blizzard wind. When Marcus was done, he looked once more at the mountain at the end of the driveway. It had grown bigger, and since this was the beginning of winter, it would continue to grow, and underneath it were already many things: a shovel, a basketball, a portable CD player and ear phones, a *Rolling Stones* CD, a copy of *Lolita*, and a suffocating boy.

THE LAST SNOW

Sometimes, when the snow dissipated, you could uncover flowers from the summer still in bloom. Martha always thought this was a minor miracle. That day, deep in the Byington's woods, the ground yielded to the shovel. It didn't take long before Kevin and Martha dug a deep enough hole and filled it up. They did not speak as they worked. They did not question whether what they were doing was right or wrong. It was past that point. For Kevin and Martha, a warming calm spread through their chests and heads, melting whatever resentment still existed. Shoveling and burying was a process of healing, of starting over. They understood this, and once every minute or two, they glanced at each other and smiled or simply nodded.

When they were done, they stood there, looking at the ground. The temperature that was predicted to hover around fifty steadily dropped. Martha started to shiver, and Kevin dug his hands deep in his pockets.

"Are you thirsty?" Martha said. She wiped at her forehead. Dirt caked her jeans and sweater.

Kevin leaned against a hickory "A little hungry."

"Lunch?"

"Sure."

The both of them turned and headed toward the house, where Bill Matford was on television, announcing another storm was on its way, swooping across the lakes and reaching town about two o'clock in the afternoon. "It's going to be a doozy," he said. "Be careful."

5

Drama is very important in life: You have to come on with a bang.
You never want to go out with a whimper. Everything can have
drama if it's done right. Even a pancake.

–Julia Child

Panhandle: A Fusion

The Dishwasher

I knew all about the stars, their names and the names of the constellations, the way they moved through the night sky like runners on a track, each keeping to its own invisible and predetermined lane. When I was thirteen, I began keeping a journal of stars, and in it I tracked their movement night to night. I documented their brightness and recorded their names and their translations. Sulafat, tortoise. Arneb, hare. Muphrid, lance bearer. The names seemed otherworldly, which of course the stars themselves were, and though they were in the sky for anyone to see, I felt that the stars—the entire expanse of the sky for that matter—was mine and mine alone. All I had to do was keep looking up.

In late summer, my favorite three stars would come into view after sunset. The Summer Triangle: Vega, Denab, and Altair, all three of them in the top twenty of the brightest stars in the sky, and all three of them part of other constellations—Lyre the Harp, Cygnus the Swan, and Aquila the Eagle. The Summer Triangle usually lasts until late fall, sometimes until Halloween if we are lucky. Each night, the stars slowly edge east, a centimeter or two a day, until they simply vanish.

The first time I discovered the Summer Triangle my mother died. I was looking through the telescope when the phone rang. I had bought a book of stars with my allowance and was determined to find all the stars listed in the book, checking them off in the margins. I had located about one hundred stars that summer. I jotted each discovery in my journal and noted their position in the sky. I had been waiting for the Summer Triangle since June, but it was too early for all three stars to come into view together. But then, on the last day of July, they appeared at the lower left of the sky. I looked through the telescope, the stars large and bright, especially Vega. I looked without the telescope and traced my finger in the air. Just about when I was going to tell my father about my find, I heard him repeating a one-word question—*What? What? What?*—his voice shaking, his head shaking. My mother was in a car accident on her way back from work. My father told me it was quick. That night, I wrote in my journal: *I found the Summer Triangle.* And next to that: *Mom is dead.*

Each year, the emergence of the three stars indicated to me that the summer was nearing an end and school would start soon. They told me about the gathering winter clouds and it was almost time to pack up the telescope until late April.

Before her death, we lived an hour outside of Chicago, so the sky was clear of the city lights, and the pollution didn't disrupt my stargazing. I used to tell my father my findings, and he would pat me on the back and tell me to find a star no one has found and name it after him. Jonathan Agnes Thompson. "How would that be, huh?" Once, right after my mother's death, I told him if I ever found a new star, which the likelihood was a zillion to one with this telescope, then I would never name the star Agnes. "That's a good name," he said a little too cheery. "It's a family name." He went on about Agnes Radford, the woman who left one of the colonies in the east and came to settle in the plains by herself, which was unheard of back then. Agnes isn't a woman's name, he told me, but one that signifies power and perseverance. I told him there's an Agnes who works in the principal's office and she's old and crabby. I told him that if I found a star I would name it after my mother. Cynthia Jane. "Wouldn't it be cool to have a star named after mom?" My father smiled and said there wouldn't be a better name for a star he could think of.

Two years after my mother's death, my father got laid off. I was fifteen and my father didn't seem to take an interest in my stars anymore. When I told him I spotted Arcturus again, my father didn't say anything, but washed the dishes. I spouted off facts: Arcturus is the brightest star in the northern hemisphere and it's dying; it's thirty-seven light years away, which means the light we're getting from that star is the light from thirty-seven years ago. My father slammed a pot into the sink. He told me to stop watching the sky. "Don't waste time with stars and constellations and planets," he said. Stars were my future. I wanted to look at them for the rest of my life. I reminded him I wanted to name one after Mom. He shook his head and said, "Who's going to pay for all this schooling? How much money can stars bring in?" I didn't know. I didn't know what to say to my father, who suddenly began to cry. He jammed his palms into his eyes, as if he was ashamed of himself. I could do nothing but watch his bulky body shake.

Not long after that we moved out of our home, and into an apartment near the city where the night sky was lit up in a faint pink haze. I could barely see a star. My father got another job as a night patrolman at some factory, and I landed here, washing dishes from four to eleven each night. It pays OK. The food is all right. But I spend most of my time dreaming about stars. I see constellations in the flecks of food left on plates. I imagine bubbles and suds as universes and galaxies unfound. I never unpacked the telescope from its box when we moved, but keep it close to me, under the bed just in case Chicago blacks out and white, pulsating dots illuminate the sky. Whenever that happens, I'll be ready.

THE VALET

Lynette and I explore abandoned houses. We're collectors, in a sense. Whatever we find, we keep and store in my unused garage. Most of the time, we uncover lost letters, old receipts, forgotten kitchen utensils, or an occasional doll. If it's cool, we keep it. If it's not, we still keep it.

Lynette is a wild-haired redhead who sees the world a little differently than other people. She's twenty-something and wants to be the premier photographer of junk. It's an increasingly popular genre of photography, she tells me. She always has a digital camera with her. Often, on our journeys, she stops and takes a picture of random items. I'll ask what she saw in that couch on the curb or the rusted spray-paint can, and she'll simply say, "Art, Monty. Art," even though my name isn't Monty, but a nickname she decided to give me. When she prints her pictures, they don't look like junk. They transcend what they truly are and become a living, breathing piece of *life*, a snapshot of America's decay and wastefulness. I don't usually talk like that, but that's how I imagine art critics will talk about her work.

When we're not in abandoned houses, Lynette and I work at the restaurant. She's a busboy, but doesn't like the title. She prefers to be called the-person-who-takes-care-of shit-the-rich-people-don't-eat. Sometimes, she whips out the camera and takes a picture of the leftovers. She often wonders why she hasn't been promoted to wait staff or hostess, but we both know she's not a people person. At staff parties, she usually stands by herself and nods to some song in her head. When someone tries to engage her in conversation, she shoots him or her a look that says: *why are you talking to me?* I often save her, not because I'm as antisocial as she is, but because I know I'm her only friend and because we share this love for the things people have lost.

Lynette always finds me when she's on break. Sometimes she goes with me to park the cars, sitting in the passenger seat, chatting about houses we should hit next or rambling on about the latest artist who has a gallery showing in NYC and who, in her expert and non-judgmental opinion, is a complete hack. Our conversations never get deeper than art and abandoned homes. For example, Lynette doesn't know I'm forty-five today. She doesn't know about Martha and that I've been thinking about her because I found a black hair band, and in that band were a few strands of Martha's hair. I shoved the band in my pocket and have been playing with it the entire day, twining it around my fingers, plucking it like a banjo. But Lynette and I, we don't talk about this. We talk about junk.

Once I found vintage sketches of naked women in a house on Livingston Drive. Livingston used to be on the rich side of Chicago before the Great Fire in 1871. Now it's part of a rundown neighborhood. The house was tucked away in the shade of the El, crumbling and slanted, as if it would topple over from a mighty gust of wind. But it hadn't. It was standing there, seemingly unnoticed for over a century. When we entered the house, I began coughing because of the dust. Lynette handed me a surgical mask.

We weren't the first to enter the house on Livingston. There were gang signs spray-painted on the walls, beer cans and bottles on the floor, a few syringes scattered. Rats scurried away at the sound of our steps. We were used to these things. Abandoned houses were sites for sin, for recklessness, for human beings to do inhuman things, but Lynette and I were there to find something of its original nature, something that made us imagine the lives of those who used to live there.

I went into what I assumed was the master bedroom. Against one wall was a broken dresser. On another wall was a shattered vanity mirror. It would've been worth something if it weren't broken. I was willing to bet that under all that dust and tarnish, the frame of the mirror was silver.

I was about to see if I could take the mirror down, when something caught my eye. A loose floorboard. Paper sticking through the cracks. I went to the corner and yanked the board out of the floor. Under there, I found a stack of sketches, about half an inch thick. I sifted through them. I started laughing. Naked women. There must have been twenty of them. Some were brittle and yellow to the point you couldn't make anything out, but others weren't. Others were perfectly fine and there was no denying that on these sketches were breasts and butts of voluptuous women, not anorexic models in magazines nowadays, but ones with curves and heft.

Lynette came into the room to see what I found. I told her it was the greatest discovery yet. I showed her the sketches. "Revolting," she said, handing them back to me. She seemed to hug herself against an invisible chill, even though it was in the middle of the hottest summer to date, even though the house was like a moldy, dusty oven.

I told her she was nuts. These were sketches probably drawn by a man over a hundred years ago, and it was refreshing to know that people then were as horny as they are now. That made me feel good, like what I had found was a connection with another time, and the person who drew these had an appreciation of the body and understood the pleasures of sex. I told Lynette all of this and she turned to leave the room, but then stopped and took off her surgical mask.

"Sex is an overrated concept, Monty, meant to turn people into savage animals. As an up-and-coming artist I want to delve

beyond sex, see it for its true nature, a diabolical way to repro-
duce more of us, people who have nothing to do and no place
to go. Do you really want more us-es in the world? Because really, there are us-es everywhere and it's sad. Sad to the deepest
darkest bone and it's a problem not just affecting me and you
and everyone in this stupid city, but the world. And it's because
of sex, Monty. Sex. Think about that."

I thought about it and decided that my friendship with Lynette would go no further than our adventures into abandoned
houses. Lynette and I, we were elementally different people,
from different worlds, and it would take a lot to reconcile the
distance and time, light years really.

*

It's about eight and I've parked six cars—two Hondas, one
a stick, a BMW, a Chrysler and three Toyotas. Lynette walks
over, her hair bunned-up, a cigarette smoking in her fingers.
She has a brown-sauce stain on her white uniform.

"It's nice out," I say. "Maybe we can go to that house in the
suburbs after work."

She shrugs and flicks an ash, staring at me in a way that
begins to freak me out.

"It's slow out here," I say. "Is it slow in there?"

She doesn't shift her gaze.

"What is it, Lynette?"

"Monty," she says, "how many houses have we gone
through together?"

I tell her twenty houses, maybe thirty.

"Thirty-eight," she says. "Thirty-eight houses, Monty."
Her voice rises. The other valets—Tommy and Robby—look
in our direction. They think I'm sleeping with Lynette. I've

tried to set them straight, tried to tell them we're friends and there's nothing between us. But they're twenty-five and always thinking with their dicks.

I tell Lynette to settle down. "Please." But telling her this makes her even louder, more frantic. A Honda pulls in and I jump up to open the passenger door for a blonde and take the keys from her husband, hoping the sight of me doing work will quiet Lynette.

It doesn't.

As I jot down the license plate and give one half of the slip to the man, Lynette tells me I shouldn't tell her to settle down. I shouldn't silence her. "Women have been silenced for far too long, Monty, and if I would've known that you were like other men then I'd never take you to all these houses."

I look at the couple apologetically. They rush into the restaurant. I shake my head and play with Martha's hair band in my pocket. Lynette looks like she's ready to give me another barrage of words, but I point into the car and she gets in, slamming the door a little too hard.

"Easy," I say.

"*Easy?* Am I your horse? Do you want me to neigh for you?"

I pull the car out into the street and then take a quick right into the parking garage.

"I thought you were different, Monty. What a disappointment you turned out to be." I slam on the brakes. I blare on the horn and scream *shut up* so loud my voice cracks. I breathe hard. I breathe and breathe.

Lynette looks as if she's about to bolt out of the door. She looks as if she thinks I'll hit her or something.

"I'm sorry," I say. "I'm too old to be talked to like that. I'm forty-five today and I don't want to be talked to like I'm a high schooler."

Lynette turns to look at me. I feel she is counting all the cracks and wrinkles on my face, as if, for the first time, she has registered that I *am* older. "You don't look forty-five," she says.

"Thank you," I tell her.

"You look a lot older. I was thinking fifty." She isn't joking. Lynette doesn't joke.

I shake my head. In my pocket, my fingers stretch out the hair band. I stare at the steering wheel. It has a fuzzy cover on it, like the fur of a calico cat.

"Monty," she says. "Do you like having sex?"

How do you answer that? How do you tell her that sex is a natural human instinct? How do you tell her the greatest sex you've ever had was with Martha, third date, and it was clumsy and wonderful all at once?

"It's OK," I say.

Lynette says oh and goes silent. She appears younger now, no more than eighteen and for a second, she has the same look Martha has when she's thinking deeply, her eyes adrift, her mouth tightly shut. And for a second, I think she is Martha, and I have the urge to close my hand over hers. I have an urge to apologize for all the wrong things I've done in our relationship. I have the urge to tell her I love her and need her and in the two years she has been gone I've been in this deep dark funk and to pass the time, I enter abandoned houses and find and keep things with a red-haired girl I'm not sure I like. I want to tell Martha this right now. In this Honda Accord where a bobble head dog is bobbing on the dash. But I know she isn't here, my Martha. I know the girl beside me is Lynette.

"I'm sorry," I say, pressing the gas on the car and slowly maneuvering it around a corner.

"Monty," Lynette looks through her bangs, "do you find me to be an odd person?"

I park. "Yes," I say. "But aren't all artists?"

"I don't want to be a stereotype," says Lynette. "Do you really think I'm like other artists?"

I shake my head. "I think you give strangeness a new meaning."

"That's nice of you to say, Monty. That's the nicest thing anyone has ever said to me."

Then Lynette leans in and kisses me. I don't push her away. My eyes are open. Her eyes are open. We kiss and stare at each other. Staring like those staring contest kids play on the playground. Who can outlast the other? No blinking. We kiss and stare. We kiss and stare. To look away is to give in, to lose, to be thrust into the world we know: the lost and found. The old and discarded. We are traveling another path right now, a path neither of us is sure we want to be on. After a minute, Lynette closes her eyes and sighs into me. She whispers, "I need you, Monty."

"OK," I say.

She climbs into the back seat and takes off her busboy outfit. I look away.

"Do you want to be with me, Monty?"

"OK," I say.

"That's not an answer to my question," she says. "Do you, Monty? Do you want to be with me?"

I nod.

Lynette covers her arms over her breasts. She's in her underwear, plain and white.

"Come here," she says.

"OK," I say and climb into the back seat, my feet stumbling over the center counsel, tripping onto her naked body. She lets out a grunt when I fall on her, but I roll off quickly and we stare at each other again.

"Promise me this won't get weird, Monty. Promise me you

won't do every cliché in the book. Promise me that what we are doing is for art. For the longevity of art."

"OK," I say.

"Oh, Monty," says Lynette, "Oh, Monty."

This is wrong. Everything in my brain and body says so. But it has ceased to be about right or wrong. It is about need. I need to do this, need to get it out my system, this energy, this guilt, this weight that I feel has been gathering in my chest for the past two years. When I look at Lynette, her freckled shoulder, her pale torso, her small nipples, it's not her anymore. It's Martha naked in the Honda Accord. Martha telling me this is our world and she needs me and loves me and all the things that happened between us are forgotten and lost. We are a "we" again. I take her hair band and put it in my right hand. My pants slide down around my ankles and I'm between her legs, cramped and clumsy, my left hand cupping her bottom, Martha's bottom. And when I enter her, her fingers dig into my skin. She responds to my movement, which is slow and fast, and jerky because I don't have room, because the car is too small to hold the both of us. I am in and I am out. In and out. Out and out and out. She doesn't mind my ineptitude, but holds on tight, holds on to my shirt, my hair, my back. She's saying Monty. She's saying it in a breathy whisper. Over and over again.

My back begins to cramp.

My head hits the top of the car.

It doesn't take long.

When it's over, we both stare at the ceiling of the car.

"We don't talk of this, Monty," Lynette says. "We don't talk of this to anyone."

"OK," I say.

"We don't talk about this to each other, too, Monty. We don't. We can't."

213

"OK," I say.

"I have to get back," she says.

"OK," I say.

"Is that all you have to say, Monty? OK? For fuck's sake. Is that it?"

I stare at the car and the bobbing head dog and the condensation that has crept up the window and Martha's hair band wound around my wrist and then at Lynette, snapping on her bra, pulling up her pants. Before she moves out the door, I cup her face. I kiss her cheek. And when she tries to talk, tries to tell me what a weird cliché I am, I shush her with my finger on her lips, and I tell her my name. I tell her from now on to use my name. I need to hear it. I need her to know.

THE PASTRY CHEF

People think I'm a goody goody because I make sweets. But that's the biggest misperception in the business. Dessert chefs are notorious for being bitches. As for being the biggest bitch in the business, I take the top of the cake. Ha, I just made a pun. Laugh.

The thing is I don't look like a bitch. I'm forty-nine, married to my childhood sweetheart now balding and on disability, with three grown kids in various parts of the country, and a golden retriever named Sonny, who I love more than my husband and children put together. I wouldn't say I'm fat, but I'm bit rounder than most; it comes with the territory if you're working with chocolate and confectionary all day for the last fo years of your life. I walk with a limp, which I got from slipping on a wet floor at a restaurant I used to work at. My limp makes all the waiters and waitresses open the doors for me. Everyone in Panhandle calls me Mrs. Johnson. I wear these glasses from the sixties and my hair is done into a beehive. One of the hostesses, I believe her name is Jen—perky boobs, long legs—said to me one time, "Mrs. Johnson, you look like my second grade teacher. I loved my second grade teacher."

I didn't want to be anyone's second grade teacher, especially someone like perky-breasted Jen. What went through my mind, right then and there, was my plump fist in her pearly whites. POW! The image was so vivid I flinched, which made Jen ask if I was OK, if I needed a glass of water; they're always asking me if I need a glass of water. Instead, I said, "You would've been my favorite student, dear," and gave her a hard candy to suck on.

The thing is I'm a bitch in my mind. In-my-mind. I have the tendency of imagining what bitch-like things I could do, but in the real world, I'm Mrs. Johnson. Nice, old Mrs. Johnson, who can bake the flakiest croissants this side of the Chicago River. I'm a woman who lives in her head, who dwells on what could've been.

It has gotten worse.

I find myself, especially when I'm tired and riding the El home after hours baking and flambéing, thinking of the should'ves and would'ves, and saying out loud and out of nowhere, "You're so stupid, Mrs. Johnson." Or, "I hate you, Mrs. Johnson."

The thing is I can't stop it. I can't stop my mind. I can't stop the words forming and spilling out of my mouth. It just happens, and after it does I'm shocked and embarrassed.

Once, my husband said, "Did you say you hate yourself?" We were watching a late night talk show. Monkeys were juggling, and I was replaying the time I told Heidi Milkin I loved her new shoes in the school playground. It was a strange innocent exchange, one that shouldn't really get me going at all, but

215

then again, it doesn't take much anymore. The shoes were gorgeous. Shiny, red, two-inch heels, a white bow on top, sparkles along the sides. Mind you this was 1965 and I was fourteen. I hated Heidi Milkin for so many reasons: for those shoes, for kissing Donny, the boy I liked, and for just being Heidi Milkin. Instead of complimenting her, what I wanted to do, what I wish I had done, was push Heidi Milkin into the mud in the school playground, rip her pretty shoes off of her feet, and then bite her big toe off. CRUNCH!

But I didn't.

I told Heidi she was the coolest girl in the school and her shoes were an indication of the fabulous life she undoubtedly lived.

After the vision I said, "I hate you, Mrs. Johnson," loud and not in my head, but in the real world, the world in front of the TV at one in the morning with my very real husband next to me, who asked me whether I said I hate myself to which I wanted to reply, "Go to hell, you slimy bug of a man. I make soufflés with more shape than you."

No, instead, I told him he heard incorrectly, and because we were past the point in our relationship of really caring, he didn't question me again.

The thing is—lately—it's been getting worse. Really worse. I'm spending more time regretting and reliving that I forget where I am or what I'm doing. Sometimes my visions become so intense I have anxiety attacks. I rush off to the bathroom and try to get my breath back because I feel like a five hundred pound man is putting his entire weight onto my chest, and I feel like drowning, like crying, like yelling, but I can't. I just can't. All I can do is say: I hate you, Mrs. Johnson, I hate you, Mrs. Johnson. Over and over and over. You're stupid, Mrs. Johnson. Stupid. Stupid. Stupid. I scream: Stop it. Stop it, Mrs.

Johnson. I tell myself that things aren't that bad, Mrs. Johnson. Everyone loves you. Everyone thinks of you as Grandmother. That's a good thing. A good thing. A-GOOD-THING. Say it to yourself, Mrs. Johnson. You are a good person. You are a good person. Repeat after me. Everyone loves you. Everyone loves you. One more time, Mrs. Johnson. Everyone…everyone… everyone…

…can suck my saggy left breast! I wish "everyone" would put his face on the ground so I can smash it like a roach. SMASH! SMASH! SMASH! Fuck everyone. Fuck everyone in the darkest deepest poop hole in existence….

I'm sorry.

The thing is I've had a bad night. I was working in the kitchen preparing a series of desserts. It was a busy night and everyone in the restaurant was ordering the Creamy Coconut Custard Cake or the Green Tea Crème Brulee. Usually, I thrive in peak business hours. My limp goes away. I move like I'm on ice, flitting from one place to another. I become queen of the kitchen and my little helpers do exactly what I tell them. "Yes, Mrs. Johnson." "I'm on it, Mrs. Johnson." But tonight, my mind transported me elsewhere and I was no longer in the hot kitchen, but in France, where I've never been.

Once, I had the opportunity to study with the Jacque Fournier, one of the top pastry chefs in the world, but I was pregnant with my first son and couldn't do it. No matter. I was there now. I was twenty and beautiful, more beautiful than I had ever been, and I was sipping Chianti, wearing dark sunglasses and a pink silk scarf, and I was at an outdoor café, the Eiffel Tower in the background, and Jacque, handsome Jacque, was feeding me cheeses and tortes and petit fours. And he was telling me how talented I was, how I could be the next great dessert chef.

"*Je t'aime, ma cherie,*" he said.

217

"I love you too, Jacque," I said.

He leaned in. I leaned in. And just when our lips were about to connect—

"Mrs. Johnson, the cakes!" My mind half in the other world, I went to the oven. Jacque and I kissed and it was hot. I was hot. The oven was open. I reached into it—"Mrs. Johnson, no!" Someone yanked me back. I was on the ground. The wait staff and the chefs were staring down at me. Two of them helped me up, asking me, "Are you OK, Mrs. Johnson? Mrs. Johnson, are you OK?"

I asked them what happened. They told me. I had gone to the oven without my mitts and I was about to pull out a four hundred degree cake with my bare hands. My faux pas halted the kitchen's activity; it made the head chef, a tiny Asian woman, stop what she was doing. "Take a few days off," she said. "Take a week. Do something special for yourself, Mrs. Johnson. We're working you too hard." I nodded. I went home. My husband didn't notice I was back early. He asked if I could bake him cookies. So here I am. Baking batch after batch. Baking so much, our house smells like a cookie factory. I'm writing in red icing, BITCH, on the cookies. It looks good. It tastes better.

Don't worry about me. I'm OK. I'll get it back together. Piece of cake. Ha, another pun. Laugh!

Did you hear me? I said *laugh*.

THE BARTENDER

The longest thing I ever wrote was seven pages and it was a letter to my brother. As soon as I dropped it in the mailbox, I wanted it back. I stuck my hand in the box and groped around for my envelope.

After about ten minutes, an old woman jabbed her umbrella into my back. She was one of those ladies that take twenty minutes to cross the street and always wears rain gear no matter what the weather.

She said, "What you are doing is illegal."

I told her I just wanted my letter back.

She jabbed me again and threatened to get the cops.

"I *need* that letter," I said, my voice desperate.

This seemed to calm the old woman. She even gave me an understanding smile. "What's done is done," she said.

The old woman reminded me of my grandmother, God bless her soul. I remember when my brother and I were boys— me eight, he eleven—and he got it in his head that the best thing to do was to let Mr. Feathers, Grandmother's cockatiel, go.

Mr. Feathers had gray plumage and a yellow and orange head. I spent hours and hours just petting Mr. Feathers with my finger. He liked my touch, I could tell. He'd raise his head and make sharp but pleasant squawks. My brother, however, had a thing against the bird, and the bird had a thing against him. Mr. Feathers refused to get on my brother's arm. This bothered him. I watched him glare at Mr. Feathers from across the room, glare and chew on his nails.

One day, while my grandmother was at the mini-mart, he said, "Mr. Feathers looks like he wants to go home."

I told him Mr. Feathers was home. This was where he lived, the fifteenth floor of Addison Apartments.

My brother said Mr. Feathers' family lived in Australia. "Don't you want him to be with his family?"

I shrugged. I thought about being apart from mine. I was the biggest mama's boy in the world—still am—and I couldn't bear being apart from my mother for very long. I could barely bear it when she'd leave my brother and me at our grandmother's to go on her dates. I began to wonder whether Mr.

Feathers longed for *his* mother in Australia the way I longed for mine, and if he did, then there was no other choice but to let Mr. Feathers go.

"Does Mr. Feathers know where home is?"

My brother nodded and said it was animal instincts.

So I got Mr. Feathers. He climbed onto my finger. I patted his neck. I told him to have a nice trip, told him to come and visit us sometime. My brother opened the window and said, "See ya." I released Mr. Feathers from the fifteenth story window. He flew from tree to tree to tree until he disappeared. When my grandmother got back, she noticed Mr. Feathers' absence immediately. She asked where Mr. Feathers was. My brother said, "Teddy let him go. He's out there." He pointed out the window. He pointed at me. My grandmother jerked me onto her lap and spanked me viciously, speaking to Jesus each time her hand met my bottom. I cried. I cried and stared at my brother, whose eyes were on the window, looking at the places Mr. Feathers had flown off to.

The old woman with the umbrella asked if I wanted to join her in the park. She fed the pigeons every day. I shrugged, thinking about my brother, thinking about the letter. The old woman said the mailman came to collect the mail at precisely 2:07 pm Monday through Saturday, rain or shine or snow. "Maybe," she said, "he'll give you back that letter."

I looked at the mailbox and then back at the woman.

"You never know," she said. "People can surprise you."

OK, I told her. I'll wait for the mailman with her.

"Good," she said, "I have a new friend."

I took the old woman under the arm and guided her across the street and into the park. She used the umbrella as a walking stick. Every two steps, the tip of the umbrella came down on the concrete in a sharp click. She breathed heavily when she walked and I kept asking her if we were moving too fast. She shook her head and told me to shut up. When we got to the park bench, five pigeons swooped down from the light posts and wobbled over to us. She talked and clucked to them. They had names: Clarisse, Bumby, Derrick, Jo-jo, and Brown.

Brown was the most striking of the five. He was, indeed, brown, but had an emerald-colored ring around the neck. The old woman sprinkled breadcrumbs at her feet. Soon, a few more pigeons landed in front of us.

I never thought much about pigeons. I liked birds, ever since Mr. Feathers, but pigeons seemed to be the anti-bird. They seemed more rat than anything. But watching them, really watching them, I saw that they possessed a unique beauty that no other bird could claim.

The old woman didn't say much to me. She pointed at a few pigeons and told me their names. I asked her if she came here a lot. "I come here every day," she said. "How are they going to eat without me?"

I told her they were pigeons. They lived off the city's trash.

"Have you ever eaten trash?" she said.

I shook my head.

"I don't imagine it being good," she said.

"Depends on the trash," I said. I went on about working at a fancy restaurant downtown, and how the trash out of those dumpsters was a nice meal anywhere else.

"Do lots of pigeons go there?" she asked.

I told her I hadn't seen many. The food might be a bit spicy for the birds. The old woman started laughing like it was the funniest thing in the world. It was crazy, but she made me smile.

"You seem like a good person," the old woman said. She wanted to know why I had my entire right arm in a mailbox.

I didn't want to tell her about my brother. She was a stranger, who fed pigeons. She saw my hesitation and said, "Just trying to be friendly." Then she said, "The mail system is the biggest advancement in human history. Did you know that?"

I shrugged.

"Imagine how many letters are sent each day around the world. Imagine what those letters contain. Our lives are dictated by what we get in the mail. Bills, catalogues, cards. Do you know how mail was sent back in the day?"

I shrugged again.

"They used these." She picked up Brown the pigeon. He didn't freak, didn't flap his wings in protest. She put him on her lap and patted his brown head. "Pigeons."

I imagined having my letter sent that way. It would've taken three pigeons to deliver it, the weight of the paper making the birds fly unevenly. It was then I wondered what my brother was doing right now, if anything. I wondered what we'd be doing together. The thought made me ache. I hunched over a bit and let out a groan. I couldn't help it. I was hurting.

The old woman stared at me. She didn't say anything. She didn't try to comfort me. She simply took a cracker out of her purse and handed it to me. "Here," she said. "You look like you need this cracker more than these birds do." The cracker was a Saltine, my favorite when I was a kid. I remember how my brother and I used crumble the crackers into our soup, crumble the crackers until they were dust. Sawdust Soup, we'd called it. I took the cracker and shoved it in my mouth.

"I need that letter back," I said, my mouth full. And then I began to cry. It was a hard cry. A lot of noise. A lot of snot. I knew I should stop because I was crying in front of this old woman I've never met, but I couldn't. Crying in front of her seemed the only way I could cry.

The woman patted my back, but it was more like slapping someone who was choking. She kept repeating, "You're scaring the birds, you're scaring the birds," but it wasn't a reprimand, more like a general comment like, *look, there's a water fountain* or *that woman has on a nice blouse* or *I like your teeth*. I cried and cried until I was dry.

The old woman said, "You're like a water factory."

I told her I was sorry. I told her I hadn't cried like that in a while. She said she'd been around crying people before, but I won top prize.

I started to laugh again. The old woman laughed, too, and we laughed until joggers and passersby started looking at us.

She took Brown off her lap and held him out to me. "Hold him," she said. "Brown likes to be held."

I made a face and asked whether pigeons had diseases.

She said, "Of course not," and insisted I take him.

I took Brown. He was calm. I put him on my lap. I liked how warm he felt. I liked how I could feel his breath. He kinda purred and it vibrated through my hands and up my arms. His head jerked to the right and then left.

The old woman said, "Doesn't that feel good?"

I nodded.

"He likes you," she said.

"I like him too," I said. I stroked the top of his head, down the back of his feathers. I circled the ring of green around his neck. Then I connected the black dots on his back. I was getting lost, looking at this bird, lost holding a pigeon of all things.

The old woman pointed to the mailbox. "There he is. You can get your letter back." But I didn't move.

"What's done is done," I said. All I wanted to do was hold Brown on my lap, hold him there just a little longer before I had to let go.

The Busboy

This is my job: I gather dirty plates and glasses and silver-ware into gray industrial buckets. I scrape scraps of food into the trash. I deliver the bucket of dishes to the dishwasher. I stay out of the way of the waiters and cooks. If I break some-thing, my pays gets docked. If I break something, the head chef threatens to flambé my sac. I don't break anything.

This is what I do: I let my mind wander. Drift. It's a term me and the other bussers came up with, except for that artsy one no one likes. But even she drifts, though she wouldn't call it that. She'd say something college like, "I'm conjoining with the spiritual world," or some shit like that.

She's strange. I'm strange. We have a mutual understanding about our strangeness.

But bussers—we're the invisible bunch. We blend. At a fancy restaurant like this, we need to. No one wants to think about the busser when they are tearing apart the garlic and soy infused squab. No one wants to think about the busser when they guzzle top-shelf whiskey. This restaurant is an illusion of wealth, a paradise of excess, with their fancy glass chandelier and the Italian marble bartop and the wood floors from some poor decimated jungle. It's the reason why management tells us to wear black clothes in this near dark restaurant. They say, "Be unseen. Be nothing."

This is how I've made a living the past thirty years: I am a busboy.

This is how old I am: forty-eight.

I have never met a busser who wanted to be a busser for-ever. This is a stopover occupation, a rest stop. In my years, I've noticed that there are two types of bussers: young FOBs, looking for a way to make an easy living before moving on to something else. They are often a quiet bunch because they don't speak the language. Then there are the college students, who drift about what their degrees will buy them later in life, who have this look of boredom and disgust about their position in life. I don't fit in these categories. I'm the permanent busboy. I'm the professional. To be a good busser you need to have a relationship with trash and the disposal of it, and no one wants to spend their days dealing with garbage. Garbage is like bussers, too. It's everywhere, but you don't want to see it.

This is what I am: Stupid.

My moms used to tell me I was dropped a few times on the head. My moms said it was all that shit she smoked when I was sleeping in her. My moms—she said a lot of things and not one of them was that I could be somebody.

I don't care. I'm me.

This was my life at school those long years ago: Miserable. There was all this stuff I just didn't get, like what that math teacher said on the first day of class. "The number one is not really the number one." Or the science teacher: "There are some species of animalia that can change from male to female." Or when the English teacher instructed us on how to write a paper: "You have to organize your thoughts into five paragraphs."

This is what I remember: I raised my hand. Everyone in class looked at me. The teacher tilted her white-domed head. She didn't know I had the capabilities of speech. But I did. I do. If I'm good at something other than bussing and drifting, it's talking. What made me to raise my hand that day was this realization that I was stupid. Stupid in a major way. And it was like this big word I just learned from that strange busser—epiphany—and this epeiphany was like the winter wind here when it comes off the lake, a punch to the chest, a moment when you find yourself wide-eyed and completely aware of yourself. I am stupid. I. Am. Stupid. S-T-U-P-I-D. Stupid, I am. And—shit, this was the best part—I was OK with that. More than OK. Relieved. So I raised my hand. I wanted to share my relief, my epiphany, with everyone. When the teacher called on me, I said, "I'm stupid." Some of the class laughed and said no duh. But I ignored them because some of them were stupid too, and I pitied them for not admitting it, for trying to be something they were not. I pitied them because I wanted them to feel this epiphany I was feeling. This release of burden and expectation. I went on. "Yeah, I'm stupid. Real stupid. Because my thoughts can't be organized into five paragraphs. I don't work like that. I mean, like my head does weird things, you know? Maybe there's something wrong with me. Does everyone think like this? In five paragraphs? Because that's just impossible for me." The teacher didn't say anything. The rest of the class didn't say anything. So I kept going. I kept at it. "Thoughts are thoughts. Even stupid ones. I got lots of them. They come and they go. No order. No sense. My brain kinda drifts, you know? I let the mind do what the mind does. Like water. Like how it moves in strange ways. Like being on water and drifting. It's like you don't know where you'll end up, only you get there and then another thought takes you somewhere else."

I didn't stop talking. I couldn't. I had to get this out. I had to explain my stupidity to people. Everyone knew I was stupid. Everyone in that classroom. Everyone at that school. My moms. Everyone. Everyone knew I wouldn't be much in life. Everyone knew that in my future I would be something remedial. Like a busser. And I wanted to say something to defend my stupidness. I wanted to not blend. I wanted to be seen. I wasn't a busser yet. I was a boy. I was a stupid boy.

This was how it felt to be a stupid boy: Numb. Like my limbs were heavy. Like my hands were bowling balls. Like my brain was this swirl of syrupy goop.

"I like thinking," I said. "I like to drift, you know? So I don't think I can do this. This five paragraph thing. This school thing. I think I don't belong here. I don't think I belong anywhere. At least not anywhere where you need thoughts in five paragraphs. This place is made for people not like me. Thank you and good bye."

I stood up.

I left the classroom.

I left school.

I applied for a job.

A busboy.

This is how it feels to be a stupid man: Eh. It doesn't matter that you're stupid when you're busser, but I'm sure it's the secret thought everyone has. Look at the old man. He's a busboy. He must be stupid. Or maybe I'm not thought about at all. Maybe I'm not seen. It's OK.

Because it's me taking your food away. It's me clearing off the tables. It's me making this restaurant beautiful.

Think about it.

What if there were no bussers?

Then there wouldn't be restaurants like this. There wouldn't be places for you to forget your lives and enjoy luxurious living. We— the bussers—make that possible. I make that possible. I matter, here, in the corner no one looks at, ready to clean and clear.

THE HOST

In those days, the seventh grade boys of Oak Lawn, Illinois, were expected to get at least to second base if not farther,

227

and if they didn't then they were marked as the biggest pan-sy-asses in Simmons Middle School. All such conquests were recorded in the bathroom stalls—who did what with whom and the dates. *The Stall* was our sports section, a catalog of scores. Even I had etched my name on to *The Stall* when Jill Livicky allowed me to slide my hand down her shirt on Tuesday October 12, 1991 at 7:13 pm at her house while her parents were at her little sister's T-ball game, while Bon Jovi sang *I'll Be There For You* on MTV. It was a bad song; it was always a bad song when I got some back then: *Hanging Tough* by New Kids on the Block, *Cherry Pie* by Warrant. Jon Bon's voice was nasal and whiny and melodramatic. But Jill Livicky, she adored him. More than adored him. It seemed her heartbeat was this song. It sustained her the way air sustained us, the way fish need water, the way a bird values flight. His posters hung over every inch of her walls—Jon Bon's face, his long, stringy hair—looking at us from all angles. At night, I wondered if Jill Livicky went down there, to her spot, to the many eyes of Jon. Him giving the peace sign. Him winking. Him shouting in a mic. Him smiling while Richie Sambora humped his guitar. Most boys in Oak Lawn kept their hair trimmed and combed with the perfect over-gelled wave. Boys in Oak Lawn didn't wear leather pants or sport cross earrings. Boys in Oak Lawn beat up boys who looked like Jon Bon Jovi. But Jill Livicky—she loved him, and by the look of her you wouldn't have guessed it. She was a Puritan—blouse buttoned all the way to the top, flowery long skirt that floated above the ankles, short curly hair that domed like a helmet, and butterfly glasses. She looked like an old Blue Eyes fan. Rat Pack follower. Jill Livicky, she wasn't a girl who lived in 1990 or 91. She was a girl out of place, out of time. Not an Oak Lawn girl. Not a high hair girl, not a French roller. She was a nice girl, a smart girl, and that drove me mad, her niceness, her Puritan look. So when her parents were out watching her little sister play T-ball, as we watched Bon Jovi on TV in her Bon Jovi room, I unbuttoned her shirt and slid my hand down her front, her skin bumpy and soft, perfect and imperfect at the same time. She didn't blink, didn't stop me. It was as if I wasn't doing anything. As if I wasn't cupping her breast and squeezing. As if I wasn't there at all, but a ghost hand on a ghost boob. She stared at the TV, at Jon Bon. She sang softly, in a trance. And this I remember, this I could never forget—she was crying. Crying and singing with my hand down her shirt, thinking not about Jon Bon Jovi staring at me at all angles, not about her tears, but about my entry on *The Stall*, my addition to a world of silly Oak Lawn boys. I was thinking about getting beyond second base, thinking maybe she'll let me round third. But when the song ended, the moment was over. I told Jill Livicky thank you. It was the only thing I could say. Thank you, I said, and she smiled, a Puritan smile, bright with too many teeth. She buttoned her shirt like an afterthought, like it had accidentally come undone. He's dreamy, isn't he? Jill Livicky said. Thank you, I said again because I wanted to go home now, because there was no reason for me to stay anymore. But part of me wanted Jill Livicky to say, No. Don't go. Stay. For a little longer. Part of me wanted Jill Livicky to proclaim her love for me, to say I was on her mind night and day, that I was the boy of her dreams, and maybe we could get married and have a bunch of Puritan kids in Oak Lawn, playing within a white picket fence, living in a wonderfully suburban bi-level with a golden retriever named Ralph, and what a life this would be, what a perfect Oak Lawn life. Instead, Jill Livicky rose from her bed and opened the door. Bye, she said. Your company was appreciated, she said. Thank you, I said again. She put her hand on my shoulder like a distant friend, and I walked out of her room, her house, and immediately heard *Bad Medicine* streaming out of her window, and saw the shadow of Jill Livicky swaying behind her blinds. The sun was almost down, just a red light along the horizon. Everything seemed red. My face. My heart. My voice caught in my throat. Night was coming, and the cicadas were buzzing something fierce. I sang Bon Jovi under my breath. I sang *I'll Be There For You*, though I knew only the chorus. I sang it like a mantra that would lead me towards some sort of enlightenment, some sort of long-haired ecstasy. I sang it because I, too, was in love with Jon Bon. I loved him the way we love the last leaf of autumn, right before the descent. I loved him the way we love the monumental markers of our lives, like how I would come to love other songs and other memories attached to those songs. I loved him because there was no way of getting him out of my head—his hair, his voice, his tight pants—tonight or the nights that followed.

THE CRITIC

The other day, I was reviewing this restaurant and a close friend tagged along. I say close because she invited herself to dinner and said, "I haven't seen you in forever," which made me feel like my absence mattered. Sometime between the soup and the appetizer, I fell asleep with my eyes open, a gift I developed to combat the long hours at church. One moment my friend was speaking about simulacra and intertwined realities (she is a postmodernist and believes we are living one hundred lives all at once), and the next moment I was transfixed on my close friend's silver cross dangling at the V of her blouse. She told me she said my name over and over again. She said she shook me. All of which I do not remember hearing or feeling because while sleeping with my eyes open I was transported into the mini-van I used to drive when I was sixteen and remembered my eighty-second rejection. This is what I have been doing since the clouds have gathered—metaphorically and physically—over this city, going over every rejection of my life. Rejection eighty-two is childish. I was driving the mini-van and beside me was a boy in a tangerine sweater. At a light, I leaned in to kiss him and he turned his head and I buried my face in a tangle of thorns. Literally. My close friend would've said what happened in rejection eighty-two happened in all the other lives existing at once, and I wonder, the Buddhist part of me, whether this was metaphysical reincarnation; where one present thought ripples over and over again until we figure why we thought it in the first place. It is only a notion. But I've been thinking about it a lot lately, which might explain the cycling of rejections I am sifting through hour after hour, day after day, from one restaurant to the next. My close friend would also say that when one spends too much time in the mind what he/she is really doing is waiting to be rescued, of which she tried to do that evening to no avail. Eventually, she left me asleep with my eyes open, but scrawled a note on my arm: *The fried bananas were fantastic. Tomorrow, make an appointment with the sun.* I won't lie. Lately, even the sun distracts me.

THE HEAD CHEF

The number one rule: be aware of where you are and what you're doing. If not, disasters happen. Like the pastry chef almost grabbing a four-hundred-degree pan the other day before the interns pulled her to the ground. Could have been the end of desserts for the night. Could have cost us thousands. What about poor Mrs. Johnson, you ask? Don't give a shit. Only thing I care about is food. Perfected food. That's my business, my life.

At rush, we turn over three to four hundred tickets, which means, simultaneously, each station of my kitchen is working on hundreds of appetizers, entrees, desserts. You can't be distracted. You can't let your life—the little life you have—get in your way.

I come in at nine and make sure all the things are ready to go. I check the produce. I sign off on deliveries. I trim the fat. I chop and dice. I come up with the specials. I cook. Most importantly, I am a tyrannical bitch. It's the edge I need to keep sharp.

I don't know what to do with myself when I'm away from the shiny chrome of the countertops and my German-sharp knives. I don't know how to speak to anyone without cussing or needling their tiniest flaws or imperfections. Nights at home are quiet, and I have to admit, I'm scared of it.

I'm used to getting things done my way. I've been taught this. Because I'm the only daughter of Thai immigrants, my parents said that to survive in this country I had to be ruthless. I had to step and stab. My father was like this. His co-workers at the tile factory called him Hyena because of his nightly cackle. Once, one of his friends said, "Your pops, he'd bite the head off a bunny and laugh about it while the thing dangled in his mouth. No one dares fuck with him."

That's how I am. I'm like my father.

It's Saturday. Holiday season. Eight o'clock rush. We're lagging.

"How are we on the tenderloins?"

"Three minutes, Chef."

Chop. Sizzle. Bubble. Pans and plates. Shouts. More tickets.

"Fuck three minutes," I say over the noise. "I want that loin in now or I'm fucking roasting you, you motherfucker. You got me?"

"Yes, Chef."

My kitchen, my army. I ask, they answer. No argument.

There's a new girl on desserts. She's blonde and cheery. I know she just got her degree from some fancy culinary academy. I know she thinks she can do a better job than me. That's what all newbies do, especially the girls. They come into chaos thinking they can tame it. They look me up and down. Measure me up like a slab of beef on a freezer hook. I'm not stupid. I know what they think. This girl can't do it. She's a twig, a skeleton. Never trust a skinny chef. It doesn't bother me. They find out quick who runs this outfit. They find out they're not worth the congealed fat on cold stock.

"Where's the sesame fried bananas, Blondie?" Her name is Kim, but she hasn't earned it yet. "I need five plates. Two with honey, two without, one with chocolate sauce. I need them now. You hear me?"

She pats her hands on her apron and works like she isn't on the clock, like she's Suzie fucking Homemaker making an apple pie for hubby. I can almost hear her hum some Mary Poppins song. Her fingers dance over the plates, and I notice she has red nail polish on—nail polish! More than that, she's wearing make-up. Vivid lips. Long painted eyelashes. She belongs in a prom dress, not a chef's uniform.

"Blondie," I say, "I ask, you answer. Where are my desserts?"

She doesn't look up. She cooks like she's the only one in the kitchen. She places the bananas in a triangle formation against an oval scoop of vanilla ice cream. She waves a squeeze bottle of honey in decorative swirls. It's as if I'm not there.

"Blondie."

In a kitchen where every burner blazes, every oven in use, where fryers bubble and spit three hundred degree oil, where you sweat buckets and have to wear bandanas to keep from dripping into the food, she is perfectly composed, not one stray strand of hair poking out of her little pink scrunchy. She's a model for an acne-free commercial. My face is like the surface of the moon.

"Blondie, in my kitchen you answer as soon I ask you something."

"That's not my name," she says. She hands me my orders and smiles, like it was a simple correction. "It's Kim."

It's as if someone turned off the noise switch. The entire kitchen comes to a standstill. Here, we can work through people chopping off bits of fingers, the screams of a burn, slips and falls—and we have many, many times—but the quiet tension of an argument manages to halt everything. Someone has undermined the Head Chef and it's fuckin' church in here. The dreamy dishwasher stops in mid-spray of a stock pot. The Japanese waitress stands frozen, a tray of food balanced on her shoulder. The freaky busboy looks likes she's about to take a picture with that camera she always has with her.

No one corrects Head Chef. She can abuse you verbally any way she pleases. Cunt. Bitch. Whore. She wants to call you Blondie. She will. It's her kitchen.

I look around. We're still lagging. Pauses like this can set us back another five to ten minutes. Food temperature drops about half a degree a minute. We don't have time for this.

I glare at my staff. They know better. I bang a pot against a counter. "What the holy fuck is going on here?"

That's all it takes.

But Blondie. She's still smiling. Like the world is one big, fucking happy place.

Her desserts. Sesame-crusted fried bananas with a scoop of vanilla ice cream, our biggest seller. This is my father's favorite food. In Thailand, he told me, street vendors sold them on every block. He told me when he was a student he could eat pounds of fried bananas, the grease soaking through the paper bags onto his hands. My father, he doesn't like eating the Pan-Thai shit I cook here. Thai food is about simplicity, he says. It's about a lot of taste in little time. Why bother changing it? But the bananas, when I bring them home, when he used to live with me, he said it was like tasting Thailand again, like tasting his childhood.

I hate Blondie for making me think of my father. She's a bubble I want to pop, and I know how to do it. Cooks are all the same. We have the same weakness. It's like kicking a guy in the balls; it always hurts.

I scan her plates. I can feel her staring, waiting for me to compliment her, to tell her how wonderful she is, how she is the best pastry chef I've ever worked with, how absolutely lucky I am to have her, and maybe someday she can run a kitchen just like this. I take longer than I should. I bend down, tilting the plates from all angles. I scrutinize them the way a doctor might a blood sample under a microscope. The desserts are done to perfection.

"I'm sorry, Blondie," I say, "but these aren't good enough. This one's overcooked. This one is drowning in chocolate. The presentation of this one is like someone upchucked on the plate. This is a real kitchen, not some lab at Johnsons and Wales. You catch me, Blondie?"

And then I dump the desserts in the garbage.

There are three ways one usually responds: 1) You stand up for your work. You say, "Chef, you are a fucking bitch, and there was nothing wrong with my dishes." And then the chef fires you. 2) You cry. And then the chef fires you. 3) You apologize. You say, "Sorry, Chef. Won't happen again," and you make the dishes even more perfect than before.

Laughing, however, is not on the list.

"This is funny, Blondie?"

"Yes," she says.

"Your ineptitude is funny?"

She laughs so hard she can't answer. But here's the strange part. As she's laughing, she's cooking, her hands steady despite her heaving body.

"Have you asked yourself if you're really cut out for this, Blondie?"

Still laughing. More bananas come out of the fryer. I can tell they are perfect.

"This is a commitment, Blondie. This isn't playtime. You're not cooking on an Easy-bake oven here."

Laugh. Laugh. Laugh.

Done. The desserts. Without flaw.

If I throw these out, we lose more time. Time we don't have. But I want to. I want her to stop laughing. I want her to raise her voice, to make it easy for me. I want her to walk out of the kitchen. I want a victory. I need it, this control. That's the rush of working in a kitchen. That's why my life is this restaurant. In here, it's food. Out there, there are too many variables. You have to face it. You have to deal with things you can't deal with, like your father, Hyena, forgetting your name or how to dress himself or how to speak English, the only language you know, so some days you cry at night because the man you love so much, the man you modeled yourself after doesn't understand a thing you are saying. You feel helpless, and so you do the only thing you can, you put him in home and promise to visit every week, but it's been two months and you're working hours you shouldn't just to keep yourself busy.

I'm losing here. I'm losing out there.

Her laughter is a like a drill.

There is one way to stop it.

"Thank you, Kim."

"You're welcome, Chef. What's my next order?"

"Green Tea Crème Brûlée, five. Coconut custard over black sticky rice, four."

"On it, Chef."

In the kitchen, there is always the end of the night. No matter what. After last orders, we put our dramas behind us. I tell them, "Well done." I tell them to get drunk and laid. I tell them I'll see them tomorrow for more fun. There are no apologies. No time for it. We wash our hands clean. We go home, and for some of us, that's when the real work begins.

THE WAITRESS

I've never been a liar despite all the lies I've told. That's not something easily digestible, like most of the food here, but allow me to explain. My name is Stacy Eng, daughter of second-generation Chinese-Americans. Sometimes I go by Hoshiko or Chandani or Khanya. As a favor, I had someone on staff make me four nametags, so I could switch them at will.

I have the face and skin that transcends countries and cultures. In the winter, I am often seen as a pale Japanese. In the summer, because I spend my days at the beach, my skin becomes darker, and then I somewhat look Indian. Most of the time, because I work at an upscale Thai restaurant, the assumption is that I'm Thai. I don't mind. I belong to everyone.

When I wait on a table of Chinese or Japanese or Indian or Thai, I put on the appropriate nametag and assume the role. That way my tips are bigger. This evening, for example, a Thai couple came into the restaurant. The man had a narrow face and round-rimmed glasses that told me he was probably a professor at the university. The woman—I assumed she was his wife—wore a nice lavender dress that draped loosely over her figure. She was pretty in a plain way, but seemed somewhat distracted, looking around the restaurant. I knew I had seen her before, but couldn't place where. When Jane seated the couple in my section, I came over and said, "*Sawasdee*," putting my hands together in the traditional Thai greeting. (This was how the wait staff was instructed to greet patrons. In fact, before the restaurant opened, all hired waiters had to go through intense training. By the end of the three-day session, we were given honorary certificates that read: *Congratulations, you are Thai*. Some of us had a good laugh: Sonia the Latino, Brian the Southside Irish, Lamont the African-American. We joked that we needed to add another hyphen to our nationalities.) The man smiled and said, "Are you Thai?" He had a barely noticeable accent. I told him I was and my name was Khanya. Unfortunately, because I was born in the States, I didn't speak Thai well, only a few words here and there. The man clapped his hands. "I knew you were Thai right away. I could tell." Then he said, "My mother's from Chiang Mai," and I nodded like I knew where that was. The woman said very little but smiled politely.

Each time I came to their table, the man asked me more questions. Did I go to school? What was I studying? Have I ever been to the Thai temple in the suburb? He asked what my parents did for a living and I told him as close to the truth as possible. My father was a doctor and my mother designed clothing. The truth truth: my father is an herbalist and my mother sews for fun.

But this wasn't going to get me a good tip. Truth, with a capital T, is too sobering. People don't come to restaurants like this to be sober. They want to be drunk with food and wine and a good time. Truth is like the steamed foie gras dumplings here. You don't want it. The truth about my family is my parents don't make much of anything and they're content with that. The truth is my parents like our little house in a crummy neighborhood. The truth is I want to bust out. I have plans for the money I've earned, like moving to New York and trying to make it as an actress. It's cliché, I know, but I think I'm good. I have to be if I keep fooling people.

Except that woman tonight.

I took a quick bathroom break and there she was, washing her hands at the sink. I said, "I hope you're enjoying the meal," and she said, "I thought your name was Hoshiko." I tried to say something, but she started to laugh. "I won't tell if you won't tell," she said. Then I remembered her. She had been in last week with three other men, all in suits and ties, all Japanese. She had leaned against one of them and laughed loud at his jokes, downing glass after glass of the '92 Glenn Ellen Chardonnay. She didn't look like the same person that night. That woman wore vivid red lips, three-inch heels and a sexy sequin dress. That woman smoked with extended fingers and ordered the crispy skinned duck with a soy and citrus reduction. The Japanese man she clung to ended up giving me, Hoshiko, a two hundred dollar tip.

The woman looked at me in the reflection of the bathroom mirror. Her lips twitched, and I thought for a second she might cry, but instead she said, "You do a good job whoever you are," and she pulled out of her purse a fifty and crumpled it up in my hand. She left the bathroom with a slight smile, and I stood for a moment, frozen, not knowing what to do.

When I came to their table, the couple was ready to leave. I handed the man the bill and he paid in cash, leaving me twenty-five dollars, a good solid thirty percent tip. He said, "Good luck," and "The food and service was excellent." The woman waved with her fingers.

I don't consider what I do lying. I do what gets me by. Doesn't everybody follow this general rule? Take a look around. Is the dishwasher really a dishwasher? Is the chef really a chef? What is the bartender truly thinking about when he's making the gin & tonic with an extra slice of lime? I guess what I'm trying to get at is we live in a world of pretend, and the truth is everyone's acting. Every person who works in this restaurant, every person in the world. They may not have extra nametags, but they're wearing different ones on different days with different people. I'm sure of it.

About the Author

Ira Sukrungruang is a Thai American writer born in 1976 in Oak Lawn, Illinois, a suburb just south of Chicago. He is the author of the esssay collection *Southside Buddhist*, which won the American Book Award, the memoir *Talk Thai: The Adventures of Buddhist Boy*, and the poetry collection *In Thailand It Is Night*. he co-edited *What Are You Looking At? The First Fat Fiction Anthology* and *Scoot Over, Skinny: The Fat Nonfiction Anthology*. Now he edits *The Clever Title* and *Sweet: A Literary Confection*.

He teaches in the MFA program at the University of South Florida.

CPSIA information can be obtained
at www.ICGtesting.com
Printed in the USA
BVOW08s0847250817
492855BV00002B/191/P